W9-ARD-466

Summer Dance

Center Point
Large Print

Also by Nan Rossiter and available from
Center Point Large Print:

Nantucket
More Than You Know
Words Get in the Way

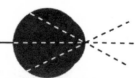

Summer Dance

Nan Rossiter

CENTER POINT LARGE PRINT
THORNDIKE, MAINE

This Center Point Large Print edition is published
in the year 2017 by arrangement with
Kensington Publishing Corp.

The text of this Large Print edition is unabridged.
In other aspects, this book may vary
from the original edition.
Printed in the United States of America
on permanent paper.
Set in 16-point Times New Roman type.

ISBN: 978-1-68324-445-5

Library of Congress Cataloging-in-Publication Data

Names: Rossiter, Nan Parson, author.
Title: Summer dance / Nan Rossiter.
Description: Center Point Large Print edition. | Thorndike, Maine :
Center Point Large Print, 2017.
Identifiers: LCCN 2017016722 | ISBN 9781683244455
    (hardcover : alk. paper)
Subjects: LCSH: Large type books. | GSAFD: Love stories.
Classification: LCC PS3618.O8535 S86 2017 | DDC 813/.6—dc23
LC record available at https://lccn.loc.gov/2017016722

For my aunt Ninfa and uncle Rich,
whose deep and abiding love for each other
will always be an inspiration!

WITH HEARTFELT THANKS . . .

To my editor, Esi Sogah, my agent, Deirdre Mullane, and the entire Kensington team, who do their very best to help make every book a success. To the men in my life—my husband, Bruce, and our sons, Cole and Noah, who fill my life with joy and inspiration.

To my friends and family, who faithfully read and share my books with friends.

And to Finn, who rests his chin on my lap every day at four o'clock and gives me a look that says it's time to stop working and go for a walk! I am truly blessed!

May

Sally Adams stood in front of her mailbox in the late-afternoon sunlight and tore open a large, padded envelope. She peered inside and felt her heart pound as she slid out the contents—a book with a sheet of folded, crisp stationery tucked inside its cover. She gazed at it in disbelief and lightly traced her finger over the title and the author's name. Then she pulled her reading glasses from their perch on top of her head, slipped out the stationery, unfolded it, and began to read. As she did, she pushed back some loose strands of her silver hair and the late-day sunlight fell across her face, illuminating crinkly smile lines around her eyes.

Ever since Coop died four years earlier, Liam had been trying to get her to write a book about her relationship with his uncle, Winston Ellis Cooper III, the salty Vietnam vet who'd raised him, but she'd just chuckled. "You're not getting any sordid details out of me."

"C'mon, Sal," Liam had cajoled. "It would make a great story."

And Sally, who'd always harbored a secret desire to write a book—maybe even sell Cuppa Jo and *become* a writer—began toying with a few words. But as she stared at the blank screen, all she could think was: *Who is fooling who? Or should it be: Who is fooling whom?* Even though she was an avid reader, she didn't know a thing about writing. She'd forgotten everything she'd learned in college, and the only lesson she could remember from high school was that the first sentence should grab the reader's attention. Sister Mary Agnes, hailing from Waltham, had swept between her students' desks in her flowing black habit and declared what she called the eleventh commandment: "Thou shalt make sure thy first sentence is a grabbah!" Sally had smiled at the memory and then remembered the old nun had also suggested they write what they know. Unfortunately, writing what *she* knew involved dredging up memories she'd spent a lifetime trying to forget; not to mention, the poor nun would turn over in her grave if she knew one of her former students was starting a memoir about a premarital relationship and an extramarital affair with a "grabbah."

Sally had looked out the window, trying to remember some of the first sentences the sister had extolled to be classics, but she'd only been able to remember the titles from which they'd come—everything from *Ulysses* to *Pride & Prejudice*, and the only sentence she'd been able to recall was from *Moby Dick*.

In that vein, she'd flippantly typed: "I am Sally." Then she'd turned the sentence over in her mind and realized her story should be told in the first person too. She'd tapped the Delete key back to "I am" and started again, and before she'd known it, she'd written a chapter. And then the words had spilled from her in a cathartic waterfall, healing her broken heart.

Sally tucked the book under her arm with the rest of the mail and leaned down to pull a weed that was sprouting next to the mailbox. She stood up, looked around, and shook her head. The gardens needed her attention, but as usual, summer had snuck up on her, and between running Cuppa Jo to Go—the breakfast and lunch hotspot, a Nantucket mainstay she'd owned for thirty years—and the countless hours she'd spent making final edits, she'd been flat out busy. But the worst was over: The edits were done and the letter brought news that her memoir, *Summer Dance*, scheduled for release later that summer, was already receiving some nice reviews.

Sally climbed the porch steps and realized Tucket and Jax were sitting inside the screen door with their tails swishing and thumping, respectively—golden retrievers' tails swish and Labs' tails thump. "Hullo, loves," she said, opening the door, and Tuck, Liam's big golden—who she'd been dog sitting for the last few days—wiggled out, followed by the smaller yellow puppy, Jax. She knelt down and they sniffed her all over and licked her cheeks. "Do I smell like bacon?" she said, laughing. "Jax, is your father teaching you all about his favorite food?"

She felt her knees start to ache, stood up, limped stiffly into the kitchen, and set the mail on the counter. The little cottage in which Sally had lived since moving to Nantucket nearly fifty years ago had been built in the late 1800s, and it had always been just that—a sturdy, rustic beach house. During its first hundred years, it saw only one improvement—running water—and every winter thereafter, the owner had had to drain the pipes because it had never been properly insulated.

Sally had bought the cottage in 1970, and over time—with Coop's help—she'd renovated and insulated it. The only room that hadn't seen a recent update was the kitchen, but that had changed the previous winter when Liam had installed beautiful white cabinets with glass-paned doors, white wainscoting, and new stainless-steel appliances—including a convection oven and gorgeous granite countertops. Now it was her favorite room.

Sally put the kettle on and looked around. She loved the little cottage and the life she'd made on Nantucket, but she'd never been able to put to rest the guilt she felt over her father's untimely death; and although she'd always worked hard—her dad's work ethic had definitely rubbed off on her—it was her dad's tireless, hard work that had made her comfortable life possible. One time, she'd told Lizzy this, and her best friend had smiled. "He wouldn't have wanted it any other way."

The kettle started to whistle and Sally poured the steaming water over the ginger turmeric tea bag in her cup—she'd recently read that turmeric was good for aching joints and she was hoping it would help her knees, which, from years of riding her bike in all kinds of weather, ached constantly. As she waited for her tea to steep, she heard a knock on the door. Tuck scrambled to his feet, barking, and Jax, giving a little warning bark, too, trotted after him. "C'mon in," she called.

Liam pulled open the door and he and nine-year-old Aidan stepped in. "Hey, Jax," Aidan said, falling to the floor and scooping the puppy into his arms. Jax thumped his wiry tail and licked Aidan's face.

"What about your other pal?" Liam reminded, watching the older dog wiggle around him too.

Aidan grinned. "Hey, Tuck," he said, putting his free arm around the golden's big neck. "I love you too."

"And . . . what about me?" Sally teased.

Aidan scrambled to his feet and almost bowled Sally over with a hug.

"Hi, hon," she said, kissing the top of his head. "Did you have fun?" Aidan nodded.

"So, how were they?" Liam asked, kissing Sally's cheek and nodding to the dogs.

"They were fine. Tuck's teaching Jax all of his tricks."

"That's what dads are for," Liam said, kneeling down to scratch the puppy's ears. "Although I'm still not convinced Tuck is really Jax's father."

"I don't know," Sally countered. "Lois Tillman said she's certain Tuck was hanging around her place when Babs was in heat."

Liam eyed Tucket. "How in the world did you get involved with a female named Babs anyway?!" He looked back at Sally. "How come the puppies don't have long hair like a golden?"

Sally shrugged. "Maybe Lab genes are stronger."

Liam shook his head. "Well, one thing's certain," he said, eyeing his big golden, "someone's going to be going under the knife."

Tuck, who was sprawled out at Sally's feet, opened one eye and swished his tail and Liam chuckled. "You won't be wagging your tail either, mister."

"Why is he going under the knife?" Aidan asked, worried.

"So we won't have any more puppies that we have to find homes for."

"A knife will do that?"

" 'Going under the knife' is another way of saying 'having surgery,' " Liam said. "It's nothing to worry about. Tuck needs to be neutered."

"What's neutered?"

"It's a type of surgery so he can't be a dad again," Liam said, hoping the answer would suffice.

Aidan frowned. "What do they do to him?"

Liam gave Sally a perplexed look and she laughed. "When a male dog is neutered, his testicles, testes, and sperm ducts are removed so he can't get a female dog pregnant."

Aidan's eyes grew wide. "You mean down here?" he asked, pointing to himself.

"Yes," Sally said with a nod.

"Oh, poor Tuck," Aidan said sympathetically, petting the dog's head.

"He'll be fine," Sally reassured him. "He'll just be a little sore for a couple days. So," she added, changing the subject, "how was Boston? How are Levi and Emma and sweet little Lily?"

"They're great," Aidan said, grinning. "Lily is so cute."

Liam nodded in agreement. "I can't believe how much she's changed since the last time we saw her—she's walking . . . and she's talking a blue streak." He laughed. "But the only one who understands her is Emma."

Aidan grinned. "Yeah, Lily will say 'we ha who ju,' and Em will say, 'Oh, you want some juice?' and Lily will nod and hold out her cup."

Sally smiled. "They're going to be good parents."

Liam nodded in agreement. "They're figuring it out."

"Just like you," Sally said, nodding toward Aidan, who was sitting on the floor with Jax again.

"Ha!" Liam said, shaking his head. "It's definitely hit or miss in our house."

"No, no, you're doing great," Sally assured, then ventured, "Do you think they'll have more kids?"

"I don't know," Liam said, shrugging. "It would be nice for Lily . . ."

"Not if Em gets Levi neutered," Aidan chimed as he stood up to see what there was to eat.

"From the mouths of babes," Sally said, pulling him into another hug. "Are you hungry, my dear?"

Aidan nodded, and when Sally pointed to a plate of freshly baked chocolate-chip cookies, his face lit up.

"Just one," Liam said. "We haven't had supper."

"Do you want one too?" Aidan asked, holding out the plate.

"No, thanks," Liam said. "Maybe Sally will let you take one ho—"

But before he could finish his sentence, Sally waved him off. "Don't be silly. I definitely don't need those cookies around here," she said, patting her belly—which was surprisingly flat for someone who owned a coffee shop and sold yummy baked goods. "That whole plate is for you."

She looked down at Tuck, who'd quietly gotten up and moved strategically over to be right at Aidan's feet with Jax sitting politely next to him. "See, I told you," she said, laughing. "Tuck has even taught Jax how to look sad." And it was true—Jax looked about as mournful and hungry as could be.

Liam laughed and shook his head. "I think you must be partly to blame, Sal, otherwise he wouldn't know there's a potential tidbit in his future."

"Noo," Sally protested, scooping the puppy into her arms. "There are no rewards for begging around here, are there, Jax?" As she said this, the little yellow Lab turned his head and licked her right on the lips.

"Nice," she said, laughing. "You got me."

"Don't worry," Liam said, grinning. "They say a dog's mouth is cleaner than the kitchen sponge." He leaned back against the counter and, feeling his hand brush against a pile of papers, turned and noticed the corner of a book sticking out from under the pile. "What's this?" he asked.

Sally watched as the look on Liam's face turned from one of puzzlement to one of realization. "Hey! Is this *it?*" he asked. "Is this your book?"

Sally took a sip of her tea and smiled. "It does have my name on it," she teased nonchalantly.

"Indeed it does," Liam said, admiring the cover and then holding it up for Aidan to see. "Look, pal, we know a real author!"

Aidan nodded approvingly. They both knew how long and hard Sally had worked on her book and how difficult it had been for her to find an agent and then a publisher. It had been a true test of patience, perseverance, and prayer. Liam turned to the first page, read the opening, and looked up in surprise. "What's this?" he asked.

"You're the one who kept after me," Sally said. "It probably would've never happened if it wasn't for you."

Liam's eyes glistened. "Wow," he said softly. "Thanks, Sal. I never expected this."

"Well, whether you think so or not, my dear, you're an inspiration to everyone who knows you."

Liam smiled and pulled her into a hug. "And the same goes for you."

She laughed. "You may not think so after you read it."

"You're going to let me read it?" he teased.

"As long as you promise you won't read too much *into* it."

"I promise," Liam said, re-reading the top of the opening page and smiling.

PART I

Blessed are those whose way is blameless,
who walk in the law of the Lord!

—Psalm 119:1

For Liam,
the boy who learned to laugh and love again,
and in so doing, taught others to do the same.

Chapter 1

I am *not* Ishmael. I'm Sally, but like the banished biblical son of Abraham, I left the only home I knew, and like the famous narrator of the Herman Melville classic, *Moby Dick*, I sought refuge on the island of Nantucket. To have a true understanding, however, of the young woman who fled Medford, Massachusetts—the town where she'd grown up, attended school, fell in love (or so she thought), and married—I must start earlier—at the beginning, or at least, close to the beginning.

Every child who grows up in Medford knows a little bit of the town's history. It's impossible to get through elementary school—public or parochial—without learning there was a famous horseback ride through Medford, or that the Christmas song "Jingle Bells" was written by a local resident who witnessed a sleigh race from Medford to Malden, or that the song "Over the River and Through the Woods" was originally a poem written by a young girl who'd traveled across the river to visit her grandparents.

The Mystic River—the river over which James Pierpont witnessed two sleighs racing, and along which Paul Revere rode, and over which Lydia Maria Child crossed—is the slate-gray ribbon of water that runs through Medford. At one time, when the land was inhabited by Native Americans and early colonists, the river ran clear and cold and teemed with fish—everything from salmon and bass to herring and carp. But decades of drainage into the river's watershed by industrial mills and homes built along the river's banks resulted in high levels of bacteria and pollution, and gradually, the clear, cold river, teeming with fish, became a turbid, greasy estuary—from which fish should not be eaten.

When I think of Medford, I think of the river.

The first time I laid eyes on Lizzy McAllister, she was standing on our front stoop. "I'm sorry for your loss, Mr. Adams," her mother said solemnly, holding out a casserole. "If there's anything I can do, please don't hesitate to ask."

My father nodded, wiping his brow with his handkerchief in the steamy August heat. "Thank you, Mrs. McAllister," he said, taking the dish.

She glanced down at me. "If Sally would like to come over and play with Lizzy sometime, she'd be more than welcome, and I'd be happy to watch her if you need to make the arrangements."

From behind my father's pant leg, I eyed the little girl standing next to her mother. She didn't seem shy at all. She had bright blue eyes, dark curls, and a sprinkle of cinnamon freckles across her nose.

"I think she'd like that," my father said, easing me in front of him and squeezing my shoulders.

"Will she be starting kindergarten next month?"

I looked up, saw my father nod, and frowned. *What's this?*

"Will she be attending St. Clement?"

"I'm not sure," my father answered. "My wife was Catholic, but I'm Protes—"

The woman frowned. "St. Clement is an excellent school," she interrupted, as if there shouldn't be any question. "It's far better than the public school."

My father nodded. "Her mother and I never had the chance to talk about it."

"Well, if you decide on St. Clement—which you certainly can since your wife was Catholic—I'd be happy to help with rides."

"Thank you. I'll have to let you know."

Mrs. McAllister nodded, reached for her daughter's hand, and turned to go, but then stopped and looked back. "I know you're overwhelmed right now, but registration is soon."

My father nodded.

I looked up at him uncertainly and then watched them walk away. It was late in the summer of 1952 and I was more than a little bewildered by everything that had happened. Why had my mom lain in bed for days, crying out in pain, and then become eerily quiet? Why had my father allowed two men to come into our house, cover her beautiful, pale face with a sheet, and wheel her out into the summer rain on a narrow bed? And why, now, was there a parade of people knocking on our door, telling my father they were sorry, and giving us food? Why didn't he tell them we didn't need any more food? Our refrigerator was full and our counters were covered.

"Your mother died," Lizzy said matter-of-factly, two days later, as she reached for a blue crayon.

"I know *that*," I said indignantly. *Does she think I don't know* anything?

"Well, why do you keep saying she's coming back?"

I bit my lip, pressed down harder on the crayon I was using, and felt it snap. Lizzy looked up. "That's okay," she said. "I didn't like Alizarin Crimson anyway." And the way she said it made it sound like she was going to throw it away just because it was broken. I looked at the flower I was coloring—I loved the rich translucent red. How could she *not* like it?

"My father didn't die," she said. "He left."

"Why?"

Lizzy shrugged. "I don't know, but my mother says he's going to rot in hell."

26

I looked up in surprise, but Lizzy seemed unfazed by her mother's words.

"Did your mother go to confession?" she asked.

"I think so."

"Did she love Jesus?"

"Yes," I answered uncertainly.

"Then you don't have to worry. She's in heaven."

"How long will she be there?"

"Once you're in heaven, you're there for good," Lizzy said matter-of-factly. "You're there for ternary."

"What's ternary?"

"Forever," she said, reaching for a green crayon.

I leaned back in my chair, looked up at the crucifix hanging in the middle of the empty wall, and tried to wrap my mind around this idea.

"You'll see her again, though," she assured, "*if* you're good."

I frowned. "Will I see her soon?"

"Not till you die and *only* if you're good."

"Do I have to be good all the time?" I asked, suddenly regretting the butter rum Lifesaver I'd taken from my dad's bureau that morning. I watched Lizzy coloring the trees in her picture. I could see the tip of her tongue sticking out of the corner of her mouth as she neatly applied the same even pressure with every stroke, never going outside the lines.

"All the time," she confirmed, nodding. "But if

27

you mess up, you just go to confession and tell the priest and he gives you pennies."

"He pays you?"

"Mm-hmm." Lizzy nodded as she concentrated on her drawing.

Well, obviously, my parents hadn't done a very good job of explaining things to me. I'd never heard any of this before. We barely went to church, never mind confession. Thank goodness for Lizzy. She seemed to be an authority on the subject.

"You don't have to worry, though," she added, exchanging green for blue again.

"Why not?"

"Because it doesn't start till after you go to confession and have Communion. You have to be the age of reason—which is seven. Then you get firmed."

I frowned. "What if you die before you're firmed?"

"As long as you're risen, you're covered."

I took a deep breath and let it out slowly, considering the wise counsel offered to me by my new friend. It was a lot to absorb, but if she knew a way for me to see my mom again, I needed to stay close to her.

Lizzy reached for a yellow crayon and started to draw a circle in the upper right-hand corner of her picture. She neatly colored it in, drew an orange smiley face in the middle of it, and then drew alternating long and short lines all around it. She held it up for me to see and I nodded approvingly —it was perfect.

In the recesses of my mind, the day of my mom's funeral has always been a confusing blur of gray clouds, damp earth, dark mahogany, and solemn, unfamiliar faces. The only things I remember with any clarity are crossing the river into Malden—where my grandparents were buried—and seeing tears stream down my father's face. In my young life, I'd never seen my father cry, and the humbling realization that my tall, handsome protector could be reduced to tears was frightening.

He was standing at the kitchen window, wearing the black dress pants and once crisp—but now wilted—white shirt he'd been wearing all day. It had finally stopped raining and raindrops were glistening on every surface as the sun streamed through the wet leaves.

"Dad?" I ventured softly.

He turned and quickly wiped his eyes. "What is it?" he asked, moving his jacket to sit in a chair and pulling me onto his lap.

"Why are you crying?" I asked.

"I'm not."

"Yes, you are," I said, trying to see his face. "We'll see Mom again," I said matter-of-factly, "if we're good."

"Who told you that?"

"Lizzy," I said, still trying to see him.

He wiped his eyes again. "Maybe."

I played with the buttons on his cuff. *Maybe? How could he not know this?* "Don't you think so?"

"I'm not sure," he said in a tired voice. "I'm not sure of anything," he added softly.

"Lizzy said if we mess up, we just go to confession and the priest will give us pennies."

"Pennies?"

"Mm-hmm," I said, nodding.

"Interesting," my dad mused.

"Was I risen?"

"Risen?"

"Lizzy says if you're risen you're covered till you're firmed."

"I think she means *christened*."

I frowned uncertainly. "Was I?"

"Yes."

"Were you firmed?"

"If you mean *confirmed*, then yes, but not in the Catholic Church."

"Was Mom?"

"I imagine."

"Did she go to confession?"

"Not often."

"Because she was good?"

He sighed. "You certainly ask a lot of questions."

"Was she?"

"Yes, your mom was a very good person."

"Am I going to St. Clement?"

"I thought you didn't want to go to school."

"I want to go with Lizzy."

"We're not Catholic."

"Mom was. I heard you say so."

My father was quiet for a few minutes before he spoke again. "If you go to St. Clement, Sally, it's because Mrs. McAllister said you can stay at her house until I get home from work. It's not because we believe everything the Catholic Church teaches."

"I know," I said, nodding, even though I didn't know but would've said anything to go to school with Lizzy.

"We'll see," he said, lifting me off his lap.

As I grew older, I realized that this was my dad's new way of making decisions—he didn't always consider what was best for me, but as a single parent, he determined what worked best logistically to keep our household running smoothly. That was why we never had a dog— although I begged, pleaded, and cajoled, he just shook his head. We were rarely home, he said, and it wouldn't be fair to the dog. It was also why I never had a swing set or a bike—after all, why should he spend money on these things when I spent most of my time at Lizzy's and she already had a swing set *and* an extra bike? It didn't matter that the bike was old and rusty. It was also why I was never a Girl Scout. Every fall, I longed to join the Girl Scouts. The poster announcing regis-tration showed girls doing all kinds of fun activities—everything from hiking and camping to making crafts and selling cookies. Not to mention, the neat uniforms they wore and the cool patches they earned. Unfortunately, Lizzy said it looked boring and silly, and because she wasn't interested, I had no way of going to the meetings. Needless to say, I spent my childhood afternoons at the McAllister house, where the activities included a quick snack and a prompt ushering outside so Mrs. McAllister could watch her soaps on their TV—another luxury we didn't have.

One afternoon, after we'd been sent out into the late October sunshine so she could watch *The Guiding Light*, Lizzy pulled a piece of chalk out of her pocket. "Potsie?"

"Okay," I said reluctantly, and she knelt down and started to draw a hopscotch board on the sidewalk.

"I heard my mother tell Mrs. McGuiness that Mrs. Jones has cancer."

"That's what my mom had!" I said in surprise.

"I know," Lizzy said, "so I kept listening and I heard her say cancer happens when your cells grow like crazy."

"Why do they do that?"

"No one knows," she said, stepping gingerly

inside the board to draw the numbers, "but my mother thinks it's punishment."

"For what?" I asked, frowning.

"Something you've done that nobody knows about, not even the priest because it's so bad you can't tell him—she said Mrs. Jones must've done something bad."

"My mom didn't do anything bad," I said, still frowning.

"Are you sure?" Lizzy asked without looking up. "Maybe she did something before you were born . . . or when you were a baby and you didn't know it."

"Like what?" I asked doubtfully.

"Maybe she took something that didn't belong to her or kissed someone she shouldn't have or thought bad thoughts."

"You can catch cancer for thinking bad thoughts?" I asked incredulously. If that was true, I was in real trouble!

Lizzy shrugged. "No one knows what causes it." She tossed the remaining stub of chalk into the bushes. "Wanna go first?"

"Okay," I said, my head spinning with this new revelation. *What bad thing could my mom have done that God punished her with cancer? My dad had said she didn't go to confession very often— maybe that was because she did something she couldn't tell the priest. And if you could get cancer for thinking bad thoughts, would I catch it too?*

I tossed my marker—a crumble of brick I'd found next to the curb—into the "1" box and halfheartedly hopped around it. Then I turned around and started to hop back, but when I leaned down to pick it up, I lost my balance and the heel of my scuffed Mary Jane touched the line.

"My turn!" Lizzy announced happily, stepping up to throw a smooth, flat stone she'd found at the beach.

I sighed, knowing I had a long wait ahead of me. Lizzy, I'd learned, had no mercy when it came to competition—she'd already proven she could run faster, swing higher, and jump farther than me, and she was a perfectionist when it came to hopscotch.

I sat on the grass, watching her hop up and down the board, stopping each time to pick up her marker with the grace and agility of a gymnast, and all the time wondering what bad thing my mom had done. Finally, I leaned back and looked up at the blue October sky, hoping God would give me the answer. When I finally looked back at the game, Lizzy had tossed her stone into the "8" box and was getting ready to hop, but before she did, she glanced over to see if I was paying attention, and when she realized I was, she picked up her stone and said, "Your turn."

I stood up, wondering if she would've kept going if I hadn't noticed her stone was on the line. And then I wondered if she'd already cheated when I wasn't paying attention. Suddenly, I felt oddly empowered by the realization that Lizzy wasn't perfect, and with new confidence, I tossed my crumble of brick into the "2" box and kept right on going until I won.

Over the years, I've often wondered how my life would be different if Mrs. McAllister hadn't brought a tuna casserole over on that Friday afternoon. Who would've stepped up and helped me muddle through life? Who would've been my best friend? Would that friend have wanted to go hiking and camping with the Girl Scouts? Would she have been by my side all through school, explaining the things my mom wasn't there to explain? Lizzy had provided me with answers to so many of life's puzzles and mysteries—queries my father avoided—and although some of Lizzy's answers were a little misguided—because her source, her mother, was a little misguided—she always did her best.

Without Lizzy, I would've been scared silly the first time I saw a spot of blood on my underwear when I was twelve; without Lizzy, I would never have understood what the priest meant when he condemned masturbation. "Your hand does *not* fall off," she assured me in a knowing whisper; and without Lizzy and Mrs. McAllister, I never would've taken so fully to heart the Catholic Church's view of divorce—after all, Lizzy's father might be spending his afterlife rotting in hell, but her mother—who refused to give him a divorce—had her lofty sights set on heaven, where I hoped my mom was spending eternity too.

When I look back now at my childhood and consider how my life unfolded—one choice triggering another—I can't help but wonder how different it might have been if my first choice had been different. If I hadn't met Lizzy, I wouldn't have gone to St. Clement; and if I hadn't gone to St. Clement, I wouldn't have been so strongly influenced by the beliefs of Mrs. McAllister and the nuns; I wouldn't have been so consumed by guilt and not sinning.

And I never would have met Drew McIntyre.

Chapter 2

I was sixteen the first time Drew reached for my hand as we walked along the river, and I was barely seventeen the first time he lifted up my plaid uniform skirt and pressed against me, his cold hands slipping under my wool sweater, searching for more than warmth. Moments earlier, I'd been waiting for Lizzy, but then Drew had come out of the locker room, his hair wet from showering, and smiled as he pulled me outside into the darkness. He led me behind the building and I could feel the cold bricks penetrating the thin cotton of my underwear as he pulled the elastic waistband away from my stomach and slipped his hand inside.

"Not here, Drew," I whispered.

"Why not?" he murmured, kissing my neck.

"Because I want it to be somewhere special."

"This is special—behind ole St. Clement's."

"No, it's not."

"C'mon, Sal, I want you so much," he murmured.

"Lizzy's going to wonder where I am. I'm going to miss my ride."

"I'll give you a ride," he whispered, pushing his boxers down just far enough so I could feel how swollen he was. "You keep telling me you're going to, Sal, and then you never do. All the guys think I . . ."

"I don't care what the guys think."

Drew stopped and held my face in his hands and I breathed in. He smelled like soap and mint gum. "You know I love you, Sal," he said, sounding hurt. "Don't you love me?"

"Of course I . . ."

"Then show me . . ."

Through the blur of tears, I watched the last remnants of the fiery orange sun slip behind the black November horizon, and as Drew pushed himself deep and hard inside me, I felt the cold, rough bricks scraping my bare skin like sandpaper.

The first time I laid eyes on Drew McIntyre, I was sitting on the bleachers next to Lizzy, watching the boys' basketball team run suicides. "Who's that?" I asked.

Lizzy looked up from her biology textbook. "Where?"

"Over there," I said, nodding to a tall boy leaning against the wall, catching his breath. He had short dark hair and his cheeks were a swirl of ruddy Irish pink from his jawline to his cheekbones.

"Oh. That's Drew something . . . I can't remember," Lizzy said indifferently.

"Is he new?" I asked, frowning. "Because I

haven't seen him before." In a school as small as St. Clement we all knew one another—after all, we'd been going to school together since we were in kindergarten.

Lizzy nodded. "He just moved here." She frowned and then remembered I'd been out with a cold. "That's what happens when you're out sick—you miss all the excitement."

"I guess so."

"Don't waste your time, Sal. The snobs already have their claws out."

"That figures," I said, knowing exactly to whom Lizzy was referring.

She looked at me. "Seriously, Sal," she said, "you can do *so* much better."

I shrugged. "He's cute."

"He's a jock," she said dismissively, as if athletic boys weren't worth our time or consideration.

I rolled my eyes. If there was one thing Lizzy did that drove me crazy, it was label people. I don't think she even knew she did it. Jocks, nerds, snobs, and preppies—no one was above judgment. One time, after she'd neatly pigeonholed everyone in our class, I'd asked her which category I fell in, and without skipping a beat, she grinned and said, *friend*. I laughed, relieved, but still worried—after all, when you have a friend who talks about other people, and you know you have some of the same traits as those people, you can't help but wonder if your friend says stuff about you when you're not around.

To this day, she still does it, although not as much. I like to think my years of reminding her "Judge not, that ye be not judged" have rubbed off. As we've grown older, the categories have changed too. Now, with a shake of her salt and pepper head, she tags people as conservative, liberal, lush, bitch, loser—or the ultimate condemnation—*total* loser. In spite of this flaw (and sin, I affectionately remind), I thank God every day for my sweet, annoying, fun-loving, philosophical, wise, solemn friend. I cannot remember a time when Lizzy wasn't in my life. I will always contend that she is the sister my parents never gave me; she is my ally and my confidante; and I truly believe, without her, I wouldn't have survived the storms that have rumbled my way. I also have to admit that, ninety-nine percent of the time, she's right about people. She was definitely right about Drew—not only was he a jock, he was a total loser. Unfortunately, I had to find that out for myself.

When I came around the corner of the building, Mrs. McAllister's old Buick was puffing exhaust from its rusty tailpipe and Lizzy was running back into the school.

"I'm over here," I called.

She turned around. "Where the hell have you been? I've been all through the school." Then she saw Drew emerge from the shadows, too, and frowned. "What were you doing?"

"Nothing," I said, shivering as I walked past her. I got into the backseat and made sure my skirt was tucked under me—I didn't want to leave any evidence on Mrs. McAllister's light blue fabric.

"Is that Drew McIntyre?" Mrs. McAllister asked, squinting through the swirl of smoke she'd just exhaled and nodding to the figure who was standing under the streetlamp, unlocking his car.

"It is," Lizzy confirmed, sliding into the front and glaring back at me.

Mrs. McAllister looked in her rearview mirror and tamped the ashes of her cigarette into her overflowing ashtray. "You girls know better than to let a boy take you behind the building," she said casually. It was more of a statement than a question, so I pretended not to hear her; then it took all I had not to let the tears welling up in my eyes breach the dam of my lower lids. I stared out the window, clenched my jaw, and watched the blurry taillights of Drew's car as he pulled out of the parking lot.

When I'd turned sixteen, I'd stopped staying at Lizzy's house after school—although I probably needed more supervision at this point in my life than I had when I was little. Mrs. McAllister, who'd recently taken a job at the new Stop & Shop, was working longer hours and picking us up later, too, so now, after she picked us up, she just dropped me off at home.

"Thank you for the ride," I said, climbing out. "See you tomorrow, Lizzy," I added, waving as if nothing had happened.

While I fumbled with my key, they waited for me to turn on the light—the signal that I was all set. Then I opened the door, waved one last time, and slid down the inside of the door with tears streaming down my cheeks. *How had I let it happen?*

Chapter 3

After that day, there was no turning back, and even though I was riddled with guilt, I never tried to stop it. On more than one occasion, Drew picked me up right after Mrs. McAllister dropped me off and we drove down to the river. Drew always tried to convince me to let him come inside instead, but I refused. *What if my father comes home?*

"I love you so much, Sal," he murmured, leaning across me to recline my seat.

"Drew, we can't keep doing this," I protested. "I'm going to get pregnant."

"No, you're not," he said, pulling a small square package out of his pocket. "Put it on for me, Sal."

I shook my head. "No, it's wrong. Everything about this is wrong."

He kissed me softly. "How can it be wrong," he whispered, "when it feels so right?"

"It just is," I said, slowly relenting and kissing him back. It wasn't that I didn't love him—he was sweet and handsome and all the girls in school—all except Lizzy—would kill to be where I was and I didn't want to lose him.

"*You're* crazy," Lizzy whispered in the library one day when I finally admitted what was going on. "You, of all people. You've lived your whole life with the goal of getting into heaven so you can see your mom again, and now you're going to let it all go . . . for what? For *him?*"

"I'll just go to confession," I countered, even though my faith was on pretty shaky ground. I was sure God would see right through my insincere repentance, but I didn't care. I'd be intimate with Drew again in a heartbeat.

"Are you at least being careful?"

"Most of the time."

Lizzy's eyes grew wide. "*Most* of the time?"

"It's a sin to use birth control too," I said dismissively. "You're damned if you do and you're damned if you don't."

"You'll be damned if you get pregnant!" she hissed.

I rolled my eyes. What else could I do? She was right, of course, but I didn't want to hear it. I felt like I'd been disappointing myself my whole life. How could a person live completely without sin? It was impossible, and yet I was consumed with the effort. I had finally reached a point where I didn't even feel like trying. Life was a struggle with little joy. The feeling of well-being was so elusive and no amount of prayer made it less so. After my mom died, I'd watched my dad grow old, the years slipping by; he never seemed happy again. He got up every morning, ate a bowl of cold cereal or a piece of toast, and drank a cup of black coffee; he dropped Lizzy and me off at school, went to his accounting job in Boston, and when he came home, we ate one of five alternating dinners: chicken potpie, Swanson frozen dinners—Salisbury steak for him, macaroni and cheese for me—hamburgers fried in a pan, fish sticks, spaghetti, or, on rare occasions, pizza. Afterward, he washed the dishes, and while I dried, we talked briefly about our day. Then he watched the news (we'd finally gotten a small black-and-white TV) or read the paper while I did homework. The next day, he (we) did it all over again. He never dated or went out with friends. He never read the Bible or went to church (I went to mass and confession with Lizzy every week). He didn't drink or enjoy fine food, and we never went on a vacation. I had no idea how he would react if he found out about Drew. In my whole life, he'd never raised his voice or his hand to me—probably because I was always trying to be good—but this was different. All he knew about Drew was that he was one of my class-mates. He had no idea what was going on after school, and when I tried to imagine his reaction, I saw his tired face shadowed with disappoint-ment—which would be worse than if he raised his voice.

Lizzy and I began our senior year with high hopes—she was on track to be valedictorian, and although colleges all over New England were sending her letters, she had her heart set on our very own Lawrence Memorial Hospital School of Nursing. I was interested in becoming a teacher, and maybe even a writer someday. I was not far behind Lizzy in class rank—our school may have been small, but we were competitive—and although I was applying to several schools in New England, I was praying I'd get into Boston College. Sister Mary Agnes had said it was a really good school, and if I went there I could save money by commuting with my dad.

In late March, acceptance letters started to trickle in. Lizzy had already been accepted to Lawrence, so she didn't even open her letters; if it came in a large envelope—and all of them did—she knew she'd gotten in. The white and maroon envelope from Boston College was last to come for me, and along with it, a generous scholarship. For the first time in my life, I felt truly happy. My life was finally coming together—I had a boyfriend I loved, and who loved me, and now, I had a future full of hope and promise.

One month later, I missed my period. "What the heck?" I muttered anxiously every time I went to the bathroom.

"I warned you," Lizzy said. "If you play with fire, you're gonna get burned."

"Is that all you've got?" I asked in dismay.

"What more do you want?"

"I don't know, how about some friendly reassurance or consolation?"

She searched my eyes. "The only way you're going to know for sure is if you go to the doctor . . . or wait."

Neither was feasible. There was no way I could go to my doctor, and I didn't want to wait—I was terrified and I wanted to know now! All I could think was that everything I was hoping for—going to college and teaching and writing—was being taken from me. And it was all because of my own foolishness. "Maybe this is God's way of punishing me," I said sullenly.

Lizzy didn't reply. She didn't have to—I could see it in her eyes. It was as if I'd taken the words right out of her mother's mouth.

"It'll be okay, Sal," she said, pulling me into a hug. "You've been under a lot of pressure with applications and waiting to hear. You're probably just late."

Chapter 4

"This cannot be happening," Drew said angrily. "We used protection."

"Not every time."

"Well, you can't go through with it."

"What am I supposed to do?"

"I don't know," he said, staring out the window. "It'll ruin everything. I have a full scholarship and my future is riding on it."

"I have plans too."

"C'mon, Sal," he said, his voice growing softer. "We don't have to go through with this. Joe knows a doctor. . . ."

"I'm *not* having an abortion," I said. "I'm not heaping another sin on top of everything else I've done."

He stared out the window. "I'm not ready to be a father. Please think about it, Sal. No one will ever know and we can just get on with our lives."

"God will know."

"Yeah, and after we go to confession, He'll forgive us."

"It's not that simple, Drew, and besides, if we go to confession, the priest will know, so you can't say 'no one will know.' "

Drew shook his head. "Sally, please. Just say you'll think about it. If we end this now, you'll be able to go to Boston like you want and I'll be able to go to Villanova . . . and we can still be friends."

I looked up in surprise. "Is that what you want—*to be friends?* I thought you loved me. I thought you wanted to get married."

"I *do* want to get married," he said, stroking my cheek. "Just not yet. In fact, I thought we might take a break while we're in college. You know, see other people—make sure we're making the right decision. Even though I know you're the one." But the way he said it made me think he was just trying to get me to cooperate. Unfortunately, it was too late—for the first time, I was seeing right through him.

I shook my head. "I can't believe you're saying that," I whispered, tears stinging in my eyes. I looked out the window, feeling utterly alone.

"I don't mean forever, Sal," Drew said softly. "Just a break. I'm sure we'll get back together."

I bit my lip and then looked him straight in the eye. "I am *not* having an abortion. I will have this baby on my own if I have to."

He slammed his hand down on the steering wheel, making me jump. "I can't believe you're doing this to me."

"I'm not doing anything to you," I said. "We've done this together. We've created a new life, and I'm just as terrified as you are. I'm just as disappointed that our dreams will have to be put on hold, but our baby deserves dreams and a future, too, and I truly believe, if your parents knew, they'd agree."

"Don't be so sure about that," he said angrily.

Drew was right—his parents were livid. They couldn't believe I'd duped their only son into marriage by getting pregnant, and to make things worse, he let them believe it. They told him I had humiliated him—*and* them—and they offered no assistance except to say he could keep the old car they'd passed on to him.

My father, on the other hand, took the news better than anyone. Although he was concerned and disappointed that I'd have to put off college, he seemed almost happy at the prospect of being a grandpa.

Soon after graduation, Drew and I were married in a quiet midweek ceremony. There was no fanfare, no flowing white gown or dashing black tux, no festive reception or sunny honeymoon. Every-thing about it was discreet—as if discretion was a lesson we both needed to learn.

My father cleaned out the cramped, dusty apartment above our garage he'd been using for storage and helped Drew find a job at the accounting firm where he worked, but when he offered to carpool, Drew declined. He preferred to drive himself—it was his time to think. But as the weeks dragged by, I realized he really meant it was his time for freedom, especially since he came home long after I'd gone to bed.

The first two months of our fragile marriage were rocky at best, but halfway through the third month we hit rock bottom. It was a hot morning in early August and I was standing at my register at Stop & Shop where Mrs. McAllister had gotten Lizzy and me jobs, when I felt a sharp pain in my abdomen. I clutched my belly, crying out in pain, and Lizzy looked over from her register. "What's the matter, Sally?" she shouted, but I couldn't even speak, and afterward, all I could remember was feeling white-hot pain, as if someone was stabbing me, and then seeing the blur of Lizzy's blood red uniform jacket floating above me.

When I finally came to, I was lying in a hospital bed.

"Hey, kiddo," my dad said softly.

"Hey," I replied weakly.

"How're you feeling?"

"Not so good."

"You just missed Lizzy," he said. "She's been here all afternoon. She said she'd come back tomorrow."

I nodded and then noticed the look in my dad's eyes. "What's the matter?" I asked, frowning. All I could remember was the excruciating pain—which had been dulled by a heavy dose of medicine.

He bit his lip. "You lost the baby, Sal."

"I did?" Tears sprang to my eyes as I ran my hands over my abdomen. "Why?"

"It just happens sometimes," he said softly. "Your mom had two miscarriages before she had you."

"She did?"

He nodded.

"Does Drew know?"

My father shook his head. "I don't know where he is."

Tears streamed down the sides of my cheeks and trickled into my ears. "Why do bad things keep happening to me?" I whispered.

My dad sat on the edge of the bed. "Everyone has things happen, Sal—it's not just you. It's part of life. It may feel like the end of the world, but it's not. This will pass, like all things, and your body . . . and your heart will heal."

I looked out the window, tears still streaming down my cheeks. "I already loved it, Dad," I whispered. "I couldn't wait for it to come. Nothing else mattered."

"I know," he said, gently pushing back my hair. "I know just how you feel."

He cleared his throat and looked away and I sensed there was more. "What?"

He swallowed. "The doctor said there's a chance you won't be able to have children."

Fresh tears welled up in my eyes and I clenched my fists. How could this be? Obviously, I'd brought it *all* on myself. God was punishing me, and my sentence was lifelong. I had callously committed one sin after another, and now, God was unleashing His fury on His selfish, wayward child. Everything that was happening to me was exactly what had been drilled into my head all through school: My sin—compounded by weeks of skipping confession and Communion—was finally being answered with punishment.

"God is punishing me," I whispered.

"What?" my dad asked, frowning.

"For everything I've done."

"That's not how He works, Sal."

"How do you know? You don't even go to church."

"I may not go to church, but it doesn't mean I don't believe."

I shook my head. "I'm sorry, Dad," I said tearfully.

"It's okay, Sally," he said earnestly, squeezing my hand. "Life's a journey, kiddo," he said softly. "We all make mistakes. Hopefully, we learn and move on . . . and God forgives us."

I nodded, although I wasn't convinced. At the tender age of eighteen, I'd already made a mess of my life and there was no way God was going to forgive me.

When Drew finally showed up, he made a veiled attempt at being sympathetic, but it seemed more like he was hiding his glee . . . and then it hit me—if I was no longer pregnant, he must think he's free. It was only August; maybe he was hoping he could still go to college.

"You can try," I said wearily when he finally got up the courage to ask. I was tired of trying to make things work. Besides, if I let him go, maybe he'd stop acting like a caged animal . . . and maybe he'd come home ready to be married.

Drew called Villanova that afternoon, but they told him it was already too late. They explained that he could reapply for the spring semester, but because he wasn't playing basketball that winter, he wouldn't be eligible for an athletic scholarship.

Drew was despondent. I hadn't realized his scholarship was the only way he could go to college. I knew his father had lost his job—that was why they'd moved to Medford—and although his dad had found a new job, his parents hadn't recovered from the lost income and they hadn't been able to set anything aside for college.

Needless to say, Drew and I were in the same place we'd been before. The only difference was that the fragile thread that had held us together— our baby—was gone. I tried to put things in a positive light. I tried to tell Drew—as my father had told me—that this would pass, that things would get better, but he didn't want to hear it.

In the weeks that followed, he barely looked

at me. I was the reason his world had come crashing down and he felt nothing but resentment toward me . . . and he made it very clear he wanted his freedom.

Unfortunately, in the eyes of the church—and in *my* heart—divorce was a sin.

Chapter 5

Drew approached the church about having our marriage annulled but was told that, for couples who'd been married in the church by a priest, annulment was not an option. As the Bible says: *"What God has joined together, let no man put asunder."*

I struggled with this. Why did we have to spend our lives legally bound to each other when we would never have a future together? It made no sense. Finally, I decided if this was God's punishment and my penance—not pennies like Lizzy had told me when we were little—I would just have to deal with it. I was so disillusioned by relationships and marriage anyway, I didn't think I'd ever fall in love again, never mind get married.

Drew and I separated soon after. He moved to an apartment with two high school friends and started working at the textile mill, and I moved out of our apartment over the garage and back into my old bedroom. I continued working at the grocery store and I saved every penny. After learning that scholarships could be rescinded, I wasn't taking any chances. If I ever had the opportunity to attend college again, I was going to have some money saved.

"You are freakin' kidding me!" Lizzy exclaimed as each injustice was served.

"It's what I deserve," I muttered miserably.

"You don't deserve this," she countered angrily.

Although Lizzy was overwhelmed with schoolwork and hardly ever went to mass anymore (I went every week without fail), we usually spent Saturday nights together. Sometimes we went to a movie, and other times we made popcorn and snuck a bottle of Boone's Farm up to her room—although it wasn't very hard to sneak anything past Mrs. McAllister anymore. Her failed marriage —and her obsessive hatred for her husband—had made her increasingly cynical and bitter, and she'd not only taken up smoking, she'd also graduated from an occasional glass of wine to drinking vodka and tonic every night. Lizzy tried to get her to ease up, but that only seemed to make her more determined to drink. I watched her slow, steady decline in amazement. Mrs. McAllister— who'd once been so pious, perfect, and self-righteous—was now sad, self-absorbed, and consumed by hatred and bitterness.

"Maybe we should've tried to get our parents together when we were younger. Then they wouldn't be so alone and unhappy now," Lizzy mused, sipping the flavor of the night—*Tickled Pink*.

"Ha!" I said, leaning back on a stack of pillows.

"That would never have happened. Your mother is still married to your father, so she could never get involved with someone new—she'd be committing adultery."

Lizzy shook her head. "It's the same with you and Drew. What are you going to do? Stay married to him your whole life and never fall in love again?"

"I guess so," I said, reaching for the popcorn.

"How do you know you won't meet someone?"

"I don't, but I made my bed—literally—so now I have to lie in it."

"That is such a load of crap," Lizzy said, pouring more wine into our cups. "The church is wrong."

"What?" I said, feigning shock. "Did I just hear you question the Catholic Church?" With mock concern, I looked at the ceiling. "Watch out for lightning."

Lizzy rolled her eyes. "They should give you an annulment."

"Well, they're not," I said, dropping a piece of popcorn into my mouth.

"Then you should get a divorce."

"I can't do that," I said resignedly. "If we get divorced, we'll be shunned."

"God will forgive you."

"How do you know?" I asked.

"Because I honestly don't think He's the mean, unforgiving ogre the church makes him out to be. The regimented rules of the church are based on the teachings of the Old Testament. After Jesus came along, everything changed—the New Testament is about love, acceptance, kindness, *and* forgiveness."

I took a sip of my wine. "So you're saying we should turn our backs on everything we've been taught?"

"Not everything, just the things that are ridiculously outdated."

"Sounds risky," I teased. "What would your mother think if she heard you say that?"

Lizzy waved her hand dismissively. "My mother is a perfect example of how the church can ruin someone's life. I don't think people are meant to live guilt-ridden lives and confess to a priest every time they do something wrong."

"You're such a free thinker," I teased.

"Someone has to do it," Lizzy said with a grin as she dropped a piece of popcorn into her mouth.

"How are your classes going?"

"Okay," she said. "Although I'm going to fail anatomy."

"No, you're not," I said, rolling my eyes. Lizzy had always been overly dramatic when it came to grades. She'd never scored anything lower than an A-minus, but if she even had one point taken off, she insisted she was failing.

"I am," she countered.

"Well, if it's the male part of the anatomy, I have a little experience with that."

"Ha! No! It's the *inside* part of the anatomy."

"Ah," I said with a laugh. "The heart—well, mine is broken, so I can't help you with that."

"Speaking of male parts, though," she said with an impish grin. "There's a guy in my class who's kind of cute."

I sat up in surprise. Lizzy had never taken an interest in any boy—*ever*. "No way!"

"Way," she said, still grinning.

"Tell me more."

"That's all."

"There must be more. Does he have a name?"

"Simon . . ." she said, and I raised my eyebrows. She took a sip of her wine and tried to suppress a wicked grin. "Simon Cohen."

I shook my head. "*You* are going to put your mother in an early grave."

Chapter 6

Lizzy and I received First Communion on Mother's Day, 1954. We were both the age of reason—seven—just as Lizzy had predicted. A prerequisite to receiving Communion is to have first participated in a Sacrament of Penance (or *pennies,* as I continued to tease Lizzy). I will never forget my first confession. I can still feel the perspiration trickling down the sides of my face as I knelt in the hot, dimly lit confessional, trying to remember what I was supposed to do . . . and the order in which I was supposed to do it. My heart pounded as I waited. Finally, I heard the swish of heavy fabric, followed by a whoosh and a click as the little window above my head slid open. I swallowed, my heart racing as I crossed myself.

"Forgive me, Father, for I have sinned," I whispered.

"What are your sins, my child?"

I felt my face flush with shame. "I-I . . . sometimes think bad thoughts . . . and I often take a cookie without asking."

On the other side of the screen, there was silence as my heart continued to pound—I was certain I was damned to hell. Finally, the priest cleared his throat. "Is that all?"

"Yes, Father."

"Are you truly sorry?"

"Yes."

"I would like you to say one rosary."

I nodded, then remembered he couldn't see me. "Yes, Father," I said.

"You may go."

"Thank you," I whispered, and as I started to stand up, I suddenly realized what I'd forgotten. I fell back to my knees and crossed myself and then nervously fumbled with the latch on the ancient wooden door before escaping into the light and breathing again.

The following Sunday, Mrs. McAllister ushered Lizzy and me to the back of the church, where all the second graders were lined up to receive First Communion. As we waited, I tried to hide behind Lizzy because my dress—unlike all the other white dresses and suits—was light blue. I'd begged my dad to let me get a new dress, but he said it wasn't practical to buy a dress for one occasion and never wear it again. I insisted I'd wear it again, but there was no changing his mind. He promised to come to the service, though, and then reminded me that he wouldn't be able to receive Communion because he wasn't Catholic.

I frowned—why couldn't my dad receive Communion? He believed Jesus was his savior. Wasn't he a child of God too? It was upsetting, but instead of pressing him for an answer, I nodded—I was just glad he was coming.

As we walked into the sanctuary, I scanned the sea of sober faces, looking for my one true supporter—my faithful fan—my dad. When I finally saw him, sitting in the back pew, he smiled and I waved; then he nodded for me to pay attention. I nodded and turned just in time to not bump into Lizzy and make the whole line of second graders fall like dominos. Looking back now, I realize how appropriate that would've been. I don't believe seven-year-olds have the capacity to truly grasp something as profound as the sacred meaning of Holy Communion. When I first felt the Eucharist dissolving on my tongue, I knew it was symbolic, but I was seven years old and I couldn't help but wonder what part of Christ's body had been given to me.

When the service ended, I found my dad waiting in the back of the church. Everyone else was excitedly heading off to celebrate with their families. Since it was Mother's Day, even Lizzy was going to a restaurant with her grandparents. Mrs. McAllister invited us to come with them and I looked up hopefully, but my dad just shook his head.

"No, thank you," he said. "You can go, Sal," he said, nodding to me, but I clung to his hand.

"No . . . I don't want to go without you," I said, trying to hide my disappointment.

Through all the years that followed, Lizzy and I continued to attend catechism every Wednesday afternoon—this was in addition to the religious classes we had during school. My favorite nun was Sister Mary Agnes—she was young and pretty and had a wonderful sense of humor and she was always reminding me to not take life so seriously.

I prayed I'd have her for a teacher, but I always ended up with Sister Mary Frances, who was ancient and wrinkled, never smiled, and kept a ruler tucked into the belt of her habit—which she rapped mercilessly on our knuckles when we failed to recite our most recent assignment. There were no blurred lines in Sister Mary Frances's teachings. The rules, rituals, and sacraments of the Catholic Church were not to be taken lightly. If you sinned, you would be punished. End of story.

I was blessed to have Sister Mary Agnes twice during those years. Once when I was in fourth grade, preparing for Confirmation, and again when I was in tenth grade. When I was in fourth, Sister Mary Agnes gave me a book about Joan of Arc. I went home and read it that very same night, and when I came in the next morning, I reported back that I loved the story of the young woman who, at seventeen, bravely led her French country-men in the fight to break the oppression forced on them by England . . . but, I added, it was a horrible and tragic injustice that she'd been found guilty of witchcraft and burned at the stake. I couldn't even imagine it! Sister Mary Agnes nodded in agreement and then whispered, "I think you should choose Joan for your Confirmation name." If she'd only known how appropriate it would turn out to be!

In tenth grade, I was blessed to have Sister Mary Agnes again—this time, for English, the class in which I was introduced to books like *Ulysses* and *Moby Dick* and *Pride and Prejudice*.

It's also when the seed to become a writer was first planted.

Chapter 7

I started taking classes at Boston College in the spring of 1966—although it was really late winter—and commuted daily into the city with my dad. Since I was still living at home, my life didn't change very much. The only big difference in my life was triggered by a change in Lizzy's: She started dating "that Jewish boy," as Mrs. McAllister called Simon (heaven forbid she use his name), so we only saw each other when we were both working or when we went to the same mass—which wasn't often. I went every week, sometimes more than once, but Lizzy's attendance had fallen off dramatically, leaving me to sit alone with my thoughts *and* my guilt.

As the weeks slipped by, I started to feel as if Lizzy and I were growing apart. We'd been closer than sisters growing up, so her absence left a gaping hole in my life. It also left me feeling neglected and a little jealous. I missed our Saturday nights watching *The Dating Game* or *My Three Sons* or *Get Smart*. I missed losing in backgammon or Scrabble—no matter what game we played, Lizzy still won. Her mind was always plotting two moves ahead while mine was trying to solve my current dilemma. One time, we played Scrabble and she used all of her tiles to make the word *highjack* (using the *g* I'd used to make *hug*), and because she'd strategically placed her tiles over pink and blue squares—and used all of them —she scored 374 points!

I also missed sipping Boone's Farm and talking late into the night. Lizzy's progressive way of thinking was spilling into every aspect of her life—from politics to current events and from the beliefs we'd been taught to the beliefs Simon had been taught. Unlike her mother, Lizzy was accepting of everyone, no matter what their race, religion, or sexual orientation. She was well ahead of her time, and although she still labeled people on occasion, she tried not to criticize.

As the weeks slipped by, Lizzy and I both became buried in homework—she in chemistry and biology and me in English Lit and accounting (my dad's idea). The weeks turned into months, and although I met new people at college—I was even asked out a couple times—my commuter status kept me away from campus at night and on weekends, so I didn't enjoy the camaraderie of dorm life or other social events. Needless to say, between schoolwork—I was doubling up on classes to catch up on my missed semester—and not being there, I didn't have the opportunity to build any lasting friendships.

The months quickly turned into years, and before we knew it, we were graduating—Lizzy with a degree in nursing and a job at Massachusetts General, and me with a BFA in English and my boring old job at Stop & Shop.

"You'll find something," Lizzy assured me. "You just need to finish your teaching certificate."

"I know," I said, nodding. I'd been planning on getting my certificate all along, but because I'd been taking accounting and business classes, the opportunity had slipped by. "I've actually applied for a new job—it's not teaching, but hopefully it will pay a little more than being a cashier."

"What is it?" Lizzy asked.

"Waitressing at the pub down by the river."

"When do you start?"

"The week after next."

"Perfect," she said with a slow smile.

I frowned. "Why is that perfect?"

"Simon and I are going to Nantucket for a week and we want you to come."

"You are?" I asked, frowning.

She nodded. "We're celebrating graduating."

I shook my head. "Oh, I don't think I want to go," I said, resisting. "I have a lot going on and I hate being a third wheel."

"You don't have that much going on and you won't be a third wheel. Besides, if you don't come, my mother won't let me go."

I rolled my eyes. "Your mother isn't going to stop you," I said. "You're an adult . . . *and* you have a real job."

"That's not the only reason we want you to come," Lizzy countered. "It'll just be more fun if you're there."

I eyed her skeptically. "I doubt it. Besides, it'll be awkward."

"No, it won't," Lizzy assured. "Besides, you'll love Nantucket. You need to get out of this stupid town."

I shook my head, but Lizzy kept pressing until I finally agreed.

We caught the ferry from Hyannis late Saturday afternoon, and by the time the island came into view, the sun was setting. I leaned on the railing, feeling the misty spray of the ocean on my cheeks. I'd never seen the ocean beyond Boston Harbor before and now I was riding on top of its beautiful, undulating blueness. I watched two gorgeous white sailboats skimming across the waves, their sails billowing in the golden sunlight; then I turned to watch the lights blinking to life across the island. I was captivated. I'd lived my entire life in Medford, and although I'd seen pictures of other places, I never imagined the amazing beauty that existed beyond my home-town.

"It's pretty, isn't it?" Lizzy said, standing next to me, the wind whipping her long, wavy dark hair.

I nodded. "I'm going to live here someday," I said, the words spilling unexpectedly from my mouth.

Lizzy laughed and tucked her wild hair behind her ears. "There's no reason you couldn't."

As the ferry docked, Simon hitched his backpack on his shoulders, and Lizzy and I picked up our bags. We walked up the cobblestone street toward town and stopped outside a small restaurant to look at the menu. Simon said the food was really good and suggested we have dinner because he didn't know how much food—if any—was at the house. That was all the convincing Lizzy and I needed—we were starving!

We sat at a table near the window and Simon ordered a bottle of wine. Almost immediately, the waitress brought it over and opened it at our table. She poured a small amount into a glass and offered it to Simon. With a solemn expression, he swirled it, sniffed, took a sip, and nodded to the waitress. She poured a small amount into each of our glasses and then set the bottle in a chilled ceramic holder. "You're such a profes-sional," Lizzy teased.

Simon laughed and held up his glass. "To graduating!" he said, and we clinked our glasses. I took a sip—the golden wine had a pleasant oak flavor—it wasn't sweet and fruity like Boone's Farm—*and* it was in a real glass!

For the first time in my life, I wasn't drinking cheap wine out of a paper cup!

We looked at our menus and Lizzy dared me to order something I'd never had before, which was easy because I hadn't had anything that was on the menu. My experience with seafood was frozen fish sticks and canned tuna, so when our dinners came and I took a bite of the tender pan-seared "drunken" scallop—so named because it was swimming in a pool of whiskey reduction and melted butter—I thought I'd died and gone to heaven. "Oh, my," I murmured. "This is better than sex."

"That's just because you've never had good sex," Lizzy teased, and I laughed. Leave it to my old friend to speak the sad truth.

"And I probably never will," I said regretfully. "But at least I can always have drunk scallops," I added brightly.

After dinner, which included a second bottle of wine and sweet berry cobbler, Simon arranged for a taxi. I felt myself sway slightly as we waited outside, and when the driver pulled up, Lizzy helped me into the back while Simon sat in front with the driver. As we bumped along the cobblestone roads, the salty summer breeze drifted through the open windows, cooling my flushed cheeks. I looked up at the historic New England buildings and felt as if I were in a dream. I wasn't just on a vacation for the first time in my life—I was a world away from the life I'd always known.

I woke up the next morning with the same sweet breeze rustling the curtains of the lovely room that was mine for a week. I looked around, admiring the creamy white walls, and then blinked at the sunlight streaming through the two large windows. I climbed out of the bed and watched the gentle waves tumbling toward the beach.

"It's Simon's grandmother's house," Lizzy said, pouring coffee into three china cups. "Isn't it great?"

"It's unbelievable," I said, sliding a cup toward Simon and cradling the third in my hands.

"It is," Sally agreed, "but Simon says she's thinking of selling it."

"She is? Why?"

"Because she's getting older and she isn't able to come out anymore."

"Doesn't someone in your family want it?" I asked, turning to Simon.

He shook his head. "I spent every summer out here when I was a boy—I have so many wonderful memories, but I'm not in a position to buy it and my parents aren't interested—they say the ferry is a hassle and they don't want to have to maintain it."

"Maybe your grandmother will give it to you."

"Not likely," Simon said, laughing. "Little, old Jewish ladies usually don't give things away."

"That's a shame," I said, as if the little house was going to be my loss. "It's so beautiful."

"Well, hopefully the person who buys it will appreciate it as much as my grandmother did," Simon said. "We've shared many happy memories here."

I nodded thoughtfully.

As the week slipped by, we swam in the frigid ocean, walked along the beach, collected sea glass, seashells, and smooth stones—just like the one Lizzy had used when we'd played hop-scotch as girls—shopped in town, went out for ice cream, and read books we found on the shelves.

One morning I was up early, sitting on the porch, reading the book I'd found.

Lizzy peered sleepily through the screen door. "Don't you know you're supposed to sleep in on vacation?"

"I know," I said, smiling, "but this book is really good!"

"What's it about?" she asked, coming out in her nightgown and sitting across from me.

"It's about an affair between a married doctor stationed on the front lines during the Russian Revolution and a troubled young woman he meets at a party."

"Ah," Lizzy said knowingly. "The tragic affair of Yuri Zhivago and the beguiling Lara."

"You've read it?" I asked in surprise.

"I've seen the movie too."

"There's a movie?!"

Lizzy nodded.

I frowned. "You went without me?"

She laughed, trying to remember the circumstances. "I guess I did. It was last year—I must've gone with Simon. It was one of our first dates."

I nodded, immediately forgiving her. "Was it good? Did it follow the book?"

"It was wonderful. Sad, though." She looked to see where I was. "I don't want to ruin it for you," she said. "You have to finish before we can talk about it."

I nodded. "I have to finish *today* since we're leaving tomorrow."

"I know," she said gloomily. She paused. "Aren't you glad you came?"

"I'm very glad. You were right—I *do* love it here."

"I knew you would."

Chapter 8

Returning to Medford was like returning to prison—the prison that was my life. Within an hour of saying hello to my dad and unpacking my bag, I was standing at my register, ringing up groceries. I glanced over at the next register—the one that had been Lizzy's—and saw a new girl standing there. She couldn't have been more than sixteen. I sighed. No more Lizzy. No more making faces or rolling our eyes at each other when a customer came through with an overflowing cart or complaining about the price of an item. No more fun—as if working as a cashier could ever be fun, but Lizzy had, at least, made it tolerable. How would I bear it now? My life's calling couldn't possibly be ringing up groceries, and I was certain it wasn't waitressing either.

My first few nights working at the pub were weeknights, so they were slow and uneventful, but, as with any new job, it took some getting used to. Memorizing the specials was my biggest challenge. That, and remembering to make sure everyone at my assigned tables was happy. I'd rarely gone out to dinner when I was growing up, so I wasn't familiar with the little things that were expected of waitresses, but I was very glad the pub wasn't as fancy as the restaurant we'd gone to on Nantucket—I don't think I could've ever opened a bottle of wine at someone's table. I was accustomed to screw tops, not corkscrews!

On Saturday, I finished my shift at the store, slipped off my red jacket, and slipped on my black apron. I walked to the restaurant, and when I pulled open the employees' entrance, I found the kitchen already bustling. "Sally, we need you on booths four, five, and six right now!" Jill shouted as the door to the dining room swung closed behind her.

I found my time card, punched in, and reached into my apron for my notepad. "There's no time for that," Jill scolded when she came back through the doors and saw me jotting down the specials. "Memorize and get out there."

I glanced at the hastily scribbled list on the board and then hurried out to the bar, where two parties were already perusing menus and a third was being seated, but when I saw the last party, I stopped in my tracks. "Jill, I can't take booth six," I whispered urgently. "Can I please have a different table?"

"What?" she asked impatiently.

"I . . ."

But she didn't even let me finish. "No, Sally. Go take care of your tables," she commanded in an annoyed voice. I clenched my fists—I hated being ordered around and I was quickly starting to hate this job.

I took a deep breath, realized I hadn't looked in a mirror since I'd gotten up that morning, and smoothed my hair. I walked over to booths four and five, took their orders, brought their drinks, and then, with a pounding heart, turned my attention to booth six. "Hi, my name's Sally," I said. "I'm going to be your waitress tonight."

Drew was sitting the farthest in, looking at his menu, but when he heard my voice, he looked up, and although he didn't acknowledge me in front of his friends, the look in his eyes spoke volumes.

I waited patiently, feeling his eyes on me until his friends finally decided they weren't actually ready to order food, but they were ready to order beer. "Two pitchers," the one closest to me said.

"Great," I muttered as I walked away. "It's going to be a long night."

I quickly lost count of how many pitchers they ordered, but it was definitely enough to make them loud and obnoxious. The people at my other tables ordered, ate, and left, but Drew's table seemed to be settling in for the night. As the crowd diminished, Jill put me to work drying silverware. "Keep an eye on your table," she reminded. "Make sure they have everything they need." I nodded submissively and reached for a dishtowel, unable to shake the sinking feeling that this was going to be my life story—

submitting to bossy bosses. It's what I'd always done, so why should it ever change?

It was well past midnight when Drew's table finally cleared out. All of the other waitresses and busboys had already left, but since I was the low girl on the totem pole, I had to stay. I went out to the bar to clear their glasses and pitchers and wipe down the table, and as I collected my measly tip, I began to wonder if this job was even worth it. Maybe I should take up my dad's offer to work at his office—after all, I'd taken several accounting classes and they had to be worth something.

When I finally punched out, I went to the ladies' room to wash my hands. I couldn't wait to get home and take a shower—I felt sticky everywhere. I looked in the mirror and sighed—I was a sight! My tan was already fading and I looked tired and old—if that was possible for someone who'd just turned twenty-two. Drew had looked old, too—he wasn't the cute Irish boy I remembered. He was a man with a scruffy beard and unforgiving eyes.

"Good night, Saul," I said as I walked past the last cook who'd stayed to clean the grill.

"Good night, honey," he said with a friendly smile. "See you tomorrow."

I nodded, already dreading it.

As I walked outside, I felt an odd sensation wash over me—as if someone was watching, but when I turned to look, I didn't see anyone. I shook the feeling and kept walking—it was only a half a mile to my house, so I'd be home in no time, but as I turned at the corner of the building I felt a sudden chill as Drew stepped out of the shadows.

"How ya doin', Sal?" he slurred.

"I'm fine, Drew. How are you?" I started to walk more quickly and then wondered if I should run back inside.

"I've been better," he said, swaying slightly.

I nodded and tried to walk past him, but he stepped in front of me.

"Yeah, for some crazy reason, girls just aren't interested in guys who are married . . . I mean, they're interested . . . until they find out . . . and then, well, I may as well have leprosy or some other contagion."

I swallowed, barely able to breathe. He smelled like stale beer and cigarettes. All I wanted to do was get around him and go home, but when I tried, he stepped in front of me again. "Not to mention my job sucks," he said, bumping me. "Have you ever worked in a mill? Freakin' factory. Same shit every shitty day." Then his face lit up. "But I heard you went to college. How was it?"

"Fine," I said, trying to sound as if college wasn't all it was cracked up to be.

"No good jobs, though—just a sucky waitress job?"

I shrugged. His words made me feel even more like a failure.

"Any boyfriends?" he asked.

I looked away, refusing to make eye contact, but he forced my chin up to look at him. "I hope you haven't been cheating on me," he warned with venom in his eyes.

I tried to look away, but he wouldn't let me.

"Sorry I didn't introduce ya back there. Maybe I shoulda. . . . 'Hey, fellas,' I coulda said, 'this is my lovely wife.' " He laughed derisively and I shook my head and started to try to walk around him, but he stepped in front of me and leaned closer. "My wife," he whispered in my ear, his stale breath swirling around me. "You *are* still my wife, aren't you, Sal? Oh, that's right . . . you're going to be my wife *forever,* aren't you? And you damn well better not cheat on me."

I swallowed and looked away; then I heard a car start and realized Saul was leaving. I watched his headlights turn onto the street, and a moment later, he was gone.

"I need to get home, Drew," I said, trying again to walk around him, but this time he grabbed my arm.

"What's your hurry, Sal?"

"Don't do this, Drew," I said, trying to pull free.

"Don't do what?" he asked. "Don't do . . . *my*

wife?" He pressed against me and I tried to push him away, but he yanked me toward the back of the building.

"Stop it!" I cried.

"That's not what you used to say," he said, pressing against me. "You used to want it."

"I don't remember *that,*" I said defiantly.

"You begged me . . . 'C'mon, Drew,'" he said in a mockingly high voice. 'C'mon, Drew, fuck me . . . fuck me as hard as you can.'" I heard his belt buckle clink and felt him unzip his pants; then my heart pounded wildly as he lifted my skirt. "I think it's the least you can do, Sal," he whispered as he forcefully pushed down my underpants. "After all, no other girls want me, and since you're my wife, it's not a crime. In fact, now that I know where you are, I'm gonna hafta stop by more often so you can perform your wifely duties."

Hot tears streamed down my cheeks, and as Drew forced himself deep and hard inside me, I listened to the dark river swirling by.

Chapter 9

"That is *so* wrong," Lizzy said angrily. "He raped you!"

"It's not rape if I'm his wife," I said tearfully, my hands still shaking.

"*That* doesn't matter," Lizzy fumed. "Anytime a woman says no—whether she's his wife or not—it's rape. You don't lose your right to say no just because you're married. These aren't the Dark Ages, Sally. A woman isn't expected to submit to her husband just because he wants it, and besides, Drew is *only* your husband on paper."

There was that word again—*submit*. I had submitted to Drew. "I can't prove anything—it would be my word against his, and since we're married, I'm sure I'd lose."

"You shouldn't have showered."

"I *had* to shower—I felt disgusting."

"You should've gone right to the hospital," she said, shaking her head. "Sally, this is crazy—he raped you and he shouldn't get away with it!"

"Well, he's going to," I said resignedly. "And now he knows where I am, so he's going to come back so I can 'perform my wifely duties.' "

"He said *that?*" Lizzy was incredulous.

I nodded.

"Oh, Sally," she said, pulling me into a hug.

"That is *not* going to happen. Maybe your dad could pick you up after work," she said, thinking out loud.

I shook my head. "No, he goes to bed early, and besides, I don't want to tell him."

"Why not?"

"Because it will upset him and he hasn't been feeling well. I don't want to make things worse." I shook my head. "I can't believe I have to go back there."

"Don't go back," Lizzy said matter-of-factly. "Quit."

I wiped my eyes. "I don't even want to live here anymore. Nothing good ever happens to me here."

"If you don't want to live here, Sal, find somewhere else to live. No one said you have to live here. Go somewhere where Drew will never find you."

"Isn't that running away?"

"Not really. You've never been happy here, and starting fresh is a perfectly good reason to move. Go somewhere where you *will* be happy."

"What about my dad?"

"Your dad can take care of himself," she said dismissively. She had no patience for either of our parents.

I shook my head. "I'm all he has."

"That's *not* your fault, Sally. Your dad never tried to find someone new. It's not fair for him to depend on you. You only have one life, too, and you deserve to live it. Besides, if he misses you, he can move closer to where you are . . . where *you* are happy."

"Yeah," I said, laughing, my voice edged with sarcasm, "and where would that be?"

Lizzy considered for a minute and then a smile crossed her face. "There's only one place where I've seen you truly happy, Sal."

June

Liam tucked the bookmark Sally had given him between the pages, leaned back in his chair, and closed his eyes. He'd only read the first few chapters, but it was enough to realize that Sally's life hadn't been easy. He'd always thought his own life had been hard, but she had suffered just as much loss and heartache. *You never know what another person has gone—or is going—through.*

Hearing a commotion in the kitchen, he opened his eyes. "Everything okay in there, pal?"

"Yup," came a small voice, followed by a crash.

"What are you up to?"

"Can't tell you."

Liam sat up, wondering if he should go in and check.

"Don't come in," the voice called.

"I think I should," Liam said, frowning.

"Don't! It's a surprise."

Liam sighed and leaned back in his chair. Ever since he'd adopted Cadie's son, his life had been nothing short of adventure. Gone were the simple days of being Nantucket's reclusive boat builder. Cadie had changed all that when she swept back into his life after twenty-five years like a summer storm, causing him to fall in love with her all over again. Now he missed her more than ever, and although it had been two years since she died, he still couldn't believe she was gone.

He'd been so surprised to hear her voice at Levi's art show opening, and when he'd turned around, he'd barely recognized her. If he hadn't been living a life of seclusion—without a television or computer—he might've known how ravaging cancer treatments can be to the human body. And then, when she told him—out of the blue as they stood in the gallery—that Levi was his son—*their* son—it was almost too crazy to believe; in fact, he probably wouldn't have believed it if Levi hadn't looked like him.

He should've been angry at Cadie for not telling him sooner, but in the next breath, she'd introduced her other son, seven-year-old Aidan, who—with his blond hair and Caribbean Sea blue eyes—looked just like her. What followed their chance meeting— which he later learned had been choreographed by Levi—had been a whirlwind of decisions and arrangements. Cadie had known she was dying, and it was breaking her heart to know that her controlling, overbearing parents would win custody of her young son, so Liam had promised he'd do everything possible to make sure he would win custody of her little boy—including marrying her. But now, she was gone and he didn't know a thing about raising a child. For the first time in his life, he realized how overwhelmed Coop must've felt under the same circumstances.

He heard another crash and stood up. "Comin' in, pal," he announced.

"No, don't—it's almost ready!"

Reluctantly, Liam sat back down, and a moment later, Aidan pushed open the screen door with a wooden tray in his hands and set it down on the small table next to Liam.

"What have we here?" he asked, eyeing two lightly toasted, golden sandwiches.

"Grilled cheese and some of Sally's bread and butter pickles," Aidan said with a grin as he scooted Moby—their gray tiger cat—off the other chair and sat down next to him.

"Mm-mm, looks good!" Liam said approvingly.

"Thanks," Aidan said, trying to keep Tuck's curious nose off the tray.

"Lie down, Tuck," Liam said, and although the big golden clumped to the wooden floor, he continued to gaze longingly at the tray.

"I brought you something too," Aidan consoled, sliding a dog treat out from under one of
the plates and holding it out. Tuck took it
politely and wolfed it down in one gulp.

"Did you even taste it, silly?" Aidan asked,
shaking his head. He reached for half of
one of the sandwiches and held it so Liam
couldn't see the bottom.

As Liam reached for half of the second
sandwich, he couldn't help but notice the
dark brown underside.

"Don't look at the bottom," Aidan warned.

"Ah, the ole serve-the-best-side-up trick,"
Liam teased. "You're learning."

Aidan took a bite. "It still tastes good."

"Spoken like a true professional . . . con
artist!"

Aidan grinned and then his face grew
hopeful. "Can we go see Levi and Emma and
Lily this afternoon?"

"We just saw them yesterday," Liam said,
taking a bite of a pickle.

"They were only here a minute, and besides,
it would be fun to go to Tuckernuck."

"Maybe we should let them get settled
first," Liam said, knowing his older son and
his girlfriend hadn't been out to their studio
cottage since the previous summer. Since
the secluded island west of Nantucket didn't
have electricity or any of the comforts and

conveniences of the modern world, staying there with a toddler was going to be a little challenging. "Isn't there something else you'd like to do? We have lots of sanding to do at the boathouse. . . ."

"Mm-mm." Aidan shook his head with his mouth full of his sandwich.

"Is that why you made lunch today?" Liam asked, raising his eyebrows. "Are you trying to ply me with food?"

"Nooo," Aidan said, laughing.

Just then, Liam's phone—which had once been Cadie's—sprang to life, playing the B-52's raucous eighties hit "Love Shack" and Liam looked at the screen. "Speak of the devil," he said, and Aidan grinned.

"What's up? . . . Yes, we're having lunch. . . . Mm-hmm . . . Your brother made grilled cheese. . . . It is good. I could bring him out there and he could make you one. . . . Yes, just don't look at the bottom. . . Mm-hmm, you must be the one who taught him the serve-the-good-side-up trick. . . . No, you didn't learn it from me . . . you must've learned it from your mother. Yeah, what do you need? Hang on. In fact, talk to Aid while I get a pen." Liam handed the phone to Aidan and went inside, and even though he was back a moment later with a pen and a scrap of paper, he had to wait for Aidan to finish telling his older half brother all about his recent baseball game.

Later that afternoon, after picking up the supplies Levi needed, Liam stood inside the wooden doors of the old boathouse—which had looked out over Nantucket Sound for over a hundred years—and pushed a metal button on the wall. He heard the familiar click of an electrical connection, and a second later, the ancient winch housed under a heavy metal panel in the floor creaked to life and the metal cable began creeping along the floor, unwinding from a large spool that was also under the panel. Liam slowly pushed his 1955 Chris Craft Sportsman—aptly named *Cadie-did!*—out into the sunlight until the cable—straining under the weight of the runabout—became taut, and the trolley—on which the boat sat—began creeping slowly toward the water.

"Aid, grab the line," he called, and Aidan skipped the stone in his hand and trotted across the paved boat ramp.

When the gorgeous runabout finally floated free, Liam pushed the bottom button to stop the winch and Aidan pulled the boat toward the dock and secured it with a cleat hitch, just as Liam had taught him. "Can I drive, Cap?" he called hopefully, zipping his life jacket.

"When we're out of the marina," Liam said, closing and locking the boathouse doors. Whenever Aidan called him "Cap," it reminded him of how he'd always called his uncle "Coop." He looked up at the wooden sign swinging lazily in the hot July breeze. Cooper's Marine Railway—Boat Building and Restoration had been his uncle's business. Winston Ellis Cooper III—or Coop, as everyone had called him—had raised Liam after his parents, Lily and Daniel, were killed in a car accident on the snowy Massachusetts Turnpike. Liam had only been seven at the time—the same age Aidan was when Cadie died—and afterward, adjusting to life on Nantucket with his mom's older brother— the rough-around-the-edges Vietnam vet with a penchant for Jack Daniels—had been difficult, so when Aidan came into Liam's life under similar circumstances, Liam knew all too well how hard it would be.

The first time Liam saw Cadie, they were both seventeen; and when she left Nantucket without saying good-bye, she took his heart with her. Twenty-six years later, when she returned to Nantucket, they were both forty-three, and with one look, she stole his heart all over again, but this time, in exchange, she'd given him two sons—one he never knew he had, and one who would need his steady guidance for many more years to come . . . and who—after Liam told him about Nantucket's most famous literary character, Captain Ahab—started calling him "Cap"— short for Captain.

Liam gently lifted Tuck into the boat and then, one by one, handed Aidan the boxes of supplies Levi had requested—little things Levi couldn't believe they'd forgotten but couldn't live without. Liam pressed the Start button of the runabout and the engine rumbled to life, its tailpipe sputtering and spraying seawater. Then, he masterfully backed away from the dock and swung around, and after they'd made their way out of the marina, he motioned for Aidan to take over.

With a grin on his tan face, Aidan moved to the helm. In the two years he'd lived on Nantucket, Aidan had grown to be completely at ease around boats, and he knew exactly what to do when Cap asked. He'd made it his goal to learn all the nautical knots, and he tied them swiftly and deftly; he knew the difference between port and starboard, fore and aft, bow and stern; and he knew how to use the marine radio—initiating communication with other vessels as well as ship-to-coast calls using the boat's registration— "This is *Cadie-did*-Whiskey-Zulu-Five-Six-

Niner-Five" —something he'd need to know if there ever was an emergency and he had to make a distress call.

With easy confidence and hands confident beyond their years, Aidan gripped the smooth white steering wheel.

"Good thing you're better at handling the boat than you are at making grilled cheese sandwiches!" Liam teased.

Aidan shook his head and grinned. He'd never had a real dad—he didn't even know his biological father—but if he had to choose a dad, he couldn't think of anyone better than Cap. One time, he'd almost called him "Dad," and he wondered—if he did—how Cap would react. Aidan looked over and watched him. He was glad his mom had fallen in love with him and that she'd found a way for him to stay with him after she died. Lately, he'd been trying not to think about her. It made his whole chest ache, but it helped to know he wasn't the only one who missed her—Cap and Levi missed her too.

Tuckernuck came into view and as they neared Levi's dock, Aidan slowed down, expecting Cap to take over, but when he nodded for him to continue, Aidan smiled and pulled up next to Levi's boat with ease and precision. "Good job, pal," Liam said, dropping the bumpers over the side and hopping out to tie the lines.

Liam lifted Tuck out, and the big golden bounded toward Levi, who was standing on the beach with Lily, named after her paternal grandmother, in his arms.

"Hey, Tuck," Levi said softly, kneeling down so Lily could pet him.

A moment later, Aidan was beside them, carrying one of the boxes—the one with the baby formula and diapers in it. "I got the goods, Lily," he announced with a grin.

"Hey, Aid," Levi said, giving his little half brother a hug. Then he looked up at Liam. "Thanks for getting everything, Dad . . . and bringing it out."

"No problem," Liam said with a smile as he set the box of supplies down on the sand and took his granddaughter from Levi. "We're always looking for a reason to come visit Lily," he teased. "Aren't we, Aid?"

Aidan nodded as he tickled her bare feet, and Levi picked up the box and smiled. "C'mon, Em's waiting."

Aidan raced ahead with Tuck at his heels. He loved visiting the restored studio cottage Cap had given to Levi, and the fact that it didn't have electricity only made it more fun. Like most of the other houses on Tuckernuck, it had a small generator that ran the fridge and water pump, and in the evening, Levi lit propane lanterns for a rustic, cozy light. Aidan thought it was the coolest place on earth and he fully planned to live on Tuckernuck, too, when he got older.

He pushed open the gate and saw Tigger sunning himself on the front steps. "Hey, Tig," he said, kneeling down to pet the orange tiger cat.

"Hello, Aid," a voice with a distinctly British accent said.

Aidan looked in the window. "Hi, Em!"

"Are you hungry?"

He shrugged. "We just had grilled cheese, so I'm a little full."

"I made blueberry pie," Emma said.

Aidan pushed open the door and Tigger scooted in. "You did?!"

"Mm-hmm," Emma said, wiping her hands on her apron and giving him a hug.

He looked around the kitchen and she pointed.

"Mmm . . . that looks good. I'm hungry enough for that!"

"I thought you might be," she said with a warm smile. "Did you and Cap bring whipping cream?"

"I think so," Aidan said as Levi and Liam came into the kitchen.

"Cap, did we bring whipping cream?"

"We did—it's in one of these boxes." He set down the box he'd carried from the boat but kept Lily in his arms as he looked around. "The place looks great," he said, nodding approvingly. "Doesn't it, Lil?" he asked, kissing her on the nose and making her giggle and place her hands gently on his unshaved cheeks.

Liam had bought the cottage many years ago—long before he knew he had a son. He'd discovered the house when he was just a teenager. Back then, he'd loved to skip his wooden runabout—the one he and Coop had restored together—and which he'd named *Tuckernuck II*—over the waves to the secluded island and hike or go swimming. It was on one of these boyhood explorations that he discovered the little half cape almost completely hidden by a wild, overgrown rose bush. After he met Cadie, he brought her out to the island, showed her the cottage, and told her about his dream to buy it someday. Back then, it had belonged to someone who never used—or maintained—it, and Liam told her he hoped it didn't go on the market until he had enough money saved to buy it. "It has a lot of potential," Cadie had said with an encouraging smile.

"It also has a lot of sentimental value," he'd told Levi, years later when he gave him the key, hinting his oldest son had probably been conceived on the cottage's wooden floor—the same spot where Liam had knelt twenty-five years later to ask Cadie to marry him.

"Soo . . ." Levi ventured shyly, glancing at Emma before looking at his dad. "We have some news."

Liam immediately looked at Emma with raised eyebrows. "Are you?"

She smiled and Liam laughed. "Boy, you don't mess around!" Then he shook his head. "I mean, you do mess around!"

Levi laughed. "Well, it's not just that. . . ."

He looked at Emma again and she held up her left hand. "We're also going to make it legal."

"Well, it's about time!" Liam said, smiling. "Congratulations!"

Aidan frowned and looked from one to the other. "Make *what* legal?"

"We're going to get married," Emma said, pulling her little almost half-brother-in-law into a hug. "And we're having another baby."

"All right!" Aidan said happily.

"I've had the ring a while," Levi said, looking sheepishly at Em, "but I wanted to ask Em here—where you asked Mom."

"All right!" Aidan exclaimed again. "We're going to have another wedding!"

Later that evening, after Aidan was in bed,

Liam leaned back in his chair and thought about the day. He was beyond happy for Levi and Emma—they—and he—had so much for which to be thankful. Their lives were truly blessed. In the last two years he'd gone from being a reclusive, lonely boat builder who didn't pay attention to the modern world and all its trappings to being a cell-phone-carrying, Internet-savvy father of two and grandfather of one . . . and a half . . . and that was just the beginning of the potential blessings his life could hold. He smiled wistfully, reached for the book on the table, and opened it to the bookmark Sally had given him.

PART II

*For I know the plans I have for you . . .
plans to prosper you and not harm you,
plans to give you hope and a future.*

—Jeremiah 29:11

Chapter 10

"These belonged to your mom," my dad said, pulling a big suitcase and a smaller matching travel bag out of the back of his closet. "They haven't been used since our honeymoon," he said, pointing to my mom's maiden name printed neatly on the ID tag.

He carried the bags to my room and set them on my bed, and I immediately opened them. The scent of lavender drifted out as I felt around the pockets, curious to see if there were any forgotten memories inside. Almost immediately, I felt something in the back pocket of the bigger case, and when I pulled out a long, gorgeous string of pearls, my dad's eyes grew wide. "Oh, my goodness!" he exclaimed. "We always wondered what happened to those. They were my grand-mother's, and she gave them to your mom on our wedding day. Your mom wore them on our honeymoon, but when we got home, she couldn't find them." He paused and shook his head. "She was devastated." I held the necklace out to him and he lightly touched the luminous pearls as if remembering, but then he shook his head again. "You keep them. They were your mother's and your great-grandmother's before her, so now they're yours—they would want you to have them."

"Oh, Dad, I don't know," I said, frowning. "Are you sure?"

He nodded.

I searched his glistening eyes. "Thank you," I said softly. "I'll treasure them always."

"I know you will," he said, giving me a hug. "Let me know if you need anything else," he whispered.

"I will," I said, and when he turned to walk out, for the second time in my life, I saw tears in his eyes.

My dad left for work early the next morning, before I was even up. He knew I was leaving, but he must've found it hard to say good-bye. He left a note on the table: *Safe home, kiddo. Don't be a stranger.*

I smiled as I made my tea. I knew he would be all right. We both would.

"I told you I'd live on Nantucket someday," I said when Lizzy dropped me off at the ferry.

"*And,* if *you* remember, I told you there was no reason you couldn't," she said, giving me a long hug.

"It's all thanks to you and Simon," I said. Simon's grandmother had been thrilled to find someone reliable to stay in her cottage. She didn't like that it sat empty, especially in the summertime, and she didn't want to rent it—

she said there were too many family heirlooms. To my surprise, she didn't even want *me* to pay rent—Simon said she called me "her caretaker" and actually thought she should pay me!

"No, it's not thanks to us," Lizzy said. "Simon's grandmother was looking for someone and you came along at just the right moment. God's timing is perfect."

"Sometimes," I said with a wry smile. Although Lizzy no longer believed some things the church taught, she would always believe in God's timing. "You better come visit," I added.

"You know it!" she said with a grin. She looked over my shoulder as the last passenger walked up the ramp, and nodded. "You're not going to be able to find a seat."

"That's okay. I don't mind standing on the deck."

She nodded knowingly. "Okay, then, go do great things," she said, giving me one last hug.

"You too," I said.

She held me at arm's length and we searched each other's eyes. It was the moment we both knew would come someday, but somehow, it was still taking us by surprise.

"Have your Scrabble board ready."

"I'll have my hopscotch board ready too."

She smiled. "Game on."

"Game on," I said with a wistful smile. "Don't forget the Boone's Farm either."

"Strawberry Hill?"

I shook my head. "Country Kwencher."

"How 'bout Tickled Pink?"

We laughed and then a voice behind us called out, "Excuse me, miss, are you boarding?"

"I am!" I called back; then I turned to Lizzy. "Love you," I said tearfully, giving her another hug.

"Love you too," she said, brushing back her own tears.

I smiled and turned to lug my mom's heavy suitcase up the ramp; then I stood on the back deck, waving as we pulled away. To see us, you'd think I was going to England instead of to an island just thirty miles off Cape Cod, but at that moment, it felt like we would never see each other again. I waved until she was just a speck of color; then I dried my eyes and looked out across the ocean toward the life—my new life— that lay ahead.

When the ferry docked in Nantucket, I felt in my pocket for the key to the cottage, reassuring myself, and as I lugged my mom's suitcase down the ramp and began walking up the cobblestone street, I felt as if my mom was with me. Holding the handle that her hand had held last made me feel as if her touch was still there. It was the first time I'd ever felt her presence *or* had the odd feeling she was looking out for me.

Chapter 11

It was early June when I moved to Nantucket, so there were still plenty of restaurants and shops looking for help. The jobs these businesses were looking to fill, however, were for cashiers and waitresses—both of which I had experience doing, but neither of which I wanted to do.

The first few days, I walked along the sunny cobblestone streets, peering into shops and learning my way around. One morning, I encountered construction and inadvertently followed a detour down a narrow side street. At the end of the street was a long gray building with weathered cedar shakes and an attractive sign that said, NANTUCKET BREAD AND BAKED GOODS—WHERE THE DOUGH ALWAYS RISES. Underneath, a smaller sign said, HELP WANTED—INQUIRE WITHIN. I stood on the sidewalk, considering, but when I smelled the lovely aroma of freshly baked bread drifting from the shop's open windows, I felt certain I should go in—the scent reminding me of the soft honey wheat bread Sister Mary Agnes used to bake for communion. If nothing else, I could buy some bread.

I walked up the front steps and pushed open the door. Hearing the bell tinkle, a man—who looked to be in his thirties—wearing an old Red Sox cap, came out from the back, wiping his hands on his apron. "Good morning," he said with a friendly smile. "What can I get for you?"

I looked at the glass display case full of bread and muffins and then looked back at him and cleared my throat. "I-I'm inquiring about the job . . . the sign in the window," I stammered, motioning behind me.

He looked me up and down and smiled. Back then, I was lucky if I weighed a hundred pounds soaking wet—and I really wasn't dressed for a job interview. I was wearing shorts and a faded maroon T-shirt that said Boston College, and my chestnut brown hair—streaked blond from the sun—was pulled back into a loose ponytail.

"Are you a baker?" he asked.

Immediately, a quick slideshow of all the Duncan Hines and Betty Crocker cupcakes Lizzy and I had made through the years played through my mind. "Yes," I said, nodding.

"Do you know how to run a register?"

I nodded again—even though I wasn't interested in being a cashier, I suddenly had a strong feeling about this job.

"When can you start?"

"Now," I blurted.

He chuckled, his eyes twinkling. "Well, at least you have enthusiasm."

I smiled.

"What's your name?"

I hesitated. I was still using Drew's last name—it was my legal name and seemed like it always would be, but whenever I said it, it felt like an anchor hanging around my neck. "Sally . . . Sally McIntyre," I said.

"Well, Sally . . . Sally McIntyre, why don't you plan on coming in tomorrow morning at . . . say, six?"

"Yes, sir," I said, remembering to breathe again. "Thank you."

"You're welcome," he said as he extended his hand. "I'm Abe Jamison."

"It's nice to meet you, Mr. Jamison," I said, shaking it.

He smiled. "Please call me Abe—Mr. Jamison makes me think of my dad—not that that's a bad thing." He paused. "How about a blueberry muffin to hold you over? They're fresh from the oven."

I hesitated. "O-okay," I stammered. He disappeared into the kitchen, and a moment later reappeared with a wax-paper bag. I could feel the warm muffin inside and I smiled.

"You look like you could use a few extra treats," he said. "There's coffee too," he added, nodding to a row of coffeepots lined up on a wooden counter behind me.

"No . . . no, thanks," I said. "I'm not really a coffee drinker."

He nodded. "See you tomorrow."

"Yes, thank you. See you tomorrow," I replied, and as I walked out, I felt as if I were walking on cloud nine. Everything was falling into place—I had a safe place to live, a new job, *and* I was living in paradise. I reached into the bag, broke off a piece of muffin, popped it in my mouth, and the warm, juicy blueberries squirted all over the top of my mouth.

The next morning, I was up and showered before dawn. I put the kettle on for a cup of tea, and while I waited for it to heat, I pictured my dad having breakfast too. I looked at the clock—he was usually up by now, and I could see him, at that very moment, standing in the kitchen smoothing honey onto his toast.

"What would you like, Sal," he'd always called out, "honey or marm?"

"Marm," I'd answer.

All of a sudden, I wondered if, in the time I'd been gone, he'd ever accidently called to see what I wanted on my toast before remembering I wasn't there. The thought made me sad. I hoped he was managing and didn't miss me too much, but as the kettle started to sing, tears filled my eyes. The truth was, I missed *him*. I brushed back my tears and poured hot water over my Earl Grey tea bag and then put a piece of bread in the toaster. When it popped up, I buttered it and opened a new jar of honey. "I'm having honey, Dad," I said softly.

Before I left, I made sure the house was as tidy as Mrs. Cohen had left it. Ever since I'd moved into her house, I'd felt as if I had to leave everything in its proper place, just in case she showed up to give a pop inspection. I didn't think her house would ever truly feel like home, though. After all, it was filled with her belongings, but it didn't matter—it worked for now and I was grateful beyond words to have such a lovely place to stay, not to mention that there were enough books on the shelves to keep me reading for years . . . *if* I was lucky enough to live there that long.

I locked the door behind me and lifted the bicycle off the front porch—Simon had said there was a bike in the shed, and the evening before, I'd pulled it out to make sure it was ride-worthy. Both tires had been flat, but I'd found a pump, and after I pumped them up, they seemed to hold air. I climbed on and pushed off, and as I rode into town in the early morning light, I felt as if I had the whole world to myself—in fact, I passed only one delivery truck; the rest of the island was sound asleep.

It was five forty-five when I leaned the bike against the back of the bakery and pulled open the door. When Abe heard me, he looked up, smiled, and immediately stopped what he was doing and put me right to work making muffins—from scratch! As I measured flour and sugar and broke eggs, he put on three pots of coffee, set out a pitcher of half-and-half, and freshened the sugar bowl. A half hour later, he unlocked the front door. I didn't expect there to be much activity because the shop was so far off the beaten path, so I was more than a little surprised by the steady stream of customers who came in to buy freshly baked bread and muffins and a cup of coffee. Abe showed me the price list for the baked goods and gave me a quick lesson on the register. As the morning flew by, I found myself spending more time ringing up purchases than I did baking, but I didn't mind. Everyone who came in was friendly and welcoming, and I immediately felt at home.

The days quickly turned into weeks, and before I knew it, it was the end of July. I asked Abe if he thought he would need me in the wintertime and he assured me he would. I was relieved because I didn't know what else I'd do. The bakery was a convenient short ride on my bike, and within walking distance in bad weather. It was also a wonderful source of food—Abe was constantly sending me home with bread and muffins, and I also started drinking coffee— something that would definitely surprise my dad when I saw him again!

As promised, Lizzy and Simon came out for a long weekend in August. They were both working at Mass General, and although it would've made sense financially for them to share an apartment, Lizzy's mom wouldn't hear of it. There was no way her daughter was going to live with a boy—never mind a Jewish boy! Needless to say, even though Lizzy admitted they were—for all intents and purposes—living together, she and Simon continued to keep separate apartments.

I watched the ferry pull in that Thursday afternoon and felt my heart pounding—I couldn't believe they were finally here! I scanned the crowd of people lining up to disembark and saw them waving from the deck. It seemed to take them forever to make their way down the ramp and through the crowd, but when they did, Lizzy and I flew into each other's arms.

"I've missed you so much," I said, holding her close.

"I've missed you too," she said, smiling. Then she held out her left hand. "My mom doesn't know yet," she said with a grin. "I had to tell my best friend first."

"Oh, my goodness!" I cried, admiring the gorgeous diamond sparkling in the sunlight. I pulled her into another hug. "Congratulations!" I turned to Simon—who was grinning like a kid on his birthday—and hugged him too. "I'm so happy for you!" I said, and began babbling on about how perfect they were for each other.

They stood there, grinning and holding hands. "We have to go celebrate," I finally concluded. "My treat. Where shall we go?"

"You don't have to treat," Simon said. "We want to take *you* out."

"Don't be silly! I'm a working girl, too . . . *and,* thanks to you, my living expenses are next to nothing."

"Okay," Lizzy said graciously, knowing how stubborn I could be. "Why don't we go to the place we went to the first night we were here?"

"Perfect," I said. "I've always wanted to go back." I looked at my watch. "Do you want to go now, or would you rather stop at the house and get settled first?"

"I'm starving—so I could definitely eat now," Lizzy said, "but I think I'd like to change, and maybe even shower, first."

Since their bags were light, I suggested we walk—it was only a little more than a mile and I hadn't taken a cab since that first night. Now that I knew my way around, I always rode my bike or walked. We started up the cobblestone walk and Lizzy looked over and smiled.

"What?" I asked, eyeing her suspiciously.

"You look great," she said. "You're so tan and you look like you've put on a little weight—which you needed. Your cheeks aren't hollow anymore, and your hair is so blond!"

"That's island life," I said with a laugh,

"*and* eating lots of freshly baked bread and blueberry muffins."

"That's right!" Lizzy said, remembering my new job. "You have to show us where you work."

I started to answer, but Simon interrupted. "Lizzy told me you're working at a bakery—are you working at Abe's?"

"I am," I said in surprise. "Do you know him?"

Simon smiled. "Everyone knows Abe."

I laughed. "I'm not surprised—I think everyone on the island gets their bread from him."

"Everyone who knows about him does," Simon said. "Does he still send bread to the Cape?"

I looked up in surprise. "Yes . . . for the needy."

"He's done that for as long as I can remember," Simon said. "Everyone loves Abe—he's a legend on the island."

"I can see why," I said.

We turned into the driveway of the cottage and Simon stopped to look at the gardens. "Wow, Sal, the gardens look great!"

"Thanks," I said, standing next to him. "I've been reading a book about gardening that I found on your grandmother's shelf and I've learned quite a bit. I think she must've created her gardens from a plan in the book because they are very similar."

"It looks like you've been doing more than reading about it."

I nodded, but I didn't tell him how many hours I'd spent weeding and pruning to get ready for their visit.

"My grandmother *loved* these gardens. She'd be out here every morning, filling her bushel with weeds, and when I was here, putting me to work, too, so I know how much work goes into it." He smiled. "Thank you for taking such good care of it—it will make her very happy."

"You're welcome," I said. "It's the least I can do—she's letting me live here for free."

Chapter 12

"Should we order wine?" Simon asked as the hostess seated us at the same table we'd sat at the first time.

Lizzy picked up her menu. "Of course," she said, as if it was a silly question. "You pick."

Simon looked at me and I nodded in agreement.

"Soo, Sal," Lizzy asked as she perused her menu, "are you having drunken scallops?"

"You better believe it," I said with a grin.

Our waitress came over to take our drink order and Simon chose a bottle of wine, and after she returned and opened it, Simon swirled, sniffed, sipped, and nodded.

"You're such a professional," Lizzy teased.

"I *am* a professional," Simon said with a grin, squeezing her leg. "Don't you know?"

I unfolded my napkin and laughed—I loved the way they teased each other. They truly were perfect for each other—Lizzy's loud and often opinionated temperament complemented Simon's easygoing, thoughtful nature, and they were of the same mind politically and philosophically. That's why I was so surprised when I saw Simon's reaction to two men who came in and sat down at the bar. The older man had wispy gray hair and his weathered face was very tan. He looked like he spent a lot of time on the water, which made me wonder if he was a fisherman. The younger one was muscular and he wore his hair cropped short. I couldn't see his face, but I couldn't help but see Simon's.

"What's the matter?" I asked, frowning.

He shrugged and didn't answer, but his jaw was locked as he looked down at his menu. I glanced over my shoulder to see what had upset him, but the men's backs were to us, and the only other thing I could see was a tattoo on the younger man's arm: *SEMPER FI.*

When I looked back at Simon, he was glaring at his menu, so I gave Lizzy a puzzled look and she leaned forward and whispered, "He looks like he's been to Nam."

"So?"

"Simon isn't a fan of the war. He doesn't think we should be there, and neither do I."

"I still don't get why you'd hold that against him? You don't even know him." I frowned. "Besides that, he was probably drafted."

"Maybe," Lizzy agreed, "but the protests have been growing . . . in fact, there's a concert in Woodstock, New York, this weekend. They're calling it 'Three days of peace, love, and rock and roll,' and it's a protest against the war."

"I know all about the protests," I interrupted,

feeling stung that my friends would think I wasn't aware of current events, "and I heard about the concert."

"Well, things are getting worse. Soldiers are coming home and people don't want anything to do with them."

"That's not right," I whispered. "Most of the boys who are being sent to Vietnam don't have a choice."

Simon suddenly looked up. "They should refuse to go," he said angrily.

His sharp reaction was so unexpected and unlike him that I didn't know what to say.

"I'm sorry, Sal," he continued, "but everything about this war is wrong."

"You're lucky you didn't get drafted, Simon. If you weren't in school, you probably would've been, and if you refused, you'd be in jail."

Simon was silent, and thankfully, a moment later, our waitress appeared to take our order. After she left, however, the same cheerless mood hung over our table, so I tried to change the subject. "So, how do you guys like working at the hospital?"

Lizzy smiled. "I love it! I'm in the neonatal unit and the babies are so unbelievably tiny, but they've got all their parts—ten tiny fingers, ten tiny toes—and even though their immune systems aren't up to speed, they respond to human touch and it makes all the difference in the world."

She looked over at Simon—who still looked angry. "And how 'bout you, grouchy? Do you like the ER?"

Just as she asked him, the two men at the bar stood up, paid their bill, and moved toward the door, but since my back was to them, I couldn't see their faces. But I could see Simon's, and as the door closed behind them, Lizzy turned to him. "You know, Si, Sally's right—he *was* probably drafted. He probably didn't have a choice, and you have no idea what demons he has to deal with now. It's wrong to treat these boys like the war is their fault."

Simon shrugged and just stared out the window and Lizzy shook her head in frustration. She took a sip of her wine and looked back at me. "How do you like being a baker?"

I smiled. "I love it. I've learned so much about bread, and the cakes and muffins Abe makes are so much better than Betty Crocker and Duncan Hines. I don't mind working the register either—it's not like working at the grocery store. Everyone is so friendly."

Lizzy smiled. "I'm sure people who live on Nantucket are less moody than people who live in Medford."

I took a sip of my wine and nodded. "I know *I'm* in a better mood. Living here is like living in paradise. You can't help but feel blessed when you're surrounded by so much beauty."

"You're never coming back to Medford, are you?"

"I doubt it," I said, shaking my head. "If I can find another apartment that's reasonable after Simon's grandmother sells her cottage, then I'll definitely stay here."

Lizzy nodded. "How's your dad doing?"

"Okay. I talk to him every Sunday and I've been trying to get him to come for a visit, but he keeps putting me off. He says he can't take the time, but he works too much. He works more now than when I was living at home, and he still doesn't eat right. I've been after him to go to the doctor—he hasn't been to one in years—but he refuses. I have a feeling there's something going on."

"Sounds like my mother," Lizzy said. "She has to use oxygen now. I tell her she needs to quit smoking, but she just gets angry."

I nodded. "My dad never smoked, so I don't know what's going on with him. Is your mom still drinking?"

"Oh, yeah. She's three sheets to the wind every night."

I shook my head. "I don't know why people do these things to themselves—life is short enough without doing things that will create health problems down the road. I wish I could at least get him to go to the doctor."

"Next time I'm home, I'll check on him. Maybe he'll let me take his blood pressure."

"Ha! I doubt it," I said, laughing and shaking my head.

"I'll try," Lizzy said, smiling. "Maybe he'll respond differently hearing it from me and not his daughter."

"Maybe," I said doubtfully. "Maybe you could encourage him to come for a visit too."

Just then, the waitress brought our dinners. Lizzy had ordered scallops, too, and after she took her first bite, she murmured, "Mmm, you're right—these are better than sex!"

"I know! Right?" I said, laughing.

"Hey!" Simon said, looking wounded.

"I'm just kidding," she said, "but I'm glad you're engaging in conversation again."

Simon poured more wine into our glasses. "I've been listening to every word."

Lizzy nodded. "You're lucky you still have both your parents . . . and your grandmother, *and* they don't seem to have any issues."

"Oh, they have issues, all right," he said, laughing. "And besides, your dad is still alive."

"He may be alive, but he's not part of my life. He never cared enough to be."

Simon frowned and I suddenly realized he and Lizzy had never talked about her dad.

"It's his loss," I consoled. "He has an amazing, beautiful daughter and he's never made the time to get to know her. That is the biggest tragedy of all."

Lizzy smiled and took a sip of her wine. "*C'est la vie*," she said with a sigh. "I can't let it get to me."

I knew it bothered her, though. When we were little, Lizzy had always harbored a secret hope that she'd hear from her father on her birthday or on Christmas, but she never did. It was heart-breaking to see her so disappointed. When we were in high school, I tried to be supportive, knowing what was on her mind. "Maybe your dad will call this year," I offered with an encouraging smile, but as the years went by, I realized I was giving her false hope, and finally, I never mentioned him again, except to say he was a *total loser* . . . and I'm sure that didn't help either. Thinking back, I can only imagine how Lizzy must've felt. Her father made her feel as if she —her life, dreams, aspirations, and her very existence—didn't matter, and yet, she just tucked the pain away and pressed on. I'm sure that's why she had always been so competitive, why she'd been the best student in our class—the valedictorian—she'd felt she had to prove her value to herself. I also think Freud would've had a field day with both of us.

By the time we were scraping our dessert plates and finishing our second bottle of wine, Simon's cheerful mood had been restored. The waitress brought our check, and when I reached for it, he eyed me but relented. I studied the bill, worked out the tip in my head, and set several bills on the tray, and when the waitress came to take it, she left three peppermints. "The tavern hosts a dance down on the beach the second Thursday of the month—it's something new. There's a bar and some appetizers—not that you're hungry after having dinner," she added with a smile, "but if you're looking for something fun to do, it's down in back." She motioned over her shoulder and we looked through the window and saw flickering lights on the beach.

"I thought I heard music," Lizzy said, sounding as if a problem she'd been puzzling over had just been solved.

The waitress smiled. "I hope to go down when I get off work."

"Is this the first one?" I asked.

"No, we've had one the last two months. The first one was in June, and it was kind of quiet, but the word's been spreading and there's quite a crowd tonight. I don't know if there will be one next month."

"Sounds fun," Lizzy said.

As we walked outside and around the building toward the beach, I felt a sudden chill sweep over me and goose bumps on my arms. It was a beautiful night—still warm from the day's heat, so it was strange to suddenly feel cold. I could feel the dizzying effects of the wine, too, but now, the sensation that someone was watching was sobering. I jerked my head around, feeling my heart pound, and in my mind's eye, saw Drew standing in the shadows. I cried out in alarm and Lizzy turned. "What's the matter?"

I swallowed and shook my head. "I-I thought I saw something."

"What?"

"I . . ."

"What?" Lizzy asked, frowning.

I shook my head. "Nothing. It's just my imagination."

Lizzy put her arm around me. "There are no boogeymen here," she said softly.

I nodded. It wasn't the first time it had happened, so I knew it wasn't just the effects of the wine, and I realized it seemed to happen every time I walked into the shadow of a building. It had even happened at the cottage when I got home late, and I couldn't seem to stop it. I'd also been having unsettling dreams from which I'd wake up shaking and crying—my image of Drew stepping out of the shadows was so real.

I swallowed and shook my head. It had to stop, but I didn't know how to stop it—short of therapy, and I knew I wouldn't feel comfortable telling a complete stranger about my past.

As we walked down to the beach, Simon reached for Lizzy's hand, pulled her close, and kissed her. I felt a pang of sadness and envy—

was I destined to be alone my whole life? Would someone ever reach for my hand again? Would I ever have someone to make me feel safe?

We stopped at the edge of the sand to watch the festivities. Tiki torches flickered along the beach, illuminating couples sitting on blankets or dancing barefoot on the sand, while others had slipped out of their clothes and were skinny-dipping in the surf.

"Want a drink?" Simon asked, motioning to the bar set up near the DJ. We looked over and saw a long table lit with lanterns and candles and a long line of coolers underneath it.

"I'll have a beer," Lizzy said.

"Me too," I said, hoping to recapture the sweet buzz I'd felt moments earlier.

Simon walked away and Lizzy and I found a driftwood log to sit on. She sniffed the air and grinned. "Smell that?"

I frowned. "What?"

"Pot—have you ever tried it?"

I shook my head and Lizzy laughed. "Well, we'll just have to fix that! I'm pretty sure Simon brought some."

A moment later, Simon came back with three frosty cans of beer, but just as he started to sit down with us, Elvis Presley's unmistakable voice singing "Can't Help Falling in Love with You" drifted from the speakers, and he reached for

Lizzy's hand instead. She turned to me and grinned. "This is our song."

I sipped my beer and watched the sparks from the torches spiral up into the sky, and when the song ended, I looked to see if Lizzy and Simon were coming back, but the DJ was playing another slow song and Simon was pulling Lizzy closer and softly kissing her lips. They looked as if they were in a world all their own. I smiled sadly—I was happy for Lizzy, but sad for myself—and with a sigh, I stood up and walked toward the water with my beer. It was then that I noticed the young man from the restaurant leaning against the bar. He was looking away, but when I walked past him, he turned, and for the first time I saw his face . . . and his blue eyes. He nodded to me and I smiled.

"How come you're not dancing?" he asked.

"I don't have anyone to dance with," I said, finding it hard to not notice his chiseled jaw and fine aristocratic features. He was tall, and although his T-shirt was tight around his shoulders, his faded jeans hung loosely from his hips.

"Dance with me," he ventured shyly.

I shook my head. "I'm not very good."

"I'm not neither," he said, holding out his hand. I put down my sandals and beer, and without saying a word, he pulled me toward him and we swayed slowly back and forth to Bob Dylan's "Lay Lady Lay."

"I love this song," I murmured.

He nodded but didn't reply, and when it ended, I heard Lizzy calling. "I better go," I said, quickly pulling away and picking up my things. "Thank you for the dance."

He nodded.

I started to walk away, but when I looked back, I saw the sad half smile that I would never forget.

Chapter 13

The weekend flew by and before we knew it, I was giving Lizzy and Simon hugs and watching them walk up the ramp to the ferry. Although their visit hadn't been nearly long enough, we'd had enough time to catch up on each other's news, and before they'd left, Lizzy had asked me to be her maid of honor.

"Of course!" I cried, and she said she'd let me know the date as soon as they'd set one.

"I still have to tell my mother," she reminded, "and I'm sure it's going to go over like a lead balloon. We can't get married in the church, so I don't know what we'll do. I don't even want to tell her in person," she said, laughing. "Maybe I'll send her a letter."

I shook my head. "Your poor mom."

"I know," Lizzy agreed. "She really needs to lighten up."

We gave each other one last hug; then I stood on the dock waving until they were specks of color. I turned, adjusted my bag on my shoulder, and dragged my heavy heart up the cobblestone street. I'd been looking forward to their visit for so long, and now the much-anticipated weekend was over. All I had left to look forward to was a quiet supper and work the next morning. Most days, I loved being at work more than I loved being off. I was always off on Sundays because the shop was closed so Abe could go fishing, but every other day, the shop was a lively place filled with the lovely aroma of baking bread, and since I'd found a taste for coffee, too—light with cream—I always had a cup nearby when I worked—it was my new source of comfort.

I turned onto Water Street and stopped in the little shop on the corner that sold newspapers and coffee. I ordered a large cup of coffee, poured in a generous amount of cream, put the lid on, and went outside to sit on a sunny bench—I was in no hurry to go home to my empty house.

I'd just taken my first sip when an old pickup truck slowed in front of me. I looked up and saw the man I'd danced with behind the steering wheel, and when he saw me, he smiled. "Where's mine?" he teased, nodding toward my cup.

"In there," I said, laughing and motioning over my shoulder. He smiled and continued driving slowly by, and as I sat there, I couldn't help but wonder if he might find a parking spot and come back. In fact, for several hopeful minutes, I looked expectantly up the street, waiting for him, but he didn't come and I felt disappointed and wished I'd asked him his name. If he had a truck on the island, chances were pretty good he lived here—but where? Nantucket isn't very big and all the locals know each other. Still, I didn't have much to go on—just that he drove an old Chevy pickup truck and had some tattoos on his arms. I'd have to ask Abe if he knew anyone fitting that description—he probably did. Between owning the bakery and faithfully attending mass every Saturday (so he could go fishing on Sunday), Abe knew everyone.

I finished my coffee, stood to throw it in a nearby trashcan, and then started to walk home, still hoping I'd see his truck. As I walked away, I pictured the way he'd looked on the beach—tall and slender and wearing faded jeans that hung loosely from his hips. He'd also been wearing a white T-shirt that made his copper skin look even darker, and although his hair was short, it looked like he might've been letting it grow out. I shook my head. The whole thing was crazy! I was still married, so I shouldn't even be thinking about someone else, and a short haircut didn't mean he'd been in the service—lots of guys wore their hair short—that was just something Simon had guessed at, and he'd been wrong to make assumptions based on his appearance and judge him without knowing him.

As I walked along the sun-dappled street, I began to wonder what I would have for dinner that night and then I remembered I still had leftovers. Simon had made dinner Friday night, explaining that Jewish people were not supposed to do any work on Saturday—Shabbat, the Jewish

Sabbath —so they had to do their cooking before sunset on Friday. Needless to say, the sweet scent of simmering beef had joined the scent of cannabis, which Lizzy had insisted I try that Friday after-noon, and by the time dinner was ready, we were ravenous. I don't know if it was the effects of the pot or Simon's cooking, but I don't think I've ever tasted anything so delicious.

Brisket, Simon had explained, is actually made from one of the toughest and least expensive cuts of meat; it's the endless hours of simmering in a broth of savory herbs, vegetables, brown sugar, and dried apricots that make it a tender, melt-in-your-mouth dish; and when it's coupled with kugel—a traditional potato or noodle casserole—you end up with a very filling—and fulfilling—meal. As I walked home, I realized I still had some left *and* I even had some snowflake rolls from the bakery with which I could sop up the yummy gravy. My stomach rumbled just thinking about it!

I climbed the cottage steps, pulled open the screen door, walked into the kitchen, and saw a bottle of wine and a new corkscrew on the table. There was also a hastily scribbled note in Lizzy's illegible handwriting:

Thank you for the lovely weekend . . . not to mention the celebratory dinner on Thursday! We loved seeing you. Enjoy the wine—no more Boone's Farm for us! We're grownup girls now!

xoxo

Lizzy and Simon

I reached for the bottle and smiled; it was the same kind of wine we'd had at the restaurant—Gan Eden, a kosher chardonnay. I fiddled with the corkscrew, trying to remember how the waitress had opened our wine. Just as I pierced the top, I heard a knock on the door and frowned. I'd just watched Simon and Lizzy off, so I knew it wasn't them, and although I knew all the customers who came into the bakery, I wasn't really friends with any of them, so that only left Abe—but why would he be here? He was supposed to be fishing.

I peered down the hall. No one had ever knocked on my door before. Suddenly, a shadow fell over my heart as another possibility filled my mind: Drew must've followed Lizzy and Simon out to Nantucket and then waited for them to leave. My heart pounded. Simon had told me I should lock the door every time I went out, even when I was home, and now I'd been out for hours and I hadn't even closed the door, never mind locked it. I tried to see a reflection in the mirror, but I couldn't see *anything*.

I swallowed, and with the corkscrew in my hand, walked down the hall and peered through the screen. A tall figure was standing on the porch, looking at the gardens.

"May I help you?" I asked.

The figure turned. "Oh, hey."

I smiled. "Hi," I said, feeling relieved. And then, just as suddenly my smile changed to a puzzled frown. "How do you know where I live?"

He smiled sheepishly. "Don't worry, I'm not stalking you," he said as if reading my mind. "After I finished running some errands, I went back to the coffee shop to see if you were still there . . . and, of course, you weren't, but this was." He held up my bag. "You left it on the bench." I pushed open the door and he held it out to me. "That's how I know where you live—your address was on an envelope. I didn't go *through* your bag," he added. "I just saw the envelope and wondered if it might have your address on it . . . and it did, so I thought I'd bring it to you. . . . You know, before you started to worry."

"Thanks," I said in surprise. "I hadn't even missed it."

"Good," he said. "I mean, I'm glad you weren't worried. There's enough to worry about in life without worrying about losing stuff."

"That's true," I said.

He noticed the corkscrew in my hand and raised his eyebrows. "Were you planning to use that in self-defense, or are you moving right from coffee to alcohol?"

I looked down and laughed. "Well, I might've used it as a weapon if I had to, but actually, my friends left it on my table with a bottle of wine and I was trying to figure out how to use it."

"So you *are* moving right from coffee to alcohol," he teased.

I laughed. "Well, actually, I'm used to screw tops—you know, the kind of wine you can open in the woods or upstairs in your friend's bedroom without worrying about having a corkscrew."

"I know just what you mean," he said, smiling. "Like Boone's Farm."

"Exactly," I said, laughing.

"I prefer good ole number seven myself—it has a screw top, too . . . and it works much faster." I gave him a puzzled look and he continued. "You know . . . Jack Daniels Tennessee Whiskey—it works much faster than wine."

"Ah," I said, nodding, "I guess so . . . if your goal is getting drunk as fast as you can."

"Yeah, that . . . and it's just so smooth. Fire in your belly," he added, patting his stomach.

I nodded, and as I looked at him, I remembered how strikingly blue his eyes were—they were the same color as the summer sky—and yet, there was still a measure of sadness in them.

"Do you need a lesson on how to use that thing?" he asked, motioning to the corkscrew.

I looked down. "I . . . I, um . . . yes, I guess I

could use a refresher," I said. "Otherwise, I might hurt myself."

He smiled. "Do you want to bring the bottle out here . . . or may I come in?"

I suddenly remembered my manners, and throwing caution to the wind, stammered, "Of . . . Of course. Come in." He followed me into the kitchen and I handed him the corkscrew and gestured to the bottle.

"Well, first you have to take the wrapper off," he said, grinning and pointing to the pinhole I'd made in the top. "It looks like someone was going to try to get the cork out with the wrapper still on," he teased, eyeing me.

"I might've been thinking of giving that a try."

"That would've been fun to watch," he said with a grin as he peeled away the heavy foil.

"Not as much fun as actually doing it," I said, laughing.

He handed the corkscrew back to me. "The best way to learn is by doing." He told me to start the tip of the screw and then twist it with one hand while holding the neck of the bottle with the other. "Make sure you screw it all the way in."

"Is that what *she* said?" I said, laughing and then blushing at my own boldness.

He raised his eyebrows in surprise. "Hmm, you're not as innocent as you look."

As I twisted the corkscrew into the cork, its arms rose and I suddenly remembered how it worked. "Oh, I've got this!" I said, setting the bottle on the counter and pushing down on the arms.

"Careful," he warned, "don't break the cork."

I nodded and, biting my lip, continued to slowly work the cork out until, finally triumphant, the entire cork emerged, unbroken.

"Good job!" he said. "Now, you do know white wine is supposed to be served chilled."

"Of course," I said, "that's what they make ice cubes for."

He shook his head and laughed.

"What?" I asked.

"Well, I don't want to sound like a know-it-all— because I'm definitely not—I've just been told that a good white wine isn't served with ice cubes —it's chilled ahead of time."

"Oh," I said.

"But that's just for snooty people," he consoled. "I don't mind ice."

I looked up in surprise. "Would you like some?"

"I thought you'd never ask," he said with a grin.

I opened Mrs. Cohen's china cabinet and took out two crystal wineglasses; then I opened the freezer. "One cube or two?"

"Two," he said, looking around the kitchen. "Is this your place?"

"Oh, no," I said, clinking the cubes into the glasses. "I'm just the caretaker—the little old lady who owns it didn't want it to sit empty."

"Who's the little old lady?"

"Mrs. Cohen—she's my best friend's fiancé's elderly grandmother."

"It's nice."

"It is," I nodded. "But it could use some updating. I can't complain, though—I get to live here for free."

"Wow! That *is* nice!"

"It is until she sells it—then I'm going to have to find somewhere else to live."

"Do you work out here?"

I nodded. "At the bakery."

He smiled knowingly. "Abe's?"

"Do you know him?"

"I just met him. My friend Dimitri introduced us." He paused. "I just moved here too."

"Where are you from?"

"Boston area—Malden."

"No!"

"Have you heard of it?" he asked.

"I'm from Medford."

He shook his head and smiled. "Small world, but I should've known."

"Why?"

"Your accent."

I laughed and took a sip of my wine. "You know, I don't even know your name."

"Coop," he said, switching his glass to his left hand and extending his right.

I smiled as I shook it. "Is that short for

something, or did your parents not like you?"

"It's short for Cooper—my last name. My friends called me Coop growing up."

"What's your first name?"

"Promise not to laugh?"

I rolled my eyes. "Ye-es."

He eyed me suspiciously. "You sure?"

I nodded. "I don't laugh at people."

"Winston . . . Winston Ellis Cooper the Third."

"Why would I laugh at that? That's a handsome name."

"Nah," he said, shaking his head.

"Are you named after someone?"

"Churchill."

"Really?"

He nodded. "My dad was in the navy during World War Two—in fact, I was born the same day the Japs bombed Pearl Harbor."

"December 7, 1941. Let's see . . ." I quickly did the math in my head. "That makes you twenty-seven."

He nodded. "When were you born?"

"March 1, 1947."

"Why, you're just a kid."

I smiled.

He smiled too. "So, I know how old you are and where you're from, but I still don't know *your* name."

"Sally."

"Sally what?"

I sighed. "Sally . . . it's a long story."

"That's a funny last name," he teased.

I rolled my eyes again, and then, my stomach growled.

He laughed. "Are you hungry?"

"Starving."

He glanced at his watch. "Well, don't let me keep you from having your supper."

"I was just going to heat up some leftovers." I hesitated. "Are you hungry?"

"That depends."

"On what?"

"On what you're having."

"Oh . . . well, I'm having brisket and kugel . . . *and* snowflake rolls."

He looked skeptical. "I think I'll pass, but thank you."

"It's really good," I pressed. "And I have more than enough. In fact, if you don't stay, I'll be eating it all week."

He hesitated. "Okay," he said finally. "It has to be better than scrambled eggs."

"It definitely is," I assured him, pulling open the refrigerator door and taking out Mrs. Cohen's old ceramic Pyrex dishes, which I was sure she'd be happy to know were storing traditional Jewish dishes that her grandson had made.

"Can I do anything?" he asked, adding more ice and wine to our glasses.

"No," I said as I put a splash of water into two

small frying pans and scooped the leftovers into them. I turned the flames to low and lit the oven. "I just need to warm everything up," I said as I wrapped the rolls in foil and put them in the oven. I was surprised by how relaxed I felt—and I knew it wasn't just the wine. Coop was just so easy to talk to and I didn't feel self-conscious or awkward at all.

"Did you go to Malden High?"

"I did," he confirmed, sitting at the kitchen table.

I sat across from him. "I can't believe you were just across the river."

He smiled. "The polluted Mystic River," he said, shaking his head. "My dad used to fish that river when he was a boy—he said it used to teem with fish."

"Not anymore," I said sadly, picturing the gray river and the bridge that crossed over it. "My grandparents and my mom are buried in Malden."

"Holy Cross?"

I shook my head. "Bell Rock—my mom was Catholic, but my dad isn't."

He nodded. "We lived just up the street from Bell Rock."

"That's so unbelievable," I said, shaking my head. "My mom died when I was five . . . so you were probably out playing or riding your bike when we were at the cemetery."

"It's possible," he said. "How'd she die?"

"She had cancer."

"My mom had cancer too. She died when I was fifteen."

"I was so little I didn't understand any of it. My friend Lizzy told me people got cancer as punishment."

Coop shook his head. "I don't understand why some people get cancer and others don't, but I definitely don't think it's punishment. My mom didn't do anything wrong . . . at least that I know of."

"That's what I said." I paused. "Lizzy also told me if I was good I'd get to see my mom again in heaven, so I spent most of my childhood trying to be good. That is . . . until I stopped trying."

"Does that mean you weren't *always* good?" he teased.

I smiled. "Maybe."

"I don't believe it."

I sighed. I didn't want to think about it. "Enough about me. How about you?"

"There's nothing to tell. Besides, we just got started on you. Did you go to Medford High?"

"No," I said, shaking my head. "St. Clement."

"Ah," he said, smiling. "That explains a lot."

"What do you mean?" I asked, peering over the top of my wineglass.

"Catholic girls are predisposed to feeling guilty."

"I felt guilty, but it didn't stop me from getting in trouble."

He raised his eyebrows. "Ah . . . so you were a rebel?"

I laughed. "Maybe. But, rest assured, I'm paying for it now."

"Hmm . . . a mysterious Catholic girl with a taste for rebellion. Sounds like my kind of woman." He took a sip of his wine. "Do you go to mass?"

I shook my head. "I need to—I've just been so busy."

"My dad would say, 'That's a lame excuse.' "

"It is lame," I agreed, standing up to stir the meat and noodles. "I plan to start going again soon—I have a lot to confess if I'm going to get into heaven." I turned off the burners and reached for two plates. "Do you have a job here?" I asked as I got out the butter.

"Sort of," he said. "I'm buying an old boathouse and planning to restore and build wooden boats."

"You're a woodworker?"

"I have a little experience," he said, "but I'm mostly self-taught and still have a lot to learn."

"Where do you live?"

"I bought a little beach house off Madaket Road—it needs work, but it's on five beachfront acres."

"Nice," I said, scooping our dinner onto the plates.

He stood to help and I handed him the plates and then opened the oven for the rolls. "Hot!

Hot!" I exclaimed, tossing them onto the table. He laughed and took the top off the butter. "You should wait," I warned, but he unwrapped the rolls and didn't even flinch as he broke them open and spread the butter between the two halves.

"What did you do before you moved here?" I asked, opening the freezer for more ice cubes.

"I was in the Marines," he said.

I looked up in surprise—somehow, during our whole conversation, I'd forgotten all about Simon's observation. "Were you in Vietnam?"

"I was."

"Were you drafted?"

"No, the draft hadn't started yet. My dad—who, as I said, was in the navy—encouraged me to enlist. He said I'd have a better chance of becoming an officer."

"And did you? Become an officer?"

He nodded, took a long sip of his wine, and looked out the window. A shadow fell across his face and I could tell he didn't want to talk about it.

He looked back at me. "Are these friends the ones I saw you with out at the beach the other night?"

I nodded as I took a small bite of the brisket.

"So you were at the tavern with them too?"

"Yes," I said, surprised he'd made the connection.

"Well, your friend's fiancé . . . what was his deal?"

"Simon? What do you mean?" I asked, pretending I didn't understand.

"I don't know. When Dimitri and I walked out, I nodded to him, but he looked right past me—as if he didn't even see me."

"Maybe he didn't."

"He *saw* me," Coop said, taking another sip of his wine.

"I don't know," I said with a shrug; then I immediately felt guilty for not being honest. "He and Lizzy are wonderful people. Lizzy and I have been best friends our whole lives. She's always there for me." I took a bite of my roll. "They just got engaged. In fact, she asked me to be her maid of honor."

Cooper dipped his roll into his gravy and took a bite. "Mmm, this is really good. Did you make it?"

I nodded. There was no way I was going to tell him Simon made it.

The evening drifted by and we talked easily about everything—from growing up in neighboring towns to our families; then he helped me clean up, and before we said good night, he asked me if I'd go out sometime.

"Thank you," I said with a sad smile. "I really had fun tonight, but, unfortunately, I can't go out with you." I didn't know what else to say and he just nodded. As he drove away, I realized I wanted nothing more than to see him again.

Chapter 14

I didn't deserve to love again, and I certainly didn't deserve to *be* loved again—but that was only part of the reason I turned Coop down. The other part was I didn't want to give him false hope or start something I couldn't finish. He was really nice—just the kind of guy I'd love to spend time with—but I didn't want to hurt his feelings. He'd already looked so crestfallen when I said no.

I stood on the porch, watching the taillights of his truck disappear into the summer night, and felt miserable. I went inside and dumped out the rest of the wine bottle. Coop—as I'd quickly learned to call him—had definitely had more to drink than I had, and even though I had a buzz, he seemed unaffected; even so, I worried about him driving and prayed he'd get home safely.

Over dinner, we'd talked about the renovations he'd been making to his house—he was basically gutting it and starting over. And we talked about our families—he didn't really keep in touch with his dad, but he had a sister, Lily, whom he thought the world of; and she'd just married a fellow named Daniel, who Coop admitted was a good guy, but he wasn't convinced he was good enough for his little sister. The subject of his military service didn't come up again; nor did the subject of my last name. The similarity of our lives was remarkable, though. I couldn't believe we'd grown up in neighboring towns, and it made me wonder how many times we'd passed each other over the years. And now, we'd both moved to Nantucket—which seemed serendipitous, and although our reasons for moving were different, we were both trying to escape our past.

We all have our stories, I thought as I wiped down the counters and finished tidying up. We all have our skeletons—things we've done that make us feel ashamed or embarrassed, but life goes on, and whether we address them or shut them out, they never go away. We trudge on, dragging them around like the clinking old bones they are, until we grow old and *become* clinking old bones. And then, none of it matters. So, why do we do it? Why do we torture ourselves with unhappy memories? Even when things are going well and we manage to feel happy, a memory can come rushing back, overwhelming us, and we cringe. *Did I really do that? What in God's name was I thinking?*

The Bible says if we're truly repentant, God will forgive us. It's as simple as that. No ifs, ands, or buts. God wipes our slate clean and doesn't see our sin again. But we humans can't seem to do the same. We let our sins haunt us—never letting them go and never forgiving ourselves.

That's how I continued to feel about everything that had happened with Drew. I could be kneading bread dough or mixing muffin batter on a beautiful summer morning, humming along to a song on the radio, but then another song would come on the radio that reminded me of high school and I'd suddenly be back in the passenger seat of Drew's car, letting him do things that filled me with shame.

That's why I said *no* to Cooper. I couldn't forgive myself, and I certainly didn't want to explain why. Unfortunately, however—or fortunately, as the case may be—saying no to him that first night didn't stop him from continuing to try. And I can't say I minded.

He came into the bakery the very next morning. In fact, he was the first in line! He was a little blurry-eyed as he paid for a blueberry muffin and a large black coffee, and he brought Dimitri with him—the salty old lobsterman who'd been at the tavern.

"Oh, yeah, she's cute," I heard Dimitri say a little too loudly as he winked at me. I smiled as I worked the register—he was cute himself, for an old guy. Although later on, Abe told me Dimitri was only in his thirties, adding it was hard living and too much sun that was aging him.

Standing together, they reminded me of the comic strip characters Mutt and Jeff. Not because Coop acted like the dim-witted Augustus Mutt;

it was just because height and build were so different. Coop was tall and slender and had short blond hair and solemn blue eyes, and Dimitri was short and stocky and had wispy gray hair and Grecian green eyes that sparkled with mischief. They were such an unlikely pair that I couldn't help but smile as they stood there with their coffee cups, conspiring.

I should've known right then and there that Winston Ellis Cooper III was trouble, *and* I should've avoided him, but instead, I felt drawn to him. Why had this handsome, quiet veteran become friends with an old Greek lobsterman? What had drawn *them* together? I later learned from Abe that they weren't just friends—they were notoriously unapologetic drinking buddies, and while Coop favored Tennessee whiskey— a.k.a. Old No. 7—Dimitri loved ouzo—a.k.a. nectar of the gods, and that was why Coop was blurry-eyed and rubbing his temples that Monday morning. After he'd left my house, he'd gone looking for Dimitri, and together, they'd painted the town!

I climbed on my bike late that afternoon, and with a bag of apricot scones banging against my knee, bumped slowly along the cobblestone streets. When I reached home, I carried the bike up onto the porch and saw a bottle of chardonnay next to the front door. The note hanging around its neck said: *Thanks for dinner.*

Let me know if you need help opening this! W.C.

I smiled. Cooper obviously wasn't going to be easily deterred, and although it was really nice to be pursued, there was no way I was going to ever tell him the things I'd done. I still felt too ashamed. I brought the bottle inside and put it in the refrigerator. Then I ran the tap until it was cold, filled a glass, and went outside to sit on the porch with the most recent book I'd found on Mrs. Cohen's shelf.

I don't know why I was so captivated by *East of Eden*. Maybe it was because the author had drawn inspiration from a story with which I was all too familiar—the tragic tale of Cain and Abel—two brothers vying for their father's love. Or maybe it was simply the enduring themes of good versus evil, dark versus light, and having free will—a gift from God that causes us humans all kinds of trouble—something to which I could easily relate! Needless to say, I couldn't put the book down, and as I was drawn into the story again, I didn't think about anything else. I lost track of time until it became too dark to read, and then I looked up and realized how late it was. For a moment, I listened to the evening birds and the waves lapping on the shore and heard my stomach rumble.

I went inside to heat up the last of the brisket, and as I sopped up the gravy with the last snowflake roll, I remembered that I really needed to go food shopping—a chore that involved getting up early and walking to work with Mrs. Cohen's metal shopping cart.

I wiped down the kitchen counters, locked the doors, put on the outside lights—a new habit I'd started—washed up for bed, and curled up with my Steinbeck tome—anxious to find out what was happening in the world of Cal and Aron Trask!

Chapter 15

The next morning, I was up before dawn, and although the Trask family beckoned from the pages of my book, there was no time for reading. I showered, dressed, spread some honey on a warm apricot scone, made a cup of tea, devoured both, and headed out the door with Mrs. Cohen's shopping cart bumping along behind me.

I looked up at the early-dawn sky streaked with pink and coral clouds and sighed. Nantucket colors were so different from Medford's drab gray—at least in my mind. I could tell it was going to be another beautiful summer day. Little did I know, however, the day was also going to be one I'd never forget. I parked my cart behind the bakery and hurried inside.

"Mornin', Abe," I called.

He looked up. "Mornin', kiddo."

"Want me to put on the coffee?"

"You must need a cup," he teased.

"I'm making it for you," I said, laughing.

He looked at the clock. "Yeah, go ahead."

I separated the paper filters, tucked them into the coffeemakers, pulled open the cellophane packages of coffee and dumped them in, filled the reservoirs with cold water, and pushed all the Start buttons. A moment later, the aroma of freshly brewed Nantucket Fogbuster joined the lovely scent of warm cinnamon strudel muffins.

I went back into the kitchen. "Job me!"

"We have some ripe bananas."

"Banana chocolate-chip muffins?"

"Go for it," he said as he finished kneading the sourdough and shaping it into loaves.

I started to peel the bananas, and as I dropped them into the mixer, Abe slid the bread into the oven. "So, did you make it to mass yesterday?" he asked, wiping his hands on his apron and reaching for a new bag of flour.

I shook my head. After Abe had learned I was Catholic, he'd started pressuring me to give the little Catholic Church in town a try, but I hadn't found the time. "I will," I said. "I just have some things to work out with God first."

"There's no better place to do *that* than in church."

"Yeah, I know. . . ." I said. Hoping to change the subject, I added, "So, I'm reading *East of Eden* right now and I almost didn't come to work because I can't wait to finish it."

"Ah," Abe said, nodding knowingly. "The classic tale of sibling rivalry and family turmoil."

"You've read it?" I asked in surprise.

"Of course," he said. "I've read everything from *Cannery Row* to *The Grapes of Wrath*."

"Hmm," I said in thoughtful surprise as I broke eggs into the mixing bowl.

Just then the phone rang and Abe looked at the clock again—it was six fifty-five, almost time to open. He picked up the receiver. "Nantucket Bread—where the dough always rises." He paused, listening. "Of course," he said. "She's right here." He held the phone against his chest and motioned to me. I frowned—who was calling *me* . . . at this hour?!

I wiped my hands on my apron and took the phone. "Hello?"

The voice on the other end was panicked and urgent, and it took me a minute to figure out who it was. "Lizzy, what's the matter?" I asked; then my heart began to race as I made sense of what she was saying. "*Your* dad? Oh, *my* dad . . . is he okay?" I frowned, still trying to piece together her frantic words. "Which ER?" I swallowed, tears springing to my eyes. "No, of course, I'll leave right now." I hung up without saying good-bye . . . or thank you . . . or anything and looked frantically around the kitchen for my bag. "I'm sorry, Abe, I have to go," I blurted distractedly.

Realizing I was looking for my bag, he pointed to the hook near the door where I always hung my things. "It's my dad. Lizzy said he's had a heart attack or something. . . . She's not sure . . ."

Abe pulled me into a hug as tears streamed down my cheeks. "It's going to be all right. Do you want me to go with you?"

I shook my head. "No," I sobbed. "You have

152

bread in the oven and the shop to open . . . and I'm sorry to leave you like this."

"Don't even think about it," he said in a voice that was calm and steady. "Your dad needs you, and if you hurry, you can catch the seven-thirty ferry." He pulled some money from his pocket and handed it to me. "Take this," he commanded, pushing a wad of bills into my hand.

I nodded. "Thank you."

He wiped away my tears and kissed the top of my head. "Go," he commanded. "Call when you can."

"Okay," I said, stuffing the money in my bag and hurrying out the door.

My hands were shaking as I paid for my ticket and boarded the ferry.

I stood on the deck and as we pulled away from the dock, I felt the ocean breeze and suddenly wished I'd brought a sweater or jacket. Then I looked down and realized I was still wearing my apron. Feeling foolish and very unprepared, I pulled it over my head, rolled it in a ball, and tied the strings around it.

I looked out across the deep blue Nantucket Sound speckled with caps of snow-white foam and shivered as I thought about my dad. I prayed Lizzy was wrong—maybe he just had a stomach bug or some other ailment that was making him feel sick. How could he have possibly had a heart attack—he wasn't overweight; he was skinny, and I was sure his arteries couldn't be clogged. It had to be something else.

I watched the horizon, keeping my eyes peeled for any sign of land—this ferry was taking forever! And then it hit me—how was I going to get from Hyannis to Boston? I pulled the money Abe had given me out of my bag and counted it—there was over two hundred dollars! I'd have to work at least two weeks to pay him back, but then I realized I had more than enough to pay for a bus ticket—in fact, with that much money I could probably take a taxi all the way to Boston!

Through the blur of my tears, I looked back out across the waves and finally saw the crooked arm of land that was Cape Cod looming on the horizon. I still couldn't believe this was happening. I'd walked to work that morning, thinking about the food I needed to pick up, and an hour later, I was racing to Boston without a suitcase—it was amazing how quickly one's life can change, and as I felt the icy fingers of fear grip my heart, I closed my eyes and prayed.

I'd left Nantucket at seven-thirty, but by the time I hurried into the emergency room, it was almost noon. Lizzy was waiting for me, and as soon as I saw her, I knew something was wrong.

"I'm so sorry," she whispered tearfully.

"Why? What happened?" I asked, stunned.

She gave me a long hug and then led me

154

down the hall. I felt like I was passing through a tunnel—the flurry of frantic activity all around me was just a blur of humanity. I stood by the edge of my dad's bed and stared. He was pale and still and when I touched his hand, it was cold. I heard Lizzy behind me, weeping, but I just stood there with dry eyes, in shock and disbelief. My dad was gone.

Chapter 16

On a steamy August morning, I buried my dad next to my mom in Bell Rock Cemetery, and even though I didn't know if it was possible for him—as a Protestant who never went to church—to pass through the gates of heaven, I prayed that, by some miracle, he was finally reunited with my mom. Looking back now, however, I'm certain he was. My dad was a good man and he did the best he could with the hand he was dealt. I've also since learned that some folks just never recover from the loss of a loved one. My dad was one of those people.

The minister from the Congregational Church presided over the simple graveside service. I figured my dad wouldn't want anything fancy or expensive—he hadn't liked spending money in life, so he certainly wouldn't want it spent in death. I also expected Lizzy and Simon and Mrs. McAllister to come, but I didn't expect anyone else—nor was I prepared for anyone else. I hadn't planned a reception or anything. I was young when my mom died, and I still hadn't lost anyone else close to me, so I truly was a beginner when it came to death and all the trappings we humans find so necessary, and I was completely surprised when I saw Abe and Coop waiting solemnly by his grave.

The minister seemed familiar with my dad's life—which also surprised me. Had my dad secretly gone to church all those years when I was at mass? I doubted it—if he had, more people would've attended his funeral. When the service ended, I turned to Abe and Coop. "Thank you for coming," I said, giving them hugs. "I never expected to see you here."

They both smiled; then Abe nodded over my shoulder in the minister's direction and I realized he was waiting to talk to me. I excused myself, turned to him, and listened as he explained the best way to reach him. As he spoke, I looked over his shoulder and noticed four men standing in the distance, leaning on shovels. I frowned and then it hit me that they were waiting for us to leave so they could lower the beautiful mahogany box containing my dad's body into the ground and dump clumps of damp earth on top of it. All of a sudden, I felt like I was betraying my dad all over again—I hadn't taken care of him in life and now I was leaving him to be put in the ground, never to be seen—or heard from—again.

Why was I having such a hard time with this? Wasn't I doing what everyone did with their loved ones' bodies? Deep down, I knew I was, but as I stood there listening to the minister, I suddenly wondered if my dad would have preferred to be cremated. The option had been offered, but I'd dismissed it without even considering it—cremation wasn't allowed in the Catholic Church and I wanted my dad to have a fighting chance of getting into heaven—but now, as I thought about it, it dawned on me that he wasn't Catholic, so he could've been cremated. Why had I put what I believed ahead of what he believed? I hadn't even considered what he might have wanted, and now, as I pictured his body decaying slowly in a dark box under a pile of dirt, I wondered if I'd made the wrong choice.

"What's the matter, Sal?" Lizzy asked, coming up beside me and putting her arm around me.

I bit my lip as a tear slid down my cheek. "Do you think he would've wanted to be cremated?" I whispered.

"Oh, hon, no. I don't think he would've wanted that. He definitely wanted to be buried next to your mom. You did the right thing."

"I just keep thinking about him . . ." I nodded at the coffin.

"It's okay," she said. "His soul isn't in there. He's already gone to heaven to be with your mom."

"Do you think so?"

"I'm sure of it," she said, giving me a hug.

The minister nodded, too, and I mustered a smile. "Thank you."

"You're more than welcome," he said, squeezing my shoulder. "Your dad was a good man, and like your friend said, I'm sure he's looking down at us from heaven right now."

I nodded, smiling sadly as I brushed away my tears.

"C'mon," Lizzy said, guiding me over to where everyone was waiting.

I looked at them, suddenly remembered Simon's unfriendly reaction to Coop at the tavern, and realized they were talking to each other. I looked over at Lizzy and she smiled— she was thinking the exact same thing.

"I'm so sorry, Sal," Abe said, giving me another hug. "It's so hard to lose your dad."

I nodded and then frowned. "Who's running the shop?"

"No one," he said. "I hung up my Gone Fishin' sign and headed out—that's one of the perks of owning your own business."

"I wish my dad had hung up a Gone Fishin' sign once in a while. If he had, he might still be here."

Abe nodded. "The customers know where I am anyway, and they all feel bad. I'm sure you're gonna get a very warm welcome when you come back."

"That's just it," I said glumly, "I don't know when I'm gonna *be* back. I have so much to take care of—my dad's house, his belongings . . ." My voice trailed off—just the thought of it all overwhelmed me.

"Take as much time as you need," Abe said. "I know what you're going through—we all go through it at some point."

"Thanks, Abe," I said. "And thank you again for coming."

He put his arm around me again. "Of course, kiddo."

I smiled and looked in his eyes. "That's what my dad used to call me, you know."

He grinned. "Well, maybe I'll just have to take over for him—you probably need someone to look after you . . . especially if you're hangin' out with this guy . . ." he said, nodding in Coop's direction.

I smiled, and although I knew no one could replace my dad, I couldn't think of anyone better to give it a try.

I turned to Coop. "And *you*," I said, shaking my head. "I'm sure you had more important things to do than come all the way out here."

He smiled. "Somebody had to show Abe how to get here."

"Well, thank you," I said, giving him a hug.

Then I turned and hugged Lizzy's mom. "Thank you for coming, Mrs. McAllister."

"Of course," she said, mustering a smile. "You're like a second daughter to me, Sally. If you need anything while you're home, just let me know."

"Thank you," I said. Then I saw Lizzy's raised eyebrows and had to work hard not to smile— it was one of the nicest things either of us had ever heard her mother say.

160

Finally, I turned to Simon. "It was sweet of you to come, Si."

He nodded and I realized he had tears in his eyes. "I'm really sorry, Sal," he said in a voice choked with emotion. I nodded, a little surprised by his tears, but later, Lizzy told me he'd been one of the nurses in the ER when they rushed my dad in, and although he didn't realize who he was at the time, he'd been assisting when they tried to bring him back.

I looked around at all of them. "I'm sorry I didn't plan lunch or anything. I really didn't know what to do."

"Don't even think about it," Lizzy said. "Do you want me to go back to the house with you?"

I shook my head. "No, this is going to take some time and I really just need to go through everything myself."

She nodded and gave me another long hug. "Well, call me if you need anything."

"I will," I said, nodding.

It took two weeks to get through everything in my dad's house—the house in which I'd grown up, but the endless contents of which I'd hardly noticed. For someone who didn't like spending money, my dad had certainly accumulated a lot of stuff! Every closet, cupboard, and drawer was a new adventure. There were tickets to shows and movies dating back decades; there were folders filled with important documents—birth, death, and marriage certificates dating back generations. *And* there was cash tucked everywhere! At the end of the two weeks, I spread all the money I found tucked in drawers, socks —even under the proverbial mattress—on the kitchen table and counted it. There was over nine thousand dollars, and that didn't even include the cans of change I found in the back of the closet! Now I *really* needed to lock the door—something I'd already been doing, even during the day—because it felt strange to be there alone . . . and I worried Drew might see the obituary.

Finally, at the suggestion of my dad's attorney, I moved the things I wanted into storage and had an estate sale. After it was over, I walked through the empty rooms one last time, locked the house, and gave the key and my address to his attorney.

I called Hy-Line Cruises, made a reservation for my dad's car, which was packed with stuff, and made one last trip across the river to the cemetery. I walked through the pine trees to the sunny spot where my parents and grandparents were buried and gazed at my dad's new granite headstone glistening in the sunlight:

HAROLD JAMES RYAN
MARCH 10, 1927–AUGUST 16, 1969
BELOVED FATHER AND HUSBAND

Then I looked at my mom's sun-bleached stone . . .

CORRINE LOGAN RYAN
May 26, 1928–AUGUST 16, 1952
BELOVED WIFE AND MOTHER

. . . and caught my breath in surprise. How had I not noticed the dates before? How had I not realized that my dad had died on the seventeenth anniversary of my mom's passing? Had he been thinking about her that morning? I'd heard of people dying of a broken heart, so I knew it was possible, but why had it taken my dad seventeen years? Had he been waiting for me to spread my wings? I'd never know. I'd never know what he'd been thinking or how the date affected him. I shook my head in disbelief, and as hot tears slid down my cheeks, it dawned on me that I never fully comprehended the depth of his grief.

Tearfully, I reached into my pocket for some smooth stones and sea glass I'd picked up on the beach the last time I'd walked along the water. Then I held them in my palm before neatly arranging them on top of their headstones, pausing to lightly trace each name. "Love you *all*," I whispered softly. "Thank you for everything, Dad."

Chapter 17

Abe was up to his elbows in muffin batter when I walked in—just in time for the Labor Day rush. "Thank goodness!" he said. "It's been crazy around here. Everyone keeps asking when you're coming back—they actually think your muffins are better than mine! Can you believe that?" He gave me a hug. "How'd it go? And more impor-tantly, how're you doing?" he asked, searching my eyes.

"I'm okay," I said. "I still can't believe he's gone."

Abe nodded. "You're going to feel that way for a while." He hugged me again and then reached for the spatula to resume stirring. "Were you able to tie up all the loose ends?"

"For the most part. My dad's attorney is going to sell the house and settle the estate." I reached into my pocket. "Here's the money you lent me," I said, pulling out two hundred-dollar bills.

"I didn't *lend* it to you—I *gave* it to you. Keep it."

I shook my head. "I want to pay you back, Abe."

"Are you sure?" he asked, eyeing me.

"I'm positive," I said. "In fact, if you ever think you might like to take up fishing full time, I'd probably be able to buy this place from you with

164

all the money my dad had socked away—literally."

"Wow! I'll keep that in mind," he said. "You must've had a good dad."

"I *did* have a good dad. I just wish I'd been a better daughter."

He frowned. "I'm sure you were a wonderful daughter."

I nodded, although I wasn't convinced. "Want me to take over?" I asked, motioning to the bowl.

"I'd love it if you took over," he said, handing me the spatula. "By the way, your not-so-secret admirer has been in here every day asking if I've heard from you."

"Coop?"

Abe nodded.

I smiled and shook my head.

"How come you won't go out with him?"

I sighed. "It's a long story."

"Yeah?" he said, eyeing me, and for a brief second, I was tempted to explain, but I bit my tongue.

"Everyone has a story, Sal. If you ever want to talk, I'm here."

"Thanks," I said, stirring the batter.

He looked at the clock. "Guess I better put the coffee on—if you-know-who finds out you're back, he'll be here first thing."

I laughed as I scooped blueberry muffin batter

into the waiting pans, and after I slid them into the oven, went to get a cup of coffee. I stirred in a generous amount of cream and took a sip. "Mmm, I missed this place," I murmured, looking around at the familiar wooden walls decorated with retro metal signs that advertised all kinds of coffee and baked goods. Abe certainly had a knack for decorating, but if I ever owned it, I'd add seating —there was plenty of room for a few tables and chairs—*and* I'd expand the menu to include sandwiches. I'd probably change the name, too—Nantucket Bread and Baked Goods was a little ho-hum.

Abe unlocked the door and I looked up from sliding freshly baked loaves of bread into bags. "Did you ever think of adding sandwiches to the menu?"

"I can barely keep up with what we have. Besides, I like to keep things simple."

"I like things simple, too, but if you hired another person and added some sandwiches— even just breakfast sandwiches like bacon, egg, and cheese on a hard roll—you'd make a fortune."

He chuckled. "That doesn't sound simple to me. Besides, I'm not in it for the money." Then he looked up and smiled. "When you buy it, you can change it."

"I might," I said. "I'd have to come up with a new name, though."

"What?!" he asked incredulously. "It took me forever to come up with *Where the Dough Always Rises*. I can't possibly sell it to you if you're going to change the name."

"I'd keep that part," I said, laughing. "And I'd keep the tradition of sending free loaves of bread to the Cape too."

"Okay, I might sell it to you then," he said with a grin.

July

"Da . . . I mean, Cap," Aidan called. "How's this look?"

Liam glanced up from sanding the newly replaced bottom of the 1955 Chris Craft Barrel Back he'd found in the classified section of *WoodenBoat* magazine. The ad had said, "Needs work," but after driving all the way to Maine, Liam realized it should've said: "Needs complete restoration!" Liam had never backed away from a challenge, though, and in his mind's eye he could see the finished boat glistening in the sunlight, so he paid cash, loaded her onto his trailer, and drove all the way back to Hyannis, where he arranged—because she wasn't seaworthy— to have her transported to Nantucket.

Now, as he looked over at the spot Aidan had been sanding, he nodded approvingly. "Looks great." He watched him resume sanding, and smiled. It was the third time this week Aidan had almost called him Dad. He didn't mind being called Cap, but he wouldn't mind being called Dad either. After all, he'd come to think of Aidan as his son, and it would be nice to know he felt the same way. He had a feeling that whenever Aidan—who adored his older half brother and loved to emulate him—heard Levi call him Dad, he felt drawn to use the same moniker.

Liam recalled how hard it had been when he, at Aidan's age, had been adjusting to living with Coop, and looking back, he wondered if his uncle would've liked being called Dad, but then he decided that their situation had been different. Liam had known—and loved—his own dad, while Aidan had never known his real father, so he couldn't possibly feel the same way about him.

Liam refolded the worn sandpaper around the block of wood he was using and started sanding again. Just as he did, he heard Tuck bark. He looked up and saw him scramble to his feet and bound out of the boathouse. A moment later, Tuck and another golden retriever raced past the open boathouse doors, jumping and playing.

"Boomer's here!" Aidan shouted, dropping his sanding block and racing outside. "Hey, Boom!" he called, and the big golden, who looked just like Tuck, almost bowled him over in greeting.

"Hi, Aid," Olivia—who was Aidan's age—and T.J.—her twelve-year-old brother—called, trotting up to him.

"Hi!" Aidan said, grinning. "What are you doing here?"

"Don't you remember?" Tracey—their mom —said, smiling and ruffling his hair. "Liv, T.J., and Boomer are staying with you for a couple of days."

"Oh! I forgot!" Aidan said, then turned to the boathouse. "Ca-ap! Tracey's he-ere!"

Liam appeared in the doorway and Tracey—who was an old classmate and friend . . . and daughter of Dimitri—smiled.

"Hey," she said, walking up to him.

"Hey," Liam said, kissing the top of her head.

She held up a paper bag and cardboard tray holding two coffee cups. "I brought lunch."

"All right!" Liam said with a slow smile. "I was wondering what we were going to have."

"I wasn't sure if you would've eaten. Don't you usually bring lunch?"

"We do, but we were out of bread this morning, and you know how much I love food shopping."

"Yeah, you only go when you're out of beer," she teased.

"That's how it used to be," he said, laughing. "Now I have to go if we're out of milk." He peered in the bag. "So, what'd you bring? I'm starving."

"Chicken salad wraps for us, tuna for the

boys, and PB and J for Olivia. Please tell me Aidan likes tuna."

"He loves it—especially the way Sally makes it—with thyme and lemon juice."

"Good," Tracey said, looking relieved. "I also brought some of her blueberry muffins."

Liam grinned. "One of the many perks of working at Cuppa Jo—access to an endless supply of Sally's famous blueberry muffins."

"I don't know if it's a perk," Tracey said, patting her belly. "I've gained ten pounds since I started working there again."

"Well, you don't look it," Liam said, putting his arm around her.

They sat down at the shady picnic table next to the boathouse and Tracey handed him the coffee cup with the letter *L* scrawled on the lid. Liam frowned. "L?"

"Mm-hmm," Tracey said, taking a sip of her creamy sweet coffee. "For Liam."

"Oh," he said, laughing and taking a sip. "Mmm, this hits the spot," he added, looking up at her sparkling green eyes. "Thank you."

"You're welcome," she said, tucking her wavy salt and pepper hair behind her ears. "It's the least I can do since you're going to be watching my tribe for the next few days."

"Not a problem," Liam assured her as he watched Aidan skip stones with Olivia and T.J. "They're thick as thieves *and* they entertain each other—it makes life easier."

"Well, you'd think Jack would want to spend time with them, but he's become the epitome of a deadbeat dad," Tracey said, adding, "He's so caught up in his new life with his new family, it's as if T.J. and Olivia don't exist . . . and I know they feel hurt—T.J. especially. He tries not to show it, but I can tell, especially when he has a ballgame and all the other boys' dads are there, cheering. I can see it in his eyes."

Liam shook his head, picturing his childhood friend Jack, who was also Tracey's ex-husband. "We'd be happy to come to some of T.J.'s games. It won't be the same as having his real dad there, but I know all about growing up without my dad, and so does Aidan."

"That would be great," Tracey said, pulling all the sandwiches out of the bag. "Baseball's over for this year, but maybe in the fall, when soccer starts."

"Okay," Liam said. "I want to sign Aidan up for soccer too. Is Liv gonna play?"

"She is! Maybe we can get them on the same team."

"That would be perfect," Liam teased. "Then you can take them to all the practices."

"Ha!" she said, laughing. "Or you can!"

Liam smiled and shook his head. "If you

ever need help juggling their schedules, don't hesitate to call."

"Do I ever hesitate?" she asked, handing him his sandwich.

"When's your flight?"

"Eight forty-five in the morning," she said, glancing at her phone. "I'm staying at the airport tonight."

"How's your dad doing?"

"Not so good. My sister said he's really weak and he doesn't even try to get up. She thinks he's giving up—he misses my mom . . . and he doesn't have Coop; he misses Nantucket and he hates Florida." She sighed and shook her head. "Getting old is no fun."

"That's for sure. How old is he?"

"Eighty-one, but he looks like he's ninety-one! He's spent way too much time in the sun."

"Are you sure you don't want the kids to see him?"

"I was going to bring them, but my sister thought it would be better if they just remembered him as he was—a strong, sturdy troublemaker rather than a bedridden old man."

Liam nodded. "Yeah, Coop was lucky to go the way he did—even though it was too soon. A heart attack is quick and to the point; none of this lingering nonsense, making life hard for everyone. That's how I want to go."

"Me too," Tracey said with a wistful smile. "Oh, I keep meaning to ask you if you finished Sally's book."

"Not yet, but it's really good. It's in my truck if you want to take it with you. You're in it, you know—although I haven't gotten to that part yet."

"So I've heard," she said, laughing. "Are you sure you can part with it for a few days?"

Liam nodded. "I doubt I'm going to have time to read with the three musketeers around—not to mention two happy-go-lucky goldens."

"Well, if you're sure you don't mind, I'd love to read it. I meant to bring a book and I forgot."

"I'll get it before you go."

"Sounds good." She looked over to where the kids were playing. "C'mon, guys! Time for lunch!"

The kids skipped their last stones and ran up to the picnic table with Tuck and Boomer at their heels.

Twenty minutes later, Tracey gave each of the dogs a tidbit, scooped up all the paper plates and potato chip bags, crunched them into a ball, and tossed it at the garbage can, but it bumped the rim and fell off the side to the ground.

"Oh, epic fail!" T.J. said.

"Boy, you've really lost your touch," Liam teased with a grin, remembering all the years

Tracey had been the star forward on the girls' basketball team when they were in high school.

Tracey smiled sheepishly and reached down to pick it up. "Oh, well, I guess I have . . . but I can still slam-dunk it!" she added with a grin, slamming it straight into the can.

"All right, Mom!" Olivia cheered supportively.

"Cap, can we put the old basketball hoop up that's leaning against the back of the boathouse?" Aidan asked hopefully.

"We don't have a basketball," Liam said, trying to quickly quash the idea.

"*We* have a basketball," T.J. piped. "We just have to stop by our house. . . ."

"Or we could *buy* one," Aidan pressed.

"I'll treat you to a new basketball," Tracey said, reaching into her bag for her wallet. "Then I can remind your dad—I mean, Cap— how it's done when I get back."

"Put your money away," Liam said, eyeing her. "And that sounds like a challenge . . . so I hope you're ready."

"I was *born* ready," Tracey teased defiantly.

"Yeah!"

"The challenge is on!" T.J. said, cheering, and Aidan and Olivia, realizing the hoop would definitely be going up, cheered too.

"Isn't it time for you to get going?" Liam said, realizing he'd just been duped.

Tracey looked at her phone. "Yes, it is," she confirmed. She picked up her coffee cup, slung her bag over her shoulder, and started to walk toward her car. "Come get your stuff, guys," she called.

T.J. and Olivia trotted after her and began pulling their sleeping bags and backpacks out of the trunk and throwing them into the back of Liam's pickup truck.

"Here's the blueberry muffins," Tracey said, handing Liam a large waxed paper bag.

"All right!" he said, peering into it. "I might just have to have one of these bad boys right now."

"Aren't you full from lunch?"

"I always have room for dessert," he said, grinning. He lifted one out, took a bite, closed the bag, and stepped over to put it in his truck. "Oh, here's the book!" he said, reminded when he saw it on the seat.

"Great," Tracey said. "Thank you so much— for everything."

"You're welcome."

She turned to the kids and gave them each a hug—including Aidan. "Be good . . . and try to be helpful," she admonished, eyeing T.J. in particular.

"We will, Mom," they promised in unison.

"Say hi to Grampa," T.J. added, and Olivia nodded.

"I will." She kissed the tops of their heads. "Love you!"

"Love you too," they said. Then they turned and ran back down to the water to skip stones.

Tracey turned to Liam. "Thank you so much for doing this," she said.

"No problem," he said, pulling her into his arms. "I'm happy to do it. Have a safe trip and say hi to your dad for me too," he added softly, kissing the top of her head.

"I will," she said, tears suddenly welling up in her eyes.

"And stay as long as you need to. We'll be fine." He lifted her chin, saw her tears, and gently brushed them away with his thumbs. "Everything's going to be okay."

Tracey nodded. "I know."

Liam searched her eyes. "I hope you know this, too . . . I love you."

Tracey mustered a smile. "I love you too."

Liam leaned down and kissed her softly on the lips.

"Mmm, I remember that from a long time ago," she whispered.

"You mean the time on the beach when you got me drunk and seduced me?"

"I think it was the other way around," she teased.

"Well, maybe when you get back, I'll let you seduce me again."

"I'd like that," Tracey said. Then she looked at her watch. "I wish I could stay."

Liam nodded. "No, you better go or you'll miss the early ferry and then you'll hit all kinds of traffic."

Tracey looked down at the book. "Thanks for the book—I have a feeling it's just what I need."

He nodded and let go of her hand. "Have a safe trip and keep in touch."

"I will," she said as she climbed into her car and started it. Then she backed up and looked in her rearview mirror, and through the blur of her tears, she saw all three kids standing with Liam, waving while both dogs barked. "Bye, Mom! Love you!"

"Love you too!" she called, waving back.

As she pulled out of the boathouse parking lot, she took a sip of her coffee and glanced down at Sally's book on her passenger seat. She couldn't wait to read it and hoped it would help take her mind off everything that was going on in her life.

By the time she boarded the plane the next morning, she was already on chapter eighteen, and as soon as she stored her carry-on and sat down, she opened it back up to part three and started reading again.

PART III

For I do not do the good I want to do . . .

—Romans 7:19

Chapter 18

"What a great car," Coop said as he walked around my dad's old turquoise Bel Air.

"Want to buy it?" I asked as I swept leaves off the front steps of the bakery.

"What?! You *can't* sell it!" Coop admonished. "It's a classic."

I shrugged. "Well, I really don't need it and I don't have a garage to put it in, so it's just going to get rusty with all the salty air out here—not to mention the snow that's coming. I really should've arranged for my dad's attorney to sell it along with the house. I don't know why I went to the trouble of bringing it out here."

"Well, I'm not going to be able to buy it because I don't have the money right now, but I definitely think you should keep it. There's an empty barn down at the boatyard where you can store it."

I looked at the car, considering his offer. I really *did* want to sell it, but I knew there wasn't a big market for cars on Nantucket, and I didn't want to have to haul it back to the Cape. I had enough going on and I still didn't know how I was going to get all the stuff I'd put in storage, *if* I ever found a place of my own.

"Maybe," I said. "I'll have to think about it. By the way, did I tell you Simon's grandmother is going to be putting the cottage on the market?"

Coop looked up in surprise. "What are you going to do?"

"I don't know. I guess I'll have to look for a cheap rent."

"I'll rent you a room cheap," he teased with a grin.

"Ha! Nice try!"

"Why don't *you* buy the cottage?"

"Me?"

"Sure. Why not? When you sell your dad's house, you could probably buy it outright. You said he didn't have a mortgage, so you could probably pay cash, and that would make Simon's grandmother happy because she wouldn't have to worry about it passing an inspection."

"How do you know so much?"

"Because I just went through it. I needed financing, so the bank had to come out and make sure the house was worth the amount I wanted to borrow. They also had to make sure there wasn't anything structurally wrong with it, and because there *were* some things—rotting sills and floorboards—I had to prove I could make the repairs."

I nodded as I swept off the mat in front of the door. It would be nice to stay where I was. At the same time, it was hard to imagine what the cottage would be like with my things in it and not Mrs. Cohen's, and there were definitely some things I'd want to change. "I think I'd want to make some renovations too."

"I could help you with that."

"Don't you have enough going on? You're trying to get a business off the ground and you have your own house to work on."

"The busier I am the better," he said. "It keeps my mind off things."

I wasn't sure what Coop meant when he said *things,* but I guessed he was—like me—trying to forget his memories of the past. I'd recently read an article about how vets who were returning from Vietnam were struggling with memories of the things they'd seen . . . *and* with the way they were being received when they got home. They certainly weren't getting a hero's welcome.

"We'll see," I said, leaning on my broom. "She's not putting it on the market till spring, so I don't have to worry just yet."

Coop nodded, took a sip of his coffee, and climbed into his truck. "Come down to the boathouse later if you want to see the barn."

I nodded and waved, then went back to my sweeping. The summer crowd that lingered through Labor Day had now headed back to school and work, and the usually bustling bakery was already showing signs of slowing down. When I expressed concern about not having enough to do, Abe assured me there would be plenty to do—cleaning and sweeping and other odd jobs, not to mention baking bread to send to the Cape—and now, he wasn't only baking bread for the soup kitchens on Cape Cod, but he was also selling Nantucket Bread in several stores. He went on to say there'd be a few more busy weeks of catering to a mostly retired crowd—people who didn't have young kids or jobs—but that would be it. Nantucketers didn't mind, he added. Everyone knew the cool autumn breeze always brought a measure of peace and quiet to the island, and they all looked forward to it—it was actually the nicest time of the year.

After I finished sweeping and cleaning the kitchen, I drove down to the boathouse and parked my dad's car in the sandy parking lot next to the building. I could hear music coming from a radio and when I walked around the corner of the building, Coop looked up. "Hey!" he said, smiling. "Did you come to check out the barn?"

"I did," I said, walking over to see what he was working on. He had a wooden sign laid across two saw horses. I looked at the letters he'd neatly traced in pencil: COOPER'S MARINE RAILWAY—BOAT BUILDING AND RESTORATION. "Do you really know how to build a boat?" I asked, wondering how he'd fit that in between high school and Vietnam.

"I'm learning," he said, pointing to a pile of books on the workbench. I looked over and saw an open bottle of Jack Daniels and a plastic thermos cap cup next to it.

"It's a little early to be drinking, don't you think?" I teased.

"It's never too early," he said with a grin. "Besides, it helps keep my hands steady." He walked over and poured some into the cup. "Want some?" He looked around. "I have another glass around here somewhere."

I hesitated. "Sure," I said, throwing caution to the wind. I hadn't had a drink since the bottle of wine we'd shared a month ago, and after all I'd been through, I figured I deserved it.

He dumped some nails out of a small mason jar, blew into it, and squinted as some dust flew out. Then he poured some Jack Daniels into it. He held it out to me and I eyed the jar skeptically. "What? It's clean," he said, then refilled his own cup and held it up. "Cheers!" he said with the crooked half smile I was growing to love.

I took a sip and felt the heat of the golden liquid rush right to my belly *and* my head. "Whew!" I said. "That packs a wallop!"

"It does if you're not careful," he said, smiling. "It *is* smooth, though."

"If you say so," I said, still feeling the heat in my throat.

He frowned. "Have you ever had any hard stuff before?"

"Of course," I said. "Lizzy and I stole a bottle of

her mom's vodka one time before we went to the movies." I shook my head, suddenly recalling how hard it had been to focus on the movie screen. I'd squinted my eyes as we watched *The Graduate*, but no matter how hard I tried, I kept seeing three Dustin Hoffmans and three Anne Bancrofts; then we didn't even get to see the end of the movie because we were both in the ladies' room. It was definitely one of those cringeworthy memories.

"Well, you better go easy on it—it doesn't take much."

"I will," I said, taking another sip and feeling the warmth spiral right to my head.

He chuckled as he rinsed his paintbrush in another mason jar.

"Is that paint thinner?" I asked, eyeing the clear liquid now swirled with red.

"It is," he said, looking up. "Why?"

I held up my jar. "How do you know this jar never held paint thinner?"

"Because it had nails in it."

"And your point is . . . ?"

"I would never put nails in a jar that had held paint thinner," he said with a grin.

I eyed him skeptically.

"Promise," he said innocently as he dried his brush. "Want to see the barn?"

"That's why I came," I said, suddenly feeling very light-headed.

"C'mon," he said, motioning for me to follow.

I took another long sip, enjoying the warm sensation that trickled down my throat, set my mason jar on the workbench, and followed him out into the late-day sunlight, almost tripping on a cable that was running along the ground.

"Careful," he warned, reaching out to steady me.

I looked down, puzzling at the rail tracks running from inside the boathouse down into the water. In my mind, I immediately conjured up a shiny black train with puffing steam and ringing bells. "Is that the underwater train track to Cape Cod?" I asked with a chuckle, picturing the words *NANTUCKET EXPRESS* painted on the side. "They could definitely use one if it's faster than the ferry."

"They could use one under the Cape Cod Canal too," he said, pulling a set of keys out of his pocket. "Unfortunately, I'm afraid it's only for moving boats in and out of the water. There's a railcar under the water attached to the cable, and I can line a boat up above it and then push a button in the boathouse and the railcar will slowly come out of the water, lift the boat, and bring it into the boathouse to be worked on."

I nodded and watched as he unlocked the rusty padlock and slid open the doors. Just as he did, two swallows flew out. "Hmm," he said, looking up toward the rafters where sunlight was streaming through a broken window. "That can be fixed."

I looked around at the empty space—it was certainly big enough for my dad's car, but it seemed like it would be forgotten in here, so what was the point?

"What do you think?"

"I don't know. Why should I keep it if I'm never going to use it?"

"You might use it someday."

"You sound like my dad," I said. "That's why he left behind a house full of stuff—because he thought he might use it someday."

Coop chuckled. "Well, it's true. I don't know how many times I've thrown something away and a week later I've found a use for it."

"That must be a guy thing."

"I still think you should keep the car."

"And you don't mind storing it?"

"Nope, I don't need this space."

"Okay, well, I should probably leave it here right now since, after having three sips of Jack Daniels, I have a buzz."

"That's fine. I can give you a ride home."

"Do you want me to move it in now?"

"No," he said, sliding the doors closed and leaving the lock hanging. "I think I'll sweep it out and fix the broken window first. If you leave the keys, I'll move it."

"Okay," I said, reaching into my pocket and

realizing it was empty. "I must've left them in it."

We walked back to the boathouse and after Coop splashed more whiskey into his cup, he held the bottle over my mason jar and eyed me questioningly.

"No, no," I said. "I'll just finish what I have."

He handed it to me and screwed the top back on the bottle and reached up to turn off the radio, but just as he did, Bob Dylan's haunting voice drifted from the speakers.

"Wait," I said. "Do you remember this song?"

"I remember," he said. "You asked me to dance with you on the beach to it."

"I think it was *you* who asked *me* to dance."

"Maybe you're better at it . . . now that you've been drinking."

"Isn't everyone better at dancing when they've been drinking?"

"In their own mind," he teased, holding out his hand. "But let's see if it's true for you."

I took his hand and he pulled me close. We swayed slowly back and forth, staying in the same spot—just like we had at the beach. "I don't think it helped," I said.

"What do you mean? I've never had a better dance partner," he said softly.

I leaned back and searched his eyes. "Have you ever danced with anyone else?"

"Maybe," he said softly. "Have you?"

"Maybe," I whispered, feeling my heart fill

with sadness. When I moved here, I never expected to meet someone new, so I hadn't worried about being married, but now, not even a year later, I'd already met someone I was interested in getting to know better. *How foolish and shortsighted I'd been,* I thought sadly.

I pushed my memories of Drew away and laid my head on Coop's chest. I certainly hadn't expected to feel so safe, but with Coop's arms around me and his slender body against mine, I felt as if nothing in the world could ever hurt me. I breathed in and smelled soap and autumn leaves. "You smell good," I murmured.

"So do you," he said, pressing his nose against the top of my head. "You smell like shampoo and warm bread."

I laughed and he looked down and smiled. "But what do you *taste* like?" he asked softly. He lifted my chin and softly kissed my lips. "Mmm," he murmured. "You taste like sweet Tennessee whiskey."

"So do you," I whispered, letting him kiss me again.

Chapter 19

"Hey, did you ever find a bottle of wine on your porch?" Coop asked as he pulled into my driveway.

"I *did*," I said. "Was that you?" I asked, pretending to be surprised. I'd actually forgotten all about the wine after I'd stuck it in the fridge, because the very next day I'd had to rush off to Boston.

He nodded, eyeing me. "You didn't know it was me?"

I tried to look innocent, but I ended up laughing and he realized I was giving him a hard time. He shook his head. "Did you drink it?"

"Not yet. Your note said to let you know if I needed help opening it."

"And do you?"

The whiskey—combined with Coop's warm lips—had left my head spinning and my heart pounding. "Do you have time to help me right now?"

"*Right* now?" he teased.

I laughed again. "You know, you should probably just strike while the iron's hot and not ask so many questions," I said, opening my door.

He smiled, turned off the truck, and followed

me inside. "I don't suppose you've made that beef dish lately—what'd you call it?"

"Brisket?" I asked, opening the fridge and reaching into the back for the wine.

"Yeah, that was really good."

"Actually, it was Simon who made it," I said, bracing for a negative reaction.

"Well, he's a good cook."

"It's his grandmother's recipe."

"He and I had a chance to talk at your dad's service—I think we have a better understanding of each other now." He shook his head. "I totally get why people are upset about the war. I don't think we should be there either, but it's not like I had a choice—I was already in the military when the decision to get involved was made.

"Ever since I was a boy, my dad had encouraged me to join the service—he didn't care what branch—although I know he would've loved it if I joined the navy. He'd always tell me how his years in the service had been the best years of his life, and how proud he'd felt to serve his country. He told me I'd be proud, too—and I was, in the beginning. I'm not anymore, especially with the way vets coming home are being treated—no one thanks us for our service. In fact, they blame us. I don't even want anyone to know, although it's a little tough to hide my tattoos."

"Were you in the marines, right?"

He nodded, gesturing to his tattoos. "Semper Fi is short for *Semper Fidelis*—which means "always faithful"—it's the motto of the Marines." Then he pointed to his other arm. "The bulldog is our mascot."

"I didn't know," I said, feeling foolish. I realized, now, I knew nothing about the military. I'd always been so caught up in my own world and my own problems that I'd never given much thought to the greater world and its problems.

"I was so proud when I got my tattoos, obviously —otherwise I wouldn't have gotten them— and I'm proud of the guys I fought with—they're my brothers. It's a bond no one can take away, but I saw so many buddies get killed or maimed—it was horrific and I can't erase the images from my mind. That's why so many vets are so screwed up—the things we saw. We were just kids." He looked up. "How'd you get me to talk so much?"

"I don't know," I said, "and I'm sorry it's been so hard."

"Enough," he said. He gestured to the bottle. "Let's see what you remember."

I nodded and immediately started to point the corkscrew into the top.

"Wait a minute," he said, shaking his head. "What are you supposed to do first?"

"Oh, right!" I said, peeling back the foil from the top of the bottle. A moment later, I managed to get the cork out without breaking it and then poured wine into two of Mrs. Cohen's crystal wineglasses. I handed him one. "You must be hungry if you were asking about brisket."

"I am a little hungry," he admitted, "but you don't need to feed me. If you could ask Simon for the recipe sometime, I'd like to make it."

"I will. I know he made it in his grandmother's slow cooker, and it took all day."

"Slow cooker?"

I nodded. "It's a big pot that you plug in. It cooks at a low temp for a long time—low and slow, Simon said, makes even the toughest meat tender. I've never used a slow cooker, but that's how Simon explained it. You put everything in it in the morning and when you get home, you have a nice, hot meal."

I opened the cabinet to show him the Crock-Pot and he looked it over. "I'm going to have to get one of those. I get a little tired of scrambled eggs every night."

I laughed. "That's what I was going to offer you. It's all I have and I make pretty mean scrambled eggs."

"That's okay," he said, holding up his glass. "I'm perfectly fine with this."

We went out to sit on the porch, and as we watched the last long streaks of sunlight sink below the horizon, Coop took a sip of his wine. "It's your turn."

"*My* turn?" I asked, feeling my heart start pounding.

"Yeah, there's truth in wine," he said. "And since I told you something about myself, you need to tell me something about yourself."

I took a sip of my so-called truth serum, hoping it would give me courage, and bit my lip pensively. "I'm sorry I kissed you," I said.

"Why?" he asked, frowning. "I don't think I've ever had a kiss feel so right."

"Which means you've kissed other girls. . . ." I ventured.

"Sally, I'm twenty-seven—I've *more* than kissed them."

"Me too," I said quickly, wishing that could be the end of my admission.

"You're an adult," he said, as if whatever I'd done was completely understandable. "I know you're Catholic, Sal, but this isn't confession. I just want to get to know you. I like you—in case you haven't figured it out—and I don't care who came before me."

I swallowed, gathering my courage. "I like you, too, Coop—that's why this is so hard. I never expected to like someone again. I never expected to want to be with someone again."

I felt tears filling my eyes and Coop sat up

and reached for my hand. "What is it, Sally? What is making you sad?"

I shook my head. "I can't be with you, Cooper— ever—because I'm . . . I'm married."

"Oh," he said, leaning back in his chair but still holding my hand. "I'm sorry I pressured you— I had no idea."

"It's not your fault," I said. "And it's not like that. I'm married, but we're not together—we never will be. Drew and I were married in the Catholic Church, so we can't get a divorce—I mean, we *can,* but if we do, we won't be allowed to be part of the church. We won't be able to receive Communion or anything. We would basically be excommunicated. I know it sounds crazy, but that's how it is."

"It's okay, Sal," he said, smiling and leaning forward. "Don't be sad." He gently wiped away my tears.

"That's just it. I *am* sad because I totally screwed up my life and now I can never fall in love again. I'm stuck."

He smiled. "I don't think the church can stop you from falling in love," he said softly. "They may frown on it, but they can't stop it."

I nodded.

"If you're never going to be together, why'd you get married?"

"Because I got pregnant."

"Boy, you really were a rebel," he teased, and in spite of my tears, I laughed. Then it dawned on him that I didn't have a child. "What happened to the baby?"

"I had a miscarriage."

"Oh," he said, shaking his head sadly. "I'm really sorry."

"I was young and foolish and I thought I was in love, and I thought he loved me, too, but when all this happened, I realized he didn't love me, and after I lost the baby, he just wanted his freedom. For a long time, I thought God was punishing me for everything I'd done."

"Do you still?"

I shrugged. "Not as much. I think living out here and finding a place to live for free is a blessing, so God must still love me a little."

Coop nodded and took a sip of his wine. "Well, it's just my luck to finally find a girl I like—and can talk to—and then find out she's already taken."

"I'm not *taken* . . . except in the eyes of the church," I said. "I'm sorry I led you on. I should've explained it all to you before."

"No," he said. "You told me right from the beginning that you couldn't go out with me. It's my stubborn fault for not listening. The reasons were none of my business."

"I know, but you came to my dad's service and I could tell you were interested."

"You could tell?!" he teased.

I laughed. "A little. Anyway, I should've told you before things got out of hand."

"Things haven't gotten out of hand, Sal—it was just a dance and a kiss, and although it won't be easy, I'll survive. I've been through a few things worse than being turned down by a pretty girl." He smiled. "We can still be friends, though, right?"

"Of course," I said. "Although that won't be easy either."

"Nor should it be," he said with a grin. "Now, how 'bout some of those mean scrambled eggs you said you can make?"

Chapter 20

I loved "being friends" with Coop, but as expected, it wasn't easy, and the more time we spent together, the harder it became. We were always teasing each other, and our constant banter made Dimitri and Abe wonder why we *weren't* together, but whenever they pressed Coop for a reason, he just shrugged.

The peaceful blue-sky September days drifted by. I looked forward to seeing Coop when he stopped by the bakery for a cup of coffee and a muffin, and if he didn't come in, I worried. Abe had a knack for reading my mind—and my mood. "What's the matter, Sal?" he'd teased. "No secret admirer today?"

"I didn't even notice," I'd reply, laughing and trying to hide my disappointment.

Before we met, Coop had begun restoring an old wooden catboat he'd found in a shed next to the boathouse, and when he finally had her far enough along, he invited me to come out on her maiden voyage to see how she fared on the water.

We pushed off and Coop hopped in and pulled the rope of a two-stroke Evinrude until it sputtered to life. Then we motored out into the bay, cut the engine, and as we bobbed up and down I watched him work to untangle the line.

When he finally had it free, he raised the patched sail and the jib swung around and almost knocked him over-board. He quickly regained his balance—and his composure—and fully released the sail. It billowed out, harnessing the wind; then the boat skipped across the waves like a cloud across the sky. I hung on, enjoying the cool, salty spray on my face. I knew how the little sailboat felt after being cooped up in a dark, dusty shed for so long—it felt free!

Coop motioned for me to sit next to him and I shook my head, but he insisted, and when I did, he closed my hand around the tiller and showed me how to steer. His light touch and the nearness of his body sent a wave of electricity through me, but when I looked to see if he felt it, too, he looked away. Everything Coop did—from pouring a glass of wine to handling the boat—mesmerized me. His movements were so casual and easy and eloquent, and every time his hand or body brushed against mine, a white-hot flame shot through me—a flame no amount of ice water could cool.

One week later, when Coop stopped by the bakery, I surprised him with a gift—a brand-new Crock-Pot—and when he saw the recipe for brisket taped to it, he laughed. "Are you going to come over for dinner?"

"Of course," I said—not expecting it to be anytime soon.

The following Saturday, I pulled my old Boston College sweatshirt over my head, slid a bottle of cabernet—I'd been learning more than just how to steer a sailboat from Coop—and a bag of snowflake rolls into my backpack, hitched it over my shoulders, and climbed onto my bike. As I pedaled through town, I wondered how I was going to get home later. It had been a chilly October day, and as winter approached, I'd noticed it was getting dark much earlier. I slowed down in front of a new red mailbox with W. E. COOPER painted on the side and turned into the sandy driveway. I pedaled slowly down the driveway, admiring the beach house. Although it was still under construction, it was beautiful. I kicked down my kickstand and looked around at the overgrown gardens before realizing he was leaning on the railing, watching me. He smiled, and as I walked across the driveway, he cautioned, "Watch your step." I nodded and gingerly picked my way around the piles of stone and wood.

"This is perfect," I said as I walked up the two steps to the porch. "It's so *you.*"

"Thanks," he said. "I don't know about perfect, though. I have a long way to go, and if it's so *me,* then it's anything but perfect."

"Why's that?" I asked, pulling out the bottle of wine and handing it to him.

"Because I'm far from perfect, and if you

think I am, then you don't know me very well."

"I'm trying to get to know you better."

"I wish you could really *know* me better," he said with a smile; then he leaned forward and kissed the top of my head. "Let's get you caught up," he said, gesturing to the wine.

I followed him inside, wondering what he meant. "Mmm, it smells good in here."

"Thanks," he said, opening the wine and pouring a glass.

"Aren't you having some?"

"I'm having a horse of a different color," he said, holding up a short glass of amber liquid. "Cheers!" he said.

"Cheers," I replied, clinking his glass.

"So," he said, taking a sip and putting down his glass. "I followed Simon's recipe to a T, and then I added a little of my own flavoring." He nodded to a half-empty bottle of Jack Daniels that was sitting next to the new Crock-Pot. "I hope it doesn't ruin it."

"Is Jack Daniels kosher?" I asked skeptically.

"It might be," he said. "Is this recipe kosher?"

"It is," I said, taking another sip of my wine and watching him take the top off the Crock-Pot and giving the contents a slow stir.

"By the way, do you think you'd be able to give me a ride home tonight?"

"Sure," he said.

I suddenly noticed that his eyes looked a little

glazed and I realized what he'd meant by *caught up*—it meant he'd already been drinking and I wondered how much whiskey had actually made it into the recipe and how much he'd drunk.

"Soo, when'd you start this party?" I teased.

He looked up. "You told me 'low and slow,' so it's been cooking all day."

"I meant you," I said, motioning to his glass.

"Me?" he said innocently. "The party never starts before noon."

I shook my head and laughed, but in the back of my mind, I pictured Mrs. McAllister swirling her vodka and tonic. It was such a quick flash that it gave me pause. I frowned—Coop was nothing like Mrs. McAllister, so why had I suddenly thought of her? I shook my head and pushed the image away. Alcohol was funny—it latched on to some people and didn't let go, and on others it took no hold. Coop was the latter, I was sure. If he drank a little too much, then he was just like every other guy I'd known—except my dad, who never drank. And besides, Coop had reason to drink—it helped him forget the war . . . just like it helped me forget Drew. *Or does it?*

I took another sip and looked around the kitchen. There were no cabinets mounted yet and the countertops were just wood that had been sanded smooth and buttressed up against a new porcelain sink. "Are you going to have Formica tops?" I asked.

"I guess," he said, nodding. "Maybe you can help me pick out a color—I have a ring of Formica chips around here somewhere."

"I can do that," I said.

He looked around. "Did you say you were bringing rolls?"

"I did—they're in my backpack," I said, pulling them out.

"Want to put them in some foil and I'll warm 'em up?"

"I'd love it if you'd warm up my buns," I teased.

He shook his head as he handed me the box of foil. "Be careful what you say—we *are* alone, you know."

"Trust me—I *know* we're alone," I said, grinning and taking a sip of my wine. I tore off a piece of foil, wrapped the rolls in it, and popped them in the warm oven. Then I closed the door, and as I stood up, I noticed a photograph on the counter. "Hey, is this you?" I asked, picking it up.

"It is," he said, looking over my shoulder.

"Look at you!" I teased, admiring his dress uniform. "You were so young and serious and handsome."

"I *was* serious."

"And who's the pretty girl with her arms around you?" I asked, thinking she looked vaguely familiar and expecting him to say she was an old girlfriend.

"That's Lily."

"Your sister?" I asked, suddenly seeing the family resemblance.

"Yes, I'd just finished boot camp and she came to my graduation."

"She's beautiful."

He nodded as he spooned kugel and brisket onto two plates. "She's a good kid."

"Where does she live?"

"Boston." He handed the plates to me and then gave me a quizzical look. "I told you she just got married, right?"

"Yes—to a fellow you're not convinced is good enough for her."

"Oh, he's okay. They met in college and now they're both teachers."

"Where'd they go to college?"

"Same place as you," he said, taking out the rolls.

I frowned. "Boston College? How do you know I went there?"

"Just a guess," he said, nodding to my sweat-shirt as he poured more wine into my glass.

I looked down at the sweatshirt I'd forgotten I was wearing and laughed. "What year did they graduate?"

"I think it was a couple of years ago now, so sixty-seven?"

I frowned, trying to remember, and then it hit me. "Oh, my goodness! Your sister was Lily Cooper!"

"Yes," he said, eyeing me as he refilled his glass. "Don't tell me you've met her."

"I don't know her as a friend, but she was definitely in my English class, so I'm sure we said hi to each other."

Coop shook his head. "That's crazy."

"What's her husband's name?" I pressed.

"Daniel Tate."

I sat down across from him, sifting through my memory bank, trying to remember if I'd met someone named Daniel Tate. "He may've been in one of my business classes—is that possible?"

Coop shrugged. "I don't know what he took in college, just that they were both on the teacher track. What was your major?"

"Well, it was supposed to be teaching, but I got a little sidetracked because I really wanted to be a writer."

"A writer?"

"Yes," I said with a sigh. "But you know what they say . . . 'The best-laid plans of mice and men . . .' "

"Steinbeck."

"Burns," I corrected, and when he frowned skeptically, I explained, "Robert Burns wrote the poem from which John Steinbeck took his famous title."

"Ah," he said, buttering a roll and handing it to me. "Have you ever written anything?"

"Not anything worth sharing."

"Do you think you will?"

"Maybe," I said, breaking off a piece of my roll and dipping it in my gravy. "I actually think it would make more sense if I got my teaching certificate—then I'd have a steady income and a job I could count on, assuming I don't stay at the bakery. With writing, I might not have *any* income at all—at least for a while. Writing would take a tremendous leap of faith because I'd have to invest a lot of time and energy into something that I don't know will get published." I tasted the gravy-saturated roll and smiled. "Oh, my goodness!" I said with my mouth full. "This is amazing!"

"Yeah, I think the whiskey really added to it," he said, taking a bite of the meat.

"Mmm . . . it's delicious," I murmured. "Better than sex."

"Really?!" he said, raising his eyebrows.

I laughed and then quickly changed the subject. "Anyway, there's no need to worry—I'm not going anywhere anytime soon. I'm staying right here—Nantucket is my safe haven, and besides, I love the bakery."

"Safe haven?" Coop asked, raising his eyebrows.

I nodded. "I left Medford because I was afraid of Drew."

"Afraid?"

I nodded and then hesitated, wondering if I should tell him. "I hadn't seen Drew in a long time—the whole time I was in college—but one night he came into the pub where I'd just started working. It was really awkward—he and his friends got really drunk and stayed until closing." I paused. "When I left work, he was waiting for me behind the building." I felt tears welling up in my eyes as I recalled that awful night. "He said his life was ruined and no other girls wanted him . . . and then he said since I was his wife, I should satisfy him." I shook my head. "I-I tried to stop him."

Coop's eyes grew dark. "He raped you?"

I shook my head. "I don't think it's rape if we're married."

"Sally, if you said no or resisted in any way, he has to stop."

I swallowed. "That's what Lizzy said, but I don't know how that can be . . ."

"You're kidding, right?" Coop said, his voice rising. "You *must* know."

"I . . . I honestly think the church wouldn't view it that—"

"I don't care how the church would view it. The son of a bitch raped you."

"I shouldn't have said anything. It's just that I wanted you to know the reason—the *real* reason —I came to Nantucket. I wasn't just trying to escape my past. Drew said he was going to keep coming back so I could . . . so I could . . . perform my wifely duties and I was scared."

Coop leaned back in his chair. "Oh, man," he said, shaking his head. "I am so sorry, Sal. I can't even imagine." He swirled his drink and took a long sip. "Don't even tell me if he comes out here because I'll probably kill him."

He was quiet; then he took another sip of his drink and pressed his lips together. "So often, life isn't what we expect—or want—it to be. I know this isn't the most profound statement, but it's true—shit happens . . . and we just either have to soldier on . . . or not."

"Or not?"

"Yeah, ya know, end it all. I've heard of plenty of guys who couldn't take it anymore—they couldn't handle the horrific images that continuously play in their minds or the stress of a simple sound like a branch snapping bringing them to sudden heart-racing attention, so they finally just hold their Marine issues up to their temples. . . ." He held his hand up to his head like a gun and made the motion of pulling the trigger. "No more pain, no more anguish, no more memories, no more *anything*."

I frowned. "Have you thought about it?"

"Sometimes—before I came out here—and even after, for a spell, it was pretty bad, but then

I met Dimitri." He paused and looked at me. "And then I met you."

"Me?" I said, shaking my head. "I'm a train wreck . . . and I've even disappointed you."

"You haven't disappointed me, Sal," he said softly, searching my eyes. "You've brought light into my life. You have no idea how dark the clouds were before I met you—before you smiled at me that night on the beach when we danced. When I held you, it was like this huge weight lifted off my shoulders. You showed me that I *could* move on—that there was reason for living . . . and even if you're married and think we can't be together, that's not going to stop me from falling in love with you. I already have." He gently pulled me up and kissed the top of my head. "And I'm not going to stop because the church wants me to."

I closed my eyes and felt him softly kissing my cheek and my eyelashes, and slowly working his way down my neck and then barely brushing my lips. "Tell me if you want me to stop," he whispered, but I was hungry for him and I teased him with my tongue. "Ah," he murmured, "now you're asking for trouble."

"I am," I whispered, tasting his sweet whiskey-flavored tongue as it lightly touched mine.

He pulled back, searching my eyes. "Are you sure about this?" he asked, and I nodded. He kissed me again and then led me down the hall.

We stood in the doorway of his bedroom and I leaned against the frame and lifted my arms as he pulled off my sweatshirt. Then he wrapped his arms around me and held me close. "I want you so much," he murmured, his eyes glistening with tears.

"I want you too," I said, touching his cheek. He sat on the edge of his bed and I stood in front of him and watched as he slowly unbuttoned my jeans. Then, casting aside the sheets of his bed, he pulled me down next to him.

That night, Coop and I found each other again and again, our bodies intertwining until we were exhausted, and I realized that although I'd had sex before, I'd never truly made love. Afterward, I rested my head on his chest and listened to his heart beating steadily, deliberately, and I thought about how that same heart had raced with fear and throbbed with courage in Vietnam; the same heart had continued beating, even when the hearts of his buddies—his brothers, as he called them—had stopped. Who was this man I was falling in love with? Who was this man I was willing to turn my back on the church for . . . and my chance for eternal life? What had his eyes seen that made him so solemn and sad? And what was it that made me want him so much? I listened to his soft breathing and fell asleep.

Moments later, I was startled awake by shouting.

"Where are you?" he cried out. "Mikey, answer me! Oh God, Mikey!"

"Coop, wake up," I said, shaking him.

He turned and looked at me, his eyes wild—as if they didn't see me.

"Who is Mikey?"

Coop sat up, leaned forward, buried his face in his hands, and didn't answer. "I'm sorry," he whispered. "I'm sorry I woke you. You must think I'm crazy."

"No, I don't," I said, putting my hand on his shoulder. "I would never think that."

I paused. "Who was he? Was he a friend in Vietnam?"

"He was more than that—he was my platoon mate—we went through training together."

"What happened to him?"

Coop shook his head and pushed his hands through his hair in anguish. He sat on the edge of the bed and then pulled on his jeans and got up. I lay in bed and listened to him open the cabinet and reach for a glass.

Chapter 21

I truly believe that living in Mrs. Cohen's cottage full of books—and spending so much of my time reading—had renewed my interest in writing. Every time I finished a book, I thought: *I could've written that. I am perfectly capable of stringing words together into sentences that will eventually become paragraphs. I can create feelings, experiences, and eventually, a story. It may never get published; it may not even be good; but it's perfectly doable. How hard can it be?*

I also believed that writers lived lives of luxury—setting their own schedules, working in their pajamas, going for long walks or out for leisurely lunches whenever they wanted, drinking copious amounts of coffee and tea during the day, and wine—or something stronger—at night . . . *and* answering to no one. At least that's what I thought until I sat down and actually tried to write something. Yikes! Where to begin? How to start? There are so many words to choose from . . . or should it be *from which to choose?* The latter sounded archaic, but the former was a grammatical sin—Sister Agnes had pounded this into our heads: *Never end a sentence with a preposition.* Was this just a myth? I wondered, or was it grammatical suicide? I'd read a lot of books that seemed to ignore this rule, but since it had been pounded into my head, I always cringed when I heard someone do it.

For years, I dabbled, but the stories I made up didn't ring true, and the only story I could truly tell—based on what I "knew," as Sister Agnes suggested—involved reliving my past and dredging up memories that filled me with shame. Would telling my story help other people somehow? Would that make it worth the heartache?

I wrote in fits and starts, keeping a notebook in a drawer next to my bed, but I never got very far and I often tore out pages and threw them away—I was afraid someone might actually read them!

When I wasn't reading or trying to write, I was working at the bakery. Abe had been right, of course—the bakery never really slowed down—people always needed bread. On a couple of occasions, I went with him to the Cape to check on the stores now selling his bread. We brought big Nantucket-style baskets with *Nantucket Bread* engraved on copper plates, and I even set up displays at a couple of the stores with free samples of cubed bread that customers dipped in bowls of olive oil.

On Thanksgiving, Coop and I went to the Cape with Abe to help serve a turkey dinner with all the fixings at one of the shelters. We were put to work as soon as we got there—Abe carving turkeys, me scooping mashed potatoes, and Coop ladling gravy. When dinner and dessert—apple or pumpkin pie with whipped cream—were served, we joined the other volunteers for a dinner of our own and it was the most delicious Thanksgiving dinner I'd ever eaten. Abe—who'd been serving at the shelter for years—had promised it would be fun, but he hadn't said how delicious it would be, and although it was sad to recall all the quiet Thanksgivings I'd shared with my dad, serving at the shelter cheered me up—I couldn't imagine a better way to give thanks.

By the time we got back to Nantucket, it was snowing. We said good night to Abe; then Coop drove me home—to his house. Even though we'd been seeing each other for two months, we still hadn't told anyone. I was determined to keep our relationship secret because I was certain I'd be banished from the church . . . and from Communion, and this would break my heart. Coop seemed okay with the arrangement—as long as he could have me in private. He claimed he didn't care what the world knew—or didn't know. Loving me—and being loved by me—was all that mattered.

As soon as we got home that night, Coop poured a glass of whiskey and built a roaring fire in his old stone fireplace. "Would you like some wine?" he asked, visibly relaxed after taking a sip.

"No. No, thanks," I said, standing in front of the fire. When we'd first started spending time together, I didn't know how much he drank, but after a couple of weeks, I realized he didn't just drink occasionally, he had one or two—and maybe more when I wasn't there—every night. The realization worried me. I knew he was trying to block out his memories, but I began to think it was making things worse—it was as if the alcohol dredged to the surface all the memories he was trying to forget. On more than one occasion, he cried out in his sleep, shouting in alarm and shaking. Other times, he had trouble *falling* asleep; then he paced the floor, listening to every sound.

After a while, I suggested he try to go an evening without having a drink, but he became defensive and insisted he didn't drink too much. For a few nights after, he'd have beer or wine instead, and his mood would be less somber.

"C'mon, Sal," he pressed. "It's our first snowy night together on Nantucket—Thanksgiving, no less—with a fire in the fireplace, have a drink with me."

I pressed my lips together—a glass of wine would be nice. "Okay," I said, relenting. "A small glass."

He poured a glass of cabernet, handed it to me, and sat down next to me. "Happy Thanksgiving," he said, clinking my glass.

"Happy Thanksgiving to you," I replied, smiling and searching his blue eyes. "I have so much to be thankful for this year."

"Not nearly as much as I do," he said, smiling and softly kissing the top of my head.

I snuggled up next to him and we listened to the wind howling around the house.

"The storm's picking up," he said.

"I wonder how bad it gets out here."

"I don't know," he said. "Hopefully not too bad."

We sat quietly, watching bright sparks shoot up the chimney into the snowy night, and as the bed of embers began to glow, Coop stoked the fire and then gently pulled me down next to him on the rug. I felt the heat of his body on one side of me and the warmth of the fire on the other, and as the flickering firelight danced in his eyes, he traced his fingers along my hips, and I realized I'd never felt so safe . . . or loved.

"I love you, Winston Ellis Cooper the Third," I whispered.

"I love you, Sally Adams," he answered softly.

I smiled sadly—if only my name still was Sally Adams.

Chapter 22

My dad's attorney called the Monday after Thanksgiving to inform me that my dad's house had sold and that the closing would be before the end of the year because the buyer, who had two young kids, hoped to be in the house for Christmas. To my relief, he also said I didn't have to be there and added—somewhat gleefully—that as soon as it took place, the remainder of my dad's estate would be settled. "Congratulations," he said. "You'll receive a sizable check just in time for the holidays." I thanked him and hung up, wondering if he was happy for me or for himself, because he would be receiving a sizable check in time for the holidays too.

I looked out at the trees, now bare of leaves, and tried to picture little kids running around our old house. I wondered how old they were. Was there a boy *and* a girl? And who would claim my room? Would they paint it a different color? I tried to imagine a young girl growing up in my old room, and I immediately wondered if she'd notice the crack in the ceiling when she was lying in bed—as I had—and think it looked like a snowy mountain range. I also wondered if she'd notice—when she was sitting at her desk—the beautiful pink blossoms on the ancient dogwood just outside the bedroom window? I suddenly wished I'd asked my dad's attorney more questions about the family.

I filled the kettle for a cup of tea, and while I waited for it to heat, I thought of my mom, remembering how she'd suffered and cried out in that house before finally succumbing to cancer. The new owners would probably never know, but it's the type of thing I'd want to know. It's macabre, but I can't help it, especially if it's an old house. Now, I looked around the beach house again—it was so old it was on the historic registry —and I decided the odds were good that someone had died there. I pictured an old man lying in the room where I now slept, taking his last breath. What was his name? What had he done for a living? Had he been a fisherman? Had he been married? Was his wife holding his hand and comforting him when he died . . . or had he died alone?

The kettle started to whistle and I turned to pour hot water over my tea bag. I shook my head and thought: *This is why I need to be a writer!*

I picked up the book I was reading, settled into the chair in the corner of the living room, and took a sip of my tea. I opened to my bookmark, a tattered business card from the bakery, and picked up where I'd left off. I was captivated by the story of aspiring architect Howard Roark, expelled from school for refusing to conform to conven-tional teaching, but still designing buildings that incorporated the surrounding landscape into their progressive designs. Howard had no regard for what was commonly accepted and he had no concern for success or how his buildings would be received. He was true to himself, and this was a lesson *I* needed to learn. I needed to stop worrying about what other people thought of me and just be true to myself.

Unfortunately, it would be years before I found the courage.

Chapter 23

We're just friends—that's what I planned to say if anyone asked when Coop and I went out to dinner for his birthday. It never once occurred to me that my stubborn determination to keep our relationship a secret was hurting Coop. After all, he'd assured me he was fine with it. That's why I was so surprised—and worried—when we got back to my house after dinner and he shook his head when I asked him if he was going to model his birthday suit for me. "What's the matter?" I asked, reaching for him, but he held my hands so I couldn't touch him. I frowned. "Did I say something wrong?"

He shook his head again, ever so slightly, and then let go of my hands and turned to pour himself a drink. He gestured questioningly, but I shook my head, and he walked over to the fireplace, set his glass on the mantel, and opened the damper. Then he struck a match, lit the newspaper and kindling under the pile of logs he'd built before we left, and fanned the flame until the fire was roaring. Then he stepped back, reached for his glass and took a sip, and the way he watched the flames licking the back of the firebox made me think he'd forgotten I was there.

"I'm sorry," I said uncertainly. "I wish you'd

tell me what's wrong." But he just gazed at the flames. It wasn't the first time Coop had grown inexplicably silent in my presence, and I'd learned it was best to leave him alone. He'd come around eventually, but it didn't stop me from worrying that it was somehow my fault.

The next day, I realized his somber mood had had nothing to do with me and had everything to do with the anniversary of the bombing of Pearl Harbor—which I'd forgotten had happened the same day he was born. Cooper was intensely aware of it, though. He didn't just share the same month and day with the tragic event—he was born hours before the attack took place—hours before countless young, unsuspecting servicemen were killed—an occurrence that always made him feel less than celebratory on his birthday. He didn't just hold the men who'd fought beside him close at heart—he held all veterans from all wars close . . . and this made me love him all the more.

Two weeks later, Coop announced that Lily and Daniel were coming for Christmas. It was their first visit to Nantucket and I knew he was looking forward to it. I could also tell he didn't realize that their visit meant *we* wouldn't be spending Christmas together. When I mentioned this, he frowned and pressed me to change my mind. He insisted Lily would never tell anyone about us, but I shook my head. I didn't want his sister—or anyone else—to think we were more than friends, and if spending Christmas apart was the price we had to pay, so be it. In the end, I agreed to stop by and meet them, but I declined his invitation to stay for dinner.

On Christmas morning, I walked along the snowy narrow streets to St. Mary's Church—the Catholic church Abe attended. I'd walked past the little church at least a hundred times, but I'd never stepped inside. In fact, now, I hadn't been to mass in over a year. I stood on the sidewalk and looked up at the church as if I was seeing it for the first time. The cedar shake siding blended right in with the classic architecture of Nantucket, and the gentle expression of the statue of Our Lady of the Isle was both welcoming and forgiving, but it also made me feel unworthy. I walked up the wooden steps, held my breath, and went inside— it was beautiful! I found a seat in the back and slipped a small card out of the pew rack that had the history of the little church printed on it. I read in wonder—the historic little church had celebrated its first mass in August of 1897! I looked up and, through teary eyes, gazed at the stained-glass windows, and as I listened to the young soloist sing the hauntingly beautiful "Ave Maria," I was transported back to the innocence of my childhood. Suddenly overwhelmed with guilt, I pleaded, "Oh, God, forgive me."

On my way home, I resolved to start attending

mass and confession every week and I assigned myself two rosaries, but when I sat in my chair with my beads in my hands, I felt my heart ache . . . as if prayer wasn't enough. Over and over, I whispered my plea for forgiveness: " 'Oh, my God, I am heartily sorry for having offended you, and I detest all my sins, because I dread the loss of heaven and the pains of hell; but most of all because they offend you, my God, who are good and deserving of all my love. I firmly resolve, with the help of your grace, to confess my sins, to do penance, and to amend my life. Amen.' " But the repetitive prayer didn't make me feel better and I realized there was only one thing that truly would.

The next day—a beautiful blue-sky winter day—Cooper dropped Lily and Daniel off at the ferry and came straight to my house, and pulled me into his arms. "I've missed you so much," he whispered.

"I've missed you too," I said, trying not to lose my resolve. He started to kiss me, but I put my hands on his chest and stopped him.

"What's wrong?" he asked.

I pressed my lips together, gathering my courage. "I've been doing a lot of soul-searching . . . and . . ." I looked into his eyes—now shadowed with worry—and suddenly doubted my resolve.

"What?" he asked.

"I think we should stop seeing each other," I blurted, my eyes filling with tears.

"Why?" he asked in disbelief.

"Because it's wrong. Don't you see? I'm married, Coop, and it's a sin and I can only find forgiveness if I'm truly repentant—and that means I must stop sinning." I felt hot tears spilling down my cheeks. "I'm sorry, but I don't think I can be just friends—it's too hard. When you're around, I have no self-control. I just want to be with you."

Coop looked like I'd stabbed him in the heart—which *is* what I'd done. He shook his head. "Sally, what we have is *not* wrong. Don't you see? What you had before was wrong. What *we* have is right—so right. I'm sure God doesn't want you to go through life alone. I'm sure he forgives you."

I shook my head and turned away—I couldn't even look at him. I couldn't stand to see the pain I was inflicting. "I'm sorry, Coop," I whispered, tears streaming down my cheeks. "I wish I wasn't married."

Chapter 24

I struggled to not tell Lizzy—with whom I'd shared every secret since I was five years old—about Coop, but for some reason, my relationship—or non-relationship, as it were—with him was something I couldn't bring myself to tell anyone, not even my best friend. What we had shared—albeit briefly—was too sacred, too special, and words would never do it justice.

Lizzy had news for me, though, when she and Simon came out for New Year's Eve. We sat by the fire, drinking wine and talking late into the night—long after Simon had gone to bed.

"Soo," she said, smiling over her glass, "we set a date."

"You did?! You've been here all day and you're just telling me now?"

"I know, I'm sorry. It's been kind of involved," she added softly, just in case Simon, who was snoring loudly in the next room, happened to be faking and was really listening.

She nodded toward the bedroom. "Si doesn't know the whole story."

I frowned. "Why is there a story?"

"Well, before I get into it, it's Sunday, August twenty-third—so mark your calendar. I hate to make you leave this beautiful place in the busy summertime, but the wedding's going to be in Boston."

"That's okay," I said, smiling and taking a sip of my wine. "At least you're not making me go to Medford."

"That's part of the problem," she said softly. "My mother—who should have seen this coming —just about fainted when I told her, and then, when I told her we were getting married under a chuppah, I thought she was going to have a heart attack. I'm sorry to use that scenario, Sal—with your dad and all—but she literally put her hand to her chest and gripped the table for support."

"Oh no," I said, raising my eyebrows.

"Simon doesn't know any of this," Lizzy said, shaking her head. "I don't know why she didn't realize how serious we were."

"She was probably in denial."

"Probably," Lizzy said, rolling her eyes. "Anyway, she immediately poured herself a drink—which, I found out later, was just the beginning of a three-day tear. Now, I don't even know if she'll come to the wedding—which might be just as well since she'll probably get drunk and embarrass herself . . . *and* me. God only knows what she'll do."

I nodded, suddenly realizing that my most important job as maid of honor was going to be keeping tabs on the mother of the bride. "Oh,

Lizzy, I'm so sorry," I said. "If she comes, I'll definitely keep an eye on her."

"You'll have to," she said, laughing. "Can you imagine when Simon breaks the glass? She'll probably throw down her own glass and stomp on it too!"

I raised my eyebrows. "So you're having a traditional Jewish ceremony?"

Lizzy nodded. "Yes, Simon's grandmother even gave Simon her wedding ring to give me."

"Wow! That's *nice* of her."

Lizzy nodded. "It's tradition."

I frowned, knowing the rigid rules of the Catholic Church. "I know you told me you were engaged back in the summer, but I've been wondering ever since if we're even allowed to marry someone who is Jewish."

"We're not," she said, "but it doesn't matter—I'm giving up Catholicism."

She said it so casually—like you might say you were giving up chocolate for Lent.

She saw the look in my eyes and smiled. "Just by marrying Simon, Sal, I'll be falling out of grace with the Church. I won't ever be able to receive Communion or participate in any other sacraments again, so what's the point?"

"Would Simon be willing to become Catholic?"

"No," she said, shaking her head.

"What about your children?"

She shrugged. "They'll be raised Jewish."

"What about Christmas? Won't you miss it?"

"I guess we'll celebrate Hanukkah instead."

I frowned. "Aren't you the one who always said Hanukkah was lame compared to Christmas?"

She laughed. "Probably, but I'm not a little kid anymore—I'll get over it."

I was stunned. I had altered my life—with no regard for my own happiness—just to honor the Catholic Church and its beliefs, and here Lizzy was, kicking it all to the curb. "What about all we've been taught to believe? How will your children have eternal life if they aren't raised to believe Jesus died for their sins?"

"Do you really believe that?" Lizzy asked.

"I do," I said without a shred of doubt in my heart.

"You don't think God lets Jewish people into heaven . . . after all they've been through?"

I shook my head. "I honestly don't know, Lizzy. I just know the Bible says, unequivocally, that a person must accept Christ as his or her savior to receive eternal life."

"There are a lot of good Jewish people on this planet doing wonderful things," Lizzy countered, "and I just find it so hard to believe that God doesn't love them." She searched my eyes. "There's something I haven't told you."

I frowned, waiting for her to continue.

"Simon's grandparents were in Poland during

the Nazi occupation. They were separated from one another and his grandfather was killed, but his grandmother was put on a train." She paused. "Sally, she was taken to a concentration camp."

I shook my head in disbelief.

Lizzy nodded. "Simon said she would've been killed, too, if the prisoners hadn't been freed by Allied troops."

"That's incredible—I had no idea."

Lizzy nodded again. "She is this amazing woman and she's been through one of the most horrific events in history, and yet, she has this beautiful, indomitable spirit. You'd never guess she survived the Holocaust." She looked into my eyes. "Do you really think God won't grant her eternal life?"

I swallowed. "I don't know," I said softly.

"Anyway," Lizzy continued, "Simon would never give up his faith—not after everything his grandparents went through. I love him, Sal. I love him so much I'd give up my chance at eternal life, and I honestly don't care what the church thinks—if they have to be so rigid and unaccepting of other faiths, then I don't want to be a part of it anyway. It makes no sense to me and I wouldn't want my children to be dragged down by such narrow-mindedness."

I took a sip of my wine. I didn't know what to say—Lizzy and I were suddenly on opposite ends of the spectrum when it came to our beliefs. For the love of one man, she was turning her back on everything we'd been raised to believe, and for those same beliefs, I was willing to give up the man I loved. Was the love she felt for Simon more profound than the love I felt for Coop?

Lizzy smiled as she pulled her legs up under her and took another long sip. "Oh, before I forget," she said, "we're supposed to tell you Simon's grandmother is putting the house on the market soon and she wondered if you might be interested."

Chapter 25

Coop didn't stop by the bakery after the holidays. "Trouble in paradise?" Abe teased one afternoon as we were getting ready to close.

"Ha," I said. "There's no such thing as paradise." And then the irony of my statement hit me. What if there really was no paradise—no heaven—and I was giving up my relationship with Coop for nothing?

"There is a paradise," Abe said gently. "You just have to stay on the straight and narrow to find it." He paused. "No one's perfect, Sal. You can only do your best, and when you fall short, ask God for forgiveness . . . and go to church once in a while—more than just on Christmas," he added with a smile.

I nodded, fighting back tears. It was as if he'd read my mind.

Moments later, as I was cleaning up the coffee station, Coop walked in, brushing snow off his shoulders, and I remembered—by the heat that shot through my body—what paradise was like.

"Coffee, tea, or me?" I teased, holding up the last coffee carafe.

"Why? Are you back on the menu?"

I laughed uncertainly. "No, I was just fooling."

"Well, *don't,*" he said.

"I'm sorry, Coop—you're right. That was thoughtless." I searched his face for a sign of forgiveness, but all I saw was sadness. I'd heard that he and Dimitri had painted the town on New Year's Eve, and by the strain on his face and the tiredness in his eyes, it looked like the party might've lasted all week. "How've you been?" I asked softly.

"Okay," he said, then looked around. "Where's Abe?"

"I think he's taking out the garbage."

Coop searched my eyes. "Sal, I know you said you didn't think we could just be friends, but I miss you so much, I don't think I can handle not seeing you at all."

I swallowed. "I feel the same way."

"So why can't we just spend time together? Not seeing you is driving me crazy."

"It's driving me crazy too, Coop, but I'm worried we'll end up in bed again . . . and as much as I'd love to, nothing has changed—I'm still married."

I could see him trying to suppress a smile. "We can spend time together without ending up in bed."

"Yeah," I said, laughing. "Just look at you— even the word *bed* makes you smile."

"No, it doesn't," he said, frowning. "I have willpower; it's not my fault if *you* don't."

"Very funny," I said, rolling my eyes.

The back door slammed and Abe appeared in the doorway. "Well, well, look who the cat dragged in," he teased, "the long lost lov—" He stopped and held up his hands. "Oh, I forgot—there's *nothing* going on."

"There *is* nothing going on," I assured him.

"I know," he said as he disappeared into the back, "and the sky's not blue," he called over his shoulder.

"As a matter of fact, it's looking pretty darn gray today," I called after him.

Coop watched him disappear and then looked back at me. "Are you closing soon?"

"Yeah, I just have to finish cleaning up."

"Want to go for a drink?"

I looked up from wiping the counter. "I don't know if that's a good idea—you'll just use alcohol to weaken my resolve."

"No, I won't," he said, sounding wounded. "Just a simple drink with a friend."

"Where's Dimitri?" I asked, eyeing him. "Did his wife ground him?"

"Noo," Coop said, laughing.

"I bet she did."

"Come for a drink and I'll drive you home."

"Okay," I said resignedly.

Fifteen minutes later, we were sitting in The Brotherhood of the Thieves with a beer and a glass of wine between us. "How was your New Year's?" Coop asked, and I told him all about

Lizzy and Simon's visit—including the news that Simon's grandmother was putting her house on the market.

Coop raised his eyebrows. "Are you going to buy it?"

"I might," I said. "I just got the check for my dad's house, so I could, but I could also buy something else. I don't want to rush into anything."

Coop nodded. "There are a lot of nice places out here, but Simon's grandmother's cottage has one of the prettiest settings—it's close to town, but still private, and it has a killer view. Plus, it's a solid, well-built house. If I was looking for a place, I'd pick it over my own house."

"Soo, just to clarify, you think . . . maybe I should buy it?"

He laughed. "Is that what you got out of all that?"

"Sort of," I said, laughing.

"Yeah, I guess you should."

"I don't know," I said. "It needs to be renovated and . . ."

"I told you I'd help."

I took a sip of my wine and pictured him helping. "Yeah, that's just what I need—your half-naked, tan body hammering away on projects around my house."

"If my half-naked body is too much for you, I'll keep my shirt on."

"I'll have to think about it."

"Which?" he teased. "My half-naked body or buying the house?"

"Both," I said, smiling.

He laughed and then motioned to the bartender for two more drinks.

When we walked outside an hour later, it was still snowing—hard—and when we walked to the truck, it looked like a plow had buried it. "Want to just leave it?" I asked.

"No," he said. "You might be able to walk home from here, but it's a bit far for me."

He brushed off the driver's door with his arm, opened it, started the truck, and then reached behind the seat for a snow shovel and brush. He brushed off my door and I climbed in to wait, and after he cleared the windshield, I watched him shovel and thought about his offer to help with renovations. It was hard enough watching him shovel with a heavy winter coat on—how in the world would I manage when he wasn't wearing a shirt?

He opened the driver's door, slid the shovel and brush behind the seat, climbed in, and blew on his hands. "All day, it looked like snow, but I had no idea we were going to get walloped."

"I didn't either," I said. "It's a good night for a fire."

"Mmm, that would be nice," he said, holding his hands in front of the heat vents. Finally, he put the truck in gear and, with some sliding and wheel spinning, we made our way home.

"Do you still want a fire?" he asked as he pulled into my driveway.

"You're just trying to get an invitation inside," I teased.

"No, I'm not," he said. "I'm just being neighborly."

I laughed. "Okay, if you have time."

"I have nothing but time," he said, turning off the truck. We trudged through the snow toward the dark house. "I should've left a light on," I said apologetically. "I didn't expect to get home after dark." I fumbled to unlock the door. "Someday, I'm going to move somewhere warm where it never snows."

"You're going to leave Nantucket?!"

"Yes, I'm going to find a *tropical* island."

"You're a hardy New Englander—you'll never leave."

"I might," I said, turning on the lights.

Coop looked around. "Feels like it's been forever since I was here."

I smiled but didn't say anything. He unzipped his coat, stomped his boots, and walked over to my fireplace. "You're gonna need more wood soon," he said, nodding to the half-full black iron firewood ring.

"There's enough for tonight. I'll bring more in tomorrow." I watched him stack the logs in the fireplace. "Not too big," I added. "I probably won't stay up very late."

He nodded, opened the damper, lit the newspaper, and fanned the tiny flicker until the kindling was fully engulfed and licking over the logs, crackling and spitting.

"Want a drink?" I asked, holding up the bottle of Jack Daniels he'd brought over and left behind.

"Sure," he said with the slow smile that always stole my heart.

"There's no smiling, though," I warned, "or I'll lose my resolve." I handed him the glass, and when he gave me a somber look, I ended up laughing. "Oh, Coop," I said. "You have no idea how much I wish it didn't have to be this way." I searched his eyes. "And how much I want you."

He nodded, smiling sadly, and took a sip of his drink. "You could if you wanted to."

"Don't tempt me," I said, and against my better judgement, I poured a glass of wine and joined him on the couch. "How are things at the boathouse?"

"Good," he said. "I've been commissioned to build a sailboat."

"Are you able to work when it's this cold?"

"Oh, yeah. There's a big wood stove in the back of the boathouse, so it stays pretty warm."

"Who commissioned the sailboat?"

"A guy from Boston."

"And you know what you're doing?" I teased.

"No, but I'm learning," he said with a smile, adding, "I'm not a beginner, you know. My uncle Henry was a boat builder in Maine, and Lily and I used to spend summers there."

"I didn't know that," I said in surprise.

He nodded. "Henry was my dad's older brother —he never married. He was nothing like my dad—he was more of a nature lover." He held up his drink and smiled. "He loved his whiskey too. I learned a lot from him. He even tried to talk me out of officer's school, but my dad kept warning me if I didn't choose a branch of the service, I'd get drafted."

We quietly watched the fire and listened to the wind howling around the house. "You should probably just sleep here tonight," I said, patting the couch.

"You're gonna let me sleep on your couch?" he teased, finishing his drink.

"Maybe—if you promise to behave."

He grinned. "I'm the one with the willpower, remember? Besides, I'm not going to do anything that will ruin our friendship," he added.

I nodded and felt tears welling up in my eyes. I took a sip of my drink and stared into the flames.

"Hey," he said softly, noticing a tear trickle down my cheek. "What's the matter?"

"Nothing."

"Something," he countered.

I wiped my eyes. "I just wish it didn't have to be this way."

"Sally, if this is too hard, I can go," he said.

"That's just it—I don't want you to go . . . *ever*."

He looked back at the fire. "I wish it didn't have to be this way either," he said softly, putting his arm around me and kissing the top of my head. It was an innocent gesture, but his touch and the closeness of him sent a wave of desire sweeping through me. I put my hand on his leg. "Mmm, be careful," he whispered.

"I am being careful," I said, sliding it along his thigh. I looked up, and as I slid my hand higher, he closed his eyes.

Chapter 26

After a while, I think Coop must've gotten used to having his heart broken, or maybe he just stopped believing me. I was the little *girl* who cried wolf: I'd started attending mass almost every week, and every other week I'd tell him we had to stop making love, but then a week later, we'd be all tangled up in the sheets again *and* it would be better than it had ever been before. I was a confused mess—I wanted to be good—I wanted to go to heaven . . . but I wanted Coop too! Maybe that's what Coop liked about it— he'd stand there stoically while I dealt the blow of abstinence; then he'd wait patiently until I was on fire and be ever ready to put out the flames. The longest I ever went without him was thirteen days, and forever after, he joked that it was my P.R.

In the months that followed I repeatedly repented, went to confession, declared abstinence, and resolved to do better, but I knew it was hopeless—I was a woeful sinner. It was just a matter of time before I gave in and then prayed God would forgive me.

In late April, I bought Mrs. Cohen's house, and when she inquired—through Simon—if I wanted any of her furnishings, I graciously declined. I added that I'd love to have some of her books, though, *and* her Crock-Pot. Simon assured me that I was welcome to as many books as I wanted, and she would be happy to give me her Crock-Pot. He also said he was glad I didn't want any of her furniture because he and Lizzy were buying a house, too, and they desperately needed furniture. We arranged for a mover to collect Mrs. Cohen's furnishings and valuables and to deliver them to Simon and Lizzy's new house in Somerville; then the movers drove to Medford, emptied my storage unit, which Lizzy unlocked for them, and brought my stuff to Nantucket. It was a seamless transition, and in the three days the house was empty, Coop and I painted, cleaned, ate pizza, drank beer, and made love on the bare wooden floor.

On the night before my furniture was set to arrive, Coop came up my porch steps with a box in his arms. I raised my eyebrows, but he just smiled, and when I pulled open the top, a tiny gray head popped out, blinking beautiful slate-blue eyes at me. "Oh, my goodness!" I exclaimed, scooping out the little tiger kitten. "I always wanted a kitten or a puppy, but my dad would never let me get one." I brushed the kitten's soft head against my cheek. "Where'd you get her?" I asked.

"Him," Coop corrected. "My neighbor had a sign in her yard, and when I stopped by, he was the only one left."

"You were the only one left?" I cooed, holding the kitten's nose to mine. "How can that be?" I gave Coop a hug. "Thank you so much. He's perfect."

"You're welcome. I have some other stuff in the truck—cat food, cat litter, a cat carrier to take him to the vet in—which my neighbor said you'd need to do soon."

I nodded and sat on the floor with the kitten while Coop went back out to his truck. When he came in with his arms full, I looked up. "I think we should call him Henry."

He smiled. "After my uncle?"

I nodded.

He laughed. "He'd like that."

It was the first Sunday in May, and the rest of the day, when we weren't getting the house ready, we were playing with Henry. He had a sweet personality and a motorboat purr, and when he grew tired, he curled up on my lap and promptly fell asleep.

That night, because my furniture hadn't arrived, Henry and I spent the night at Coop's, and as I lay in bed—unable to fall asleep—I thought about everything that had happened in my life —from graduating, working at Stop & Shop, and living under my dad's roof in Medford to losing my dad, becoming a home—and pet— owner, and working at a bakery on Nantucket. I never would've predicted the twists and turns my life would take in the span of a year. Nor had I imagined I'd lose my dad or fall deeply in love with a man I'd want to be with for the rest of my life. I was so richly—and undeservedly—blessed, and as I was drifting off, I thanked God for loving me so unconditionally.

Moments later, I was startled awake by shouting. "Mikey, where are you? Oh, God, Mikey!"

"Wake up, Coop," I said, shaking him. He swung his arm around in defense, almost hitting me. I ducked and shook him again. "Coop, it's okay. Wake up."

He sat up suddenly, shaking and sobbing, and I waited for him to calm down.

"You okay?" I asked softly.

He nodded. "I'm sorry."

"Don't be. I'm sorry you're so tormented by these nightmares." I bit my lip. "Are you ever going to tell me what happened?"

Coop ran his fingers through his hair, and when he spoke, his voice was choked with emotion. "Mikey was my best friend—we went through everything together—and one night, we were coming into a village when, out of nowhere, we were ambushed. It was pitch-black—no moon or stars—just darkness, and all we could see were flashes of light—gunfire and exploding grenades. Mikey was in front of me, and this V.C. stood up and tossed a grenade right in front of us. Mikey pushed me back and threw himself on top of it—he didn't even think—he just did it.

"Afterward, it was total chaos. I crawled around, trying to find him—I wanted to help him—get him to a medic, but he wasn't anywhere." Coop stopped and ran his hands through his hair again. "I felt all over the ground . . . my hands were wet and sticky . . . and then, I found his dog tags, which made me even more frantic because, if he wasn't wearing them, no one would know who he was. I kept shouting his name, but then my commander came up behind me and clamped his hand over my mouth, hissing that I had to shut up. When it finally grew light out, I looked down and realized my hands and clothes were covered in blood . . . but I didn't have a scratch on me."

Tears filled my eyes. "Oh, Coop, that's awful. I'm so sorry. Are his tags the ones you wear?"

He nodded. "I tried to give them to his mom, but she wanted me to have them." He touched the silver tags hanging around his neck. "In my dreams, I see him throwing himself on that grenade, and when I try to find him . . . he isn't there. He's gone. Just gone. He was my best friend and he was blown to bits . . . saving *me*."

My tears spilled down my cheeks. I didn't know what to say, so I just wrapped my arms around him as he sobbed.

August

Sally looked up when she heard the back door open, and wiped her hands on her apron. "Oh, Tracey, I was sorry to hear about your dad," she said, wrapping her in a hug.

"Thanks, Sal," Tracey said, her eyes filling with tears.

Sally held her at arm's length. "Are you sure you're ready to come back to work?"

Tracey smiled. "Yes, but I didn't know you were going to be closed today."

Sally nodded. "I have a lot I want to do to get ready for tomorrow, and it was the only way to get everything done and have the food be fresh."

"Well, I'd like to help—it's such a big day! And besides, if I don't keep busy, I'm going to go crazy. I see my dad at every turn in that old house."

"I know how you feel—there are so many memories in your childhood home."

Tracey nodded. "I can almost hear him calling us."

Sally squeezed her shoulder. "How're the kids taking it?"

"They're really sad." She motioned toward the door. "They're out back," she added. "They're waiting for Aidan because they all have a surprise for you. They can't wait to help, too—it will keep their mind off things. T.J. is especially heartbroken—he keeps talking about the time he went fishing with his grandfather . . . and the time they saw the whales—it's one of his favorite memories. He wishes they could've gone more often."

Sally nodded. "It's good he has that memory —it's something he'll never forget."

"The one thing that gives me comfort— even more than knowing my dad is finally reunited with my mom—is knowing he's reunited with Coop."

Sally laughed. "I am sure those two are having a grand ole time painting heaven!"

"I'm sure they are," Tracey said. "I don't know how many times my mom had to call Liam and ask him to go round them up." She paused. "I loved the book by the way."

Sally looked up in surprise. "You read it?"

"I did. Liam lent it to me for my trip—it was a godsend. I truly loved it. Sometimes life just gets you down and you start to think you're the only one who's going through stuff, but a book like yours makes you feel less alone."

"Thanks," Sally said, smiling. "I really hoped

—by writing it—that people would come away with that kind of a feeling."

The bell on the door jingled and they both looked up. "Speak of the devil!" Sally said.

Liam half smiled as he held the door open for Tuck, who bounded across the room, almost knocking them over. "Hullo, love," Sally said as he slobbered her with wet kisses.

Liam put his arm around Tracey and kissed the top of her head. "How's it going?"

"It's going," she said, trying to sound more chipper than she felt. "Is Aidan with you? The kids are waiting for him."

Liam nodded. "Yup, he's out back." Then he looked at Sally. "So, tomorrow's the big day!"

"It is," Sally said, smiling. "Mitchell's Book Corner just delivered the books, but I think they brought over too many," she said, pointing to several boxes piled in the corner. "They say they've been getting lots of calls and orders." She shook her head. "I honestly don't know what to expect."

Just then the door banged open and Aidan, wearing an impish grin, peered around the doorway.

Sally raised her eyebrows. "Hmm, you look like the cat who ate the canary. What are you up to?"

Aidan stepped shyly into the kitchen. "We made something for your book party," he said, starting to unroll a large roll of paper as he walked across the room. T.J. and Olivia stepped inside, too, holding the other end, and by the time Aidan reached the far wall, a fifteen-foot banner stretched across the room that said, *"Congratulations, Sally!— SUMMER DANCE—Congratulations, Sally!"* and on either end were drawings of two white wooden lanterns—just like the image on the cover.

"Oh, my goodness!" Sally said, covering her mouth. "You made this?!"

Beaming smiles spread across the kids' faces as they nodded. "We're going to hang it out front," Aidan said, "so everyone can see it."

"That's a wonderful idea," Sally said, smiling and giving them each a hug. "When did you find the time to make it?"

Aidan shrugged. "We've been working on it ever since T.J. and Olivia stayed at our house."

"Where in the world did you find a wall— or a floor—big enough?"

"The boathouse," T.J. answered. "I drew the covers."

"Well, you did a great job," Sally said, nodding approvingly.

T.J. beamed and Olivia chimed in, "It's been hanging up for a month!"

"Yeah, we were praying you wouldn't stop by," Aidan added, laughing.

Everyone else laughed, too; then Liam suggested they go outside and figure out the best way to hang it.

"There's a ladder in the shed if you need one," Sally said. "But be careful."

The three kids followed Liam outside and Tracey turned to Sally. "So, what's on the menu?"

"Well," Sally said with a sigh as she pushed back her hair. "I was going to keep it simple, but it's gotten a little complicated. We're having wine or sparkling water and cheese—Mitchell is taking care of that. And I'm planning to make some platters of finger food—cucumber and cream cheese sandwiches, and egg salad sandwiches, lemon squares, brownies, and mini cream puffs." She paused, frowning. "I think there's something else, too, but I can't remember what it is. . . ."

Tracey laughed. "You couldn't just stick with wine and cheese?" she teased.

Sally shook her head. "What fun would that be?"

"You're going to be so busy signing books, you're not even going to get to enjoy the refreshments."

"Maybe," Sally said skeptically. "And if that's the case, it's okay. We'll see—it might be a total flop, but if, by some miracle, it's not, do you think the kids would mind passing trays of food?"

"I'm sure they'd love to."

The front door opened and Aidan came running in. "Come see!" he said excitedly, reaching for Sally's hand. She and Tracey both followed him outside and stood in front of the long gray building Sally had bought years earlier from Abe and renamed *Cuppa Jo to Go—Where the Dough Always Rises!*

"It looks great!" Sally said, hugging them again. "I hope people come."

"I hope so too," Aidan said, grinning and hugging her back.

Liam and the boys stayed outside to sweep the walk and porch and weed the garden while Tracey and Olivia went inside to help Sally make the refreshments for the reception: enough egg salad to feed an army; chocolate frosting and a big pot of vanilla pudding—enough to frost and fill three hundred mini cream puffs—and lastly, three large trays of lemon squares.

"I wish I could remember the other thing I wanted to make," Sally said.

"I wouldn't worry about it, Sal," Tracey said, gesturing to all the food. "This doesn't even include the cucumber and cream cheese sandwiches."

"Sally, can I have a lemon square?" Olivia asked.

"Of course, Liv," Sally said, gently brushing flour off Olivia's cheek. "You've been such a big help. I don't know what I would've done without you." She kissed the top of her head. "Do you want to take some out for the boys too?" Olivia nodded and Sally expertly cut several lemon squares and put them on a plate. "Ask them if they'd like a drink."

Olivia took a big bite out of one of the squares and, with a happy confectioners' sugar grin, headed outside with the plate. Moments later, she reappeared with all three hot, tired, thirsty boys trailing her. "What have you got?" Liam asked. "Any beer?"

"As a matter of fact, I do," Sally said, opening the fridge. "What about you two?" she asked, eyeing T.J. and Aidan.

"Do you have any soda?" T.J. asked hopefully.

"You can take whatever you'd like from the cooler out front."

"All right!" they said, hurrying off with Olivia behind them to make their selection.

"Would you like a beer, too, Trace?" Sally asked.

"Sure," Tracey said, smiling.

Sally pulled three bottles out of the fridge and opened them all. She looked up at the clock and realized it was five-thirty. "I didn't realize it was so late! Would you guys like to order pizza? It's the least I can do after all your help."

"Pizza sounds good," Liam said, wiping his brow and looking over at Tracey.

"Anytime I don't have to figure out dinner is a good day," she agreed, grinning.

"Pizza it is!" Sally said, picking up the phone. "What do the kids like?"

"Olivia likes plain, but T.J. will eat anything."

"Same with Aidan," Liam said.

"And you?"

"Anything," they said in unison.

Sally dialed the phone and ordered three large pizzas—one cheese, one supreme, and one Hawaiian—and while Liam and Tracey went to pick them up—along with another six-pack of *Whale's Tale*—she and the kids set up the tables for the big event the next day.

"Sal, do you think my mom and Cap will get married?" T.J. ventured.

Sally looked up in surprise. "Oh, I don't know, hon," she said. "I've known your mom and Liam since they were young—younger than you guys and I always thought they'd make a good couple, but they went their separate ways. Sometimes, it takes a while to put the past behind you." As she said this, the truth of it wasn't lost on her and she couldn't help but smile—it had taken her forty-four years!

"I hope they do," Olivia said wistfully. "I think they'd both be happier."

"Me too," Aidan said.

"Well, with you three working on it, I bet it'll happen," she said, laughing.

"Pizza's here!" Tracey called, coming into the kitchen through the back door.

"All right!" T.J. cried. "I'm starving!"

"Me too!" Aidan said.

"Me three!" Olivia chimed in.

The kids pulled stools up around the counters while Sally pulled out the special sunflower paper plates and napkins she'd bought for the reception.

"Don't you have some plain paper plates?" Tracey asked.

"I'll just use a paper towel," Liam said, frowning and reaching for a roll.

"Yeah, you should save these for tomorrow, Sally," Tracey said. "You want to be sure you have enough."

Sally rolled her eyes. "I'm sure they'll be more than enough."

"You never know," Aidan said with a grin.

"You're right," she said, laughing. "You never do!"

"That reminds me," Tracey said, looking at Liam. "I have Sally's book in my car. You should try to finish it before tomorrow. Don't let me forget to give it to you."

Liam took a sip of his beer. "I might not be able to stay awake tonight."

"Oh, you'll be able to stay awake! It's really good!"

Liam laughed and looked over at Sally. "You can't get a better review than that."

"No, you can't," Sally agreed, smiling as she took a bite of her pizza.

PART IV

For by grace you have been saved . . .
—Ephesians 2:8

Chapter 27

"My mother isn't coming," Lizzy said matter-of-factly.

"Are you serious?" I asked in disbelief as I zipped up the back of her wedding gown.

She nodded. "She said she's going to be in St. Clement Chapel, praying for my soul."

"Oh, Lizzy, I'm so sorry," I consoled. "She's going to miss out on a truly special occasion." I felt bad for Mrs. McAllister—why was she being so stubbornly resistant to her daughter marrying someone who is Jewish? It was worse than my own stubborn resistance to publically acknowledge my relationship with Coop.

Lizzy shook her head. "It's fine. At least I won't have to worry about her getting drunk and making a scene. It'll make my whole day less stressful."

I nodded, but I knew she was disappointed. "Maybe she'll change her mind."

"I hope not! She probably won't even go to St. Clement. She'll just sit in the living room, drinking, and I don't need her to change her mind and *show up* drunk."

"She's just worried about you. She's never been truly happy and she doesn't want that to happen to you."

Lizzy put her hands on my shoulders and looked

in my eyes. "Sal, you and I both know that's a load of crap, but thanks for trying."

I smiled and hugged her. "It's not easy being you."

"It's not easy being *us*," she said, laughing.

"Did you ever hear from your dad?"

"Not a word."

"Maybe the address you have is old," I offered as I helped her put on her veil. "I'm sure he'd be here if he knew."

"No, he wouldn't. He's never cared. Why should he start now?"

"Okay, you're probably right," I said, laughing and giving up—there was no pulling the wool over her eyes! "But if he'd ever taken the time to get to know you, he'd be here."

"Maybe," she said, smiling.

We stood side by side, looking in the full-length mirror. "Oh my, Lizzy! You're the most beautiful bride I've ever seen!" I said, putting my arm around her.

"You clean up pretty good too," she teased.

"Thanks," I said, laughing. "Ready?"

She nodded confidently and then searched my eyes. "I wish you'd brought someone to dance with, Sal—it'd be so much more fun for you."

"Don't you worry about me—I'm going to have plenty of fun."

"You should've brought your friend . . . what's his name? You know—the boat builder."

"Coop?" I asked. "Nah, that wouldn't be good," I said, shaking my head, "especially if your mom came."

Lizzy eyed me. "Is there really *nothing* going on between you two?"

I jokingly feigned indignance as I walked the fine line between not lying and not telling the truth. "What?! I'm a married woman!"

"A married woman with a streak of mischief," she said, laughing.

"You forget—I'm the one who's going to heaven."

"I haven't forgotten," Lizzy said. "You *are* going to heaven, and your beautiful mom and dad are going to give you a big hug when you get there."

I smiled. "Maybe. Now, let's get out there so you can knock 'em dead."

"Okay," she said.

As she opened the door, I looked at my reflection one last time. Who had I become that I would purposely deceive my best friend? Who was I kidding? I wasn't a candidate for heaven. My life was a lie and I didn't know which sin was worse—my affair with Coop or not being honest with my friends. I hated deceiving the people I loved. Even though I had a feeling they all knew what was going on, it bothered me that I couldn't be open and honest. And that was just the beginning of my charade. Whenever one of us was invited to a special event—like Lizzy and Simon's wedding—we couldn't go as a couple. Even if we were both invited to the same social gathering, we had to attend separately, or not at all. And if we did go separately, Coop would give me a mischievous, knowing smile from across the room and I'd blush and feel a wave of heat rush through me— he knew exactly what he was doing!

"Coming?" Lizzy asked, holding the door.

"I'm right behind you," I said, shaking off my dismay.

Lizzy stepped out into the room where all the women in Simon's family were waiting, and they *oohed* and *aahed* when they saw her. Lizzy smiled, nodding politely, but her eyes seemed to search for someone in particular. Finally, they settled on a well-dressed elderly woman sitting near the window, and I immediately knew who she was.

"Oh my! Elizabeth, you look stunning," she said, taking Lizzy's hands.

I smiled—I'd never heard anyone call Lizzy *Elizabeth* before.

"Thank you," Lizzy said, politely kissing her cheek. "You look lovely, too, Bubbe."

Bubbe?

"Thank you," the older woman said graciously. Then she turned to me, her eyes sparkling. "You must be Sally."

I nodded, politely extending my hand. "It's a pleasure to meet you, Mrs. Cohen."

"The pleasure is all mine, my dear," she said, taking both my hands in hers. I felt her soft, paper-thin skin and her gnarled, arthritic fingers, and looked down; when I did, I noticed a long number tattooed on the inside of her wrist and caught my breath, but she didn't seem to notice. "I've heard so many nice things about you," she continued.

"And I, you," I said, regaining my composure.

"How's my little house?"

"It's wonderful," I said. "I love it!"

"I'm glad," she said, nodding. "I'm glad someone is enjoying it as much as I did. I hope you have a lifetime of blessings and happiness there."

"Thank you," I said. "And thank you for all the books . . . and your Crock-Pot too."

"You're very welcome, I'm sure. I've always loved to read—I think it's the best way to expand one's mind."

I nodded. "I agree and I love to read too."

Mrs. Cohen nodded and turned back to Lizzy. "So, my dear, are you ready to marry my handsome grandson?"

"I *am*," Lizzy said, smiling, and there wasn't a trace of doubt in her eyes.

Jewish weddings are steeped in traditions that honor Biblical figures—figures with which I was very familiar—from Abraham and Sarah to Isaac and Rebekah. In fact, I was very surprised to learn that the Torah is filled with the same stories in the Old Testament.

Simon wore a kippah on his head and a tailored white robe—or *kittel*—over his suit—the traditional dress of Yom Kippur, and Lizzy wore an elegant, yet modest, brocade white gown. Her veil was lovely, too, and in keeping with tradition, Simon carefully lowered it over her face after he was certain she was the bride he planned to marry—there would be no tricking the groom into marrying the wrong girl, as happened in the Old Testament when Laban tricked Jacob into marrying his older daughter, Leah, instead of his beloved beautiful Rachel!

The wedding ceremony took place on a beautiful August Sunday under a chuppah. Lizzy and Simon —the *chatan* and *kallah*—were absolved of all past sins as their souls were made spiritually pure. And as they became one with each other, Simon gently slipped the simple gold band his grandmother had given him onto the first finger of Lizzy's right hand. Afterward, there was drinking of wine, signing of the *Ketubah* (marriage contract), stomping of a glass, and lots of Jewish blessings. And in the end, although the traditions of the Jewish and Catholic faiths differ, the result is the same—a couple is married!

"Mazel tov!" I whispered as I gave my childhood friend a long hug.

Chapter 28

"Mommy's home!" Coop called as I came up the porch steps. Almost immediately, I heard soft paws on wood as Henry came sliding around the corner.

"Hey there, sweetie pie," I said, kneeling down. Henry wasn't a kitten anymore—he was a sleek, handsome cat. His every movement seemed effortless and graceful. He hopped up and lightly rested his snow-white paws on my knee, then leaned up to touch my nose with his—one of his many funny antics—as if he was nearsighted and needed to be nose-to-nose with me to be sure. "It's really me," I said, kissing the top of his head. Satisfied, he dropped down and swished through my legs, purring like a motorboat. "I missed you, too," I said, laughing.

"What about me?" Coop asked, leaning against the kitchen doorway, wiping his hands on a dishtowel.

"Maybe a little," I teased, giving him a hug.

"That's all I get?"

"What else did you have in mind?"

He looped the dishtowel around my waist and pulled me against him, and as he kissed my cheek and made his way slowly down to my neck, I could feel how aroused he was. "I've *really* missed you," he murmured, teasing my lips with his tongue.

"I've *really* missed you too," I whispered. "Especially when I didn't have anyone to dance with."

"That's no one's fault but your own," he whispered, pulling me toward the bedroom.

Twenty minutes later, I was lying naked and content in his arms when Henry leapt lightly onto the bed and eyed us curiously.

I laughed. "I guess he became acclimated to being here."

"Yep, no problem. I actually think he likes it better here."

Henry pressed his nose against Coop's and then curled up next to him.

"See?" Coop said.

I laughed. "Just because he cuddles up next to you doesn't mean he likes it better."

"I think I'm going to keep him," Coop teased, stroking Henry's head. "What do you think, Hen, want to stay with me?" Henry opened one eye, pushed his head into Coop's hand, and yawned contentedly.

Coop grinned. "I knew it."

"Don't even think about it," I said, laughing.

"Of course, *you* could come live with us too."

I snuggled closer to them. "I wish I could," I said softly.

Life went on. Coop and I worked our days and

spent our nights together. Although I had Sundays off, Coop worked *every* day. Abe told him he should slow down and take a day off to go fishing once in a while . . . and I repeatedly reminded him of the Bible's cautionary Sabbath commandment: "Thou shall not sow thy field or prune thy vine-yard!" But Coop just laughed and said if he didn't prune his vineyard, he wouldn't have any wine.

I honestly think he felt if he worked until he was bone tired and had a few drinks, he'd sleep through the night. It rarely worked, though, but I could certainly understand why he tried. I was haunted by events in my past, too, and even though it had been years, whenever Coop wasn't beside me at night, I had trouble falling asleep, certain Drew was lingering in the shadows. On nights like that, my consolation was Henry—who hopped up on the bed and put his nose up against mine, making sure it was me.

Chapter 29

It was a couple of years before Coop and I found ourselves constrained by our secret again. It happened when Coop's sister gave birth to a son and asked Coop to be little Liam's godfather. Coop was thrilled, and although I really wanted to go to the christening, I knew my presence would only raise eyebrows—*and* questions. Needless to say, Coop went alone, and when he came home, he was completely in love with his little nephew.

"Let's have a baby," he said as we lay in bed that night.

"I think that might really give us away," I teased.

"Who cares?" he said in a voice that sounded earnest. "We would make a beautiful baby. You're so pretty and I'm so handsome, he'd be a lady-killer."

"You're so modest too," I teased. "And how do you know it would be a *he?*"

"He . . . she . . . it wouldn't matter."

I felt tears in my eyes. "Coop, I'd *love* nothing more than to make a baby with you," I said softly, "but all this time . . . all this time that we haven't used birth control"—I bit my lip—"is a pretty good sign the doctor was right after I lost my baby—I can't get pregnant."

Coop grew quiet and I couldn't help but wonder if he was having second thoughts about us—about *me*. As we lay side by side, it felt as if we were worlds apart. All I could think about was the moment my dad said I might not be able to have children, but what was Coop thinking? Was he recalling past loves—loves that could have made him a dad? Was he regretting his decision to be with me? Would he leave me? I lay still for a long time, and finally, I squeezed his hand. To my great relief, he squeezed back; then he pulled me closer and kissed the top of my head. "I love you, Sal," he whispered.

"I love you, too," I said softly, feeling thankful.

In late August, Lizzy called to say she was coming for a visit. I was elated! It had been two years since their wedding, two years since Simon had taken the new position at the hospital that kept him busy all the time, and two years since they'd been able to come to Nantucket.

"Is Si coming?" I asked.

"No, he has to work," she said. "It'll be a girls' weekend," she added, "just like old times!"

"That'll be great—I can't wait!"

On Friday afternoon, I walked down to the wharf and watched the ferry pull in. As it docked, I scanned the deck, looking for Lizzy, but there was no sign of her, and as the last passenger disembarked, I began to worry. Maybe something happened. Maybe she missed the ferry.

Maybe she'd been in an accident on the way to Hyannis. I looked at my watch, wondering when the next ferry was scheduled to arrive. Then I looked back up and saw a very round woman making her way slowly toward the ramp. "Lizzy!" I shouted in surprise. She looked up and waved. Her face was beaming!

"Oh, my goodness!" I cried, hurrying over. "Look at you! How come you didn't tell me?"

She smiled. "I wanted to surprise you."

I laughed and hugged her awkwardly and then held her at arms' length. "I can't believe it! When are you due?"

"Mid-September, although it feels like she's going to make her grand entrance at any moment."

"Her?!" I asked in surprise.

Lizzy nodded. "I'm having a girl."

"Oh, Lizzy, I'm so happy for you! How're you feeling?"

"Big! I need to sit down a lot—like now—and I have to pee every five minutes. That's why I was the last one to get off the ferry—I was in the bathroom and it was so tiny I could hardly turn around."

I laughed, picturing Lizzy maneuvering in what I knew to be a closet-size room with a door that practically touched the front of the toilet—only a man could design a bathroom that had no room to sit.

"Want to sit now?" I asked, motioning to a bench. She nodded and began to waddle toward it.

I carried her bags and sat down next to her. "I can't believe you didn't tell me."

"I wanted to tell you," she said, laughing. "You don't know how many times I almost did, but I really wanted to see your face."

"Was it worth it?" I asked, laughing.

"It was," she confirmed.

I shook my head in disbelief. "Do you have a name picked out?"

"Elise—it means *'Promise of God.'* "

"I love it! It's perfect."

All of a sudden, Lizzy's lip started to tremble and tears welled up in her eyes. Within seconds, they were spilling down her cheeks.

"What's the matter?" I asked, reaching for her hands.

She shook her head again, unable to answer.

"Lizzy, what's wrong?" I asked, feeling my heart race.

She pressed her lips together. "It's *not* perfect, Sal. My baby isn't perfect. She will *never* be perfect."

I waited for her to continue, but she just wept.

"How do you know? What's the matter? What did the doctor say?"

She covered her mouth with one hand and sat up straighter, rubbing her belly. Then she closed her eyes and clenched her jaw. I had never seen her so sad, and tears filled my own eyes as I waited. "Tell me . . ." I said softly.

She nodded. "I'm trying—this is why I couldn't tell you on the phone—I knew, as soon as I saw you, I'd lose it," she said, her voice filled with frustration and anguish.

I squeezed her hands and she took a deep breath. "There's something wrong with my baby," she whispered.

"There is?" I felt my heart sink. "Are you sure? How do you know? Maybe your doctor made a mistake."

Lizzy shook her head. "He did a test—an AFP—it's a standard blood test and my numbers were really low—and he said that's an indicator that there's something wrong—that she may have Down's." She paused. "He suggested I consider terminating."

"He did?" I was horrified. "He wanted you to have an abortion?"

"He didn't *want* me to. He just said it was an option."

"Oh, Lizzy," I whispered. "I'm so sorry. Did you?" I ventured. "Did you consider it?"

She shook her head. "Not for a second," she said, searching my eyes. "I love her, Sal. I haven't even met her yet, but I love her more than life itself."

I nodded.

"Now I understand why you were so sad when

you lost your baby. I don't want anything to happen to her."

"Does your mom know?"

Lizzy nodded and then rolled her eyes. "You'll never guess what she said."

I frowned, but then, all of a sudden, I knew exactly what Mrs. McAllister had said. "She said God is punishing you for marrying Simon."

Lizzy nodded and laughed, wiping her eyes. "She's so predictable!"

"You don't believe that, do you?"

"No," she said as fresh tears filled her eyes. "I don't care what she thinks. I don't care what anyone thinks. The only thing that matters is that Elise's feelings are *never* hurt. I know kids are going to make fun of her—you know how kids are—they're mean and they're going to tease her." She shook her head again. "Life is hard enough without being different—without everyone looking at you, without everyone feeling sorry for you . . . for *us*. Sally, I don't want anyone's pity. I just want to love my baby without the world watching. If I could live out in the country and raise my baby with no one watching and judging me and feeling sorry for us, I would. I don't care what people think, but I *don't* want their pity. I won't be able to bear it if people look at us and shake their heads as if we've suffered some terrible misfortune."

I swallowed, already regretting having said

I was sorry. "I'd never pity you, Lizzy," I said as I gently brushed away her tears and searched her eyes. "Elise is going to be a beautiful baby—she's going to touch many lives with her sweet, kind ways. You just wait and see. She's going to be strong and beautiful, and she's going to fill your hearts—and the hearts of everyone she meets—with love."

Lizzy mustered a smile. "I know, Sal. I know she is."

"You're going to be a great mom too," I added, smiling.

"You think?" she said, wiping her eyes.

"Well, you already have that mother bear thing down pat," I teased.

"I do," she agreed, laughing.

We called for a taxi, and while we were waiting for it to come, Coop drove by. When he saw us, he looked surprised and waved, and I tried to discreetly wave back, hoping Lizzy wouldn't notice, but of course, she did.

"Is that your cute boat-builder friend?"

I nodded and looked up the street. "Where is that dumb taxi?"

"Maybe he would give us a ride," she suggested.

"He's probably busy," I said, although I knew he wasn't. In fact, I knew exactly where he was going. "Girls' weekend means guys' weekend, too," he'd said happily, "and Dimitri and I have some serious male bonding to do!"

Lizzy nodded. "I'm sorry I'm holding you up. I wish I could walk," she said apologetically. "I can't wait to see what you've done to the cottage."

"Don't be silly," I said. "We have all the time in the world." I sat down next to her and when she looked up and smiled, I felt a tidal wave of guilt wash over me. Not telling Lizzy about Coop suddenly seemed so silly, not to mention dishonest. After everything we'd been through together—and now, with the news she'd just shared—I felt miserable. I couldn't imagine her ever keeping anything from me—especially something like this—and if she did, I would not only be hurt—I'd be mad. "The truth is, Lizzy . . ." I began softly, but just as I started to tell her, our taxi pulled up and I immediately stood and picked up her bags, thankful for the interruption.

"Henry is such a sweetheart," Lizzy said that evening when we were sitting on the porch.

I watched her stroke his head. "He sounds like a motor boat," I said, laughing.

"He *is* kind of loud," she agreed. "Where'd you get him?"

"A lady down the road. He was the last one."

She nodded. "I'd like to get a cat or dog someday—I think it would be good for Elise."

"It would be," I agreed, smiling.

Lizzy took a sip of her lemon tea—as soon as I'd seen her coming down the ramp, I'd known we wouldn't be drinking Boone's Farm—or any other form of alcohol—that weekend, and I'd actually felt a little relieved.

"Stop saying you're sorry," I scolded when she apologized again—this time for not being able to indulge on our girls' weekend. "It's not a big deal—I hardly ever drink."

"Why's that?" she asked, frowning.

"For one thing, I don't like to drink alone—and I'm alone most of the time," I lied, "and for another, it just makes me tired and then I fall asleep when I'm reading."

The real reason, however—which I didn't share—was I'd seen firsthand what alcohol did to Coop—it made him self-absorbed and moody—and it scared me; and I hoped that, if I cut back, he would, too, but I was wrong—my *not* drinking only seemed to make him drink more . . . and I knew, at that very moment, he and Dimitri were probably three sheets to the wind.

"What are you reading now?" Lizzy asked.

"*Rich Man, Poor Man.*"

"You like those family sagas," she teased.

"I do," I said, laughing. "Have you read it?"

"No," she said, shaking her head. "I don't have much time for reading . . . and I'm going to have even less," she said, rubbing her huge belly.

"Well, I'm almost finished. You can take it with you."

She nodded and then studied me over her tea. "What were you going to say before?"

"Before when?" I asked, frowning.

"When we were waiting for the taxi."

I frowned. "I don't remember," I answered, shrugging.

"After your boat-builder friend drove by."

"Oh," I said, chuckling. "Nothing important."

"Are you sure?" she asked.

I nodded.

"Because you'd tell me."

"Of course," I lied.

Chapter 30

Whenever Lily and Daniel came for a visit, I made myself scarce, but after Liam was born, Coop would—under the guise of giving his sister and her husband some private time—bring his little nephew to the bakery for a muffin, and Liam and I became fast friends.

"Hi, Sal!" he called as soon as he came through the door; then he'd pull his hand free from Coop's and run over to give me a huge hug. Even though he was only three, he was a charmer—just like his uncle! He had a beaming smile and an outgoing personality that stole everyone's heart, including mine.

"Hi, Li!" I said, hugging him. "Where've you been? I've missed you."

"Oh, you know, home," he said with all the precious, literal honesty of a child.

I nodded, trying to suppress a smile.

"You told me to come back, so I did."

"Well, I'm glad."

He nodded and then tried to see over my shoulder. "Do you have any blueberry muffins?"

"Of course I have blueberry muffins—Coop told me you were coming."

A smile immediately lit up his sweet face.

"Coop," he called, "Sally just took some out of the oven!"

Coop's slow smile in response spoke volumes— the man who had always held his cards close to his vest had suddenly started wearing his emotions on his sleeve.

"How was the ferry?" I asked Liam as I put muffins on a plate.

"Good," he said, taking a bite and coming away with sugary cheeks. "Look at these blueberries, Coop," he said, holding up the muffin to show him all the still-warm oozing blueberries. "Sally, you make the best muffins," he swooned, making me wish I could go back in time and once again have the lovely, sweet wonder and innocence of a three-year-old.

Coop continued to press me to let him tell Lily about us. He said it was silly for me to worry, insisting she'd never say anything, nor would she judge us. She'd just be happy he'd found someone to love—and who loved him—and if he could just tell her, he added with a grin, maybe she'd stop bugging him about finding a girl. I held my ground, though.

Over the years, I almost relented several times, and I almost told Lizzy too. It was on the tip of my tongue, especially during the two weeks that I stayed with her after Elise was born. Now, Elise—born a few months after Liam—was turning three, too, and I still hadn't told her. I'm a fool, I chided myself. I should've told her years ago. Now it's too late—if I tell her now, after being involved with Coop for six years, she'll be hurt and she'll never forgive me! What had started as a simple secret about an affair had snowballed into a years-long—perhaps lifelong—deception. If I'd only known in the beginning that Coop and I would last, maybe I would've been more open.

No amount of trying to justify my actions, however, made me feel better, and seeing Lizzy only made me feel worse. When she came out to visit later that summer with little Elise in tow, she had more news to share—she was expecting again, a little boy this time—but I still stayed mum.

"We're naming him Elijah," she said, "after Simon's grandfather."

"It's a beautiful name," I replied, nodding and purposely avoiding the word *perfect*.

"This time, all is well," she said, smiling. "My bloodwork is perfect."

"I'm glad," I said, watching Elise pet Henry, who was curled up on her lap.

"Do you like Henry, El?" I asked.

"I *love* Henry," she said, looking up at me with her sweet almond eyes.

"How's it been going?" I asked, turning back to Lizzy.

"Okay," she said. "We're hoping Elise can start

preschool in the fall—we just have to get the potty figured out."

"Isn't she a little young for preschool?"

"No, they have programs for three-year-olds now—*if* they're potty-trained. We're working on that, right, Elise?"

Elise nodded, almost imperceptibly, but didn't look up, her focus entirely on Henry.

"Did you ever find a kitten or puppy?" I asked quietly, hoping Elise wouldn't hear.

"Daddy's 'lergic," Elise piped matter-of-factly.

I raised my eyebrows. "He is?"

Lizzy nodded. "Yeah, we were at a friend's house and Si just started sneezing. He's never been allergic before . . . that he knows of, but this friend has two dogs and they just set him off—his eyes running . . . the whole nine yards."

"That's too bad," I said, frowning.

"It is," Lizzy agreed. "Anyway, we're hoping Elise can figure out the potty before the end of the summer, because it would be great if she could be in school part of the day when the baby comes."

"Well, if it doesn't work out, I'd be happy to come help again," I said.

Lizzy nodded. "Thanks, Sal—it's always nice to know I can count on you."

Yeah, well, sort of, I thought miserably, *as long as it fits into my own agenda.*

"El, would you like a blueberry muffin?" I asked, changing the subject.

Elise looked up and grinned—she was another big fan of my muffins.

"Why don't we go see if you can use the potty first?" Lizzy interrupted. "Then you can have a muffin as a reward."

Elise's face fell. "I don't need to," she said softly, looking down.

"Then, no muffin," Lizzy said firmly. "When you use the potty, you can have one."

I frowned. "You sound like your mother," I said, trying to sound like I was teasing, although I really meant it. Lizzy looked stung, and I quickly added, "I'm just kidding."

"No, you're not . . . and you're right—I do sound like my mother, but you have no idea how hard it is. You don't know what it's like, Sally. You only have to be responsible for yourself . . . and you've had everything handed to you."

Now I was the one who felt stung. "Wow, Lizzy—where'd that come from?"

She swallowed, tears springing to her eyes. "I'm sorry. I shouldn't have said that."

"You should if that's what you think."

She shook her head. "I shouldn't've come. I'm way too emotional. I think my body's chemistry is completely thrown off by this pregnancy. I cry at the drop of a hat—like now," she said, wiping her eyes. "It's just Simon works all the time and I'm stuck home with Elise and I . . . I go a little stir-crazy . . . and when he is home, he can't help because his back bothers him."

"It's perfectly normal to feel tied down," I consoled, sitting next to her. "What did Simon do to his back?"

"He lifted something the wrong way and strained something—it's been going on for months."

"Maybe he should go to the doctor."

"He did and they gave him some pain meds—which he seems to take all the time." She sighed. "Sally, I don't know if I can handle having two kids at home all day—that's why I need Elise to go to nursery school."

I swallowed, trying to imagine her circumstances; then I looked at Elise and realized she was watching her mom cry and looking like she was going to cry too. "El, are you looking forward to having a little brother?" I asked.

She nodded.

"Are you gonna help Mommy take care of him?"

She nodded again. "I'm going to 'teck him."

I frowned uncertainly and then realized she meant *protect* him. "Elise says words the same way you did when you were little," I teased, eyeing Lizzy. "Do you remember saying firmed, risen, and pennies instead of confirmed, christened, and penance?"

Lizzy laughed and nodded. "I was such a know-it-all."

"You were," I agreed.

"I still am," she added.

"No, you're not. Sometimes you just need a new perspective."

She nodded. "I just feel so overwhelmed and I wish . . . I wish I had your life—it's so carefree and easy."

"Yeah," I said softly. "Well, people's lives aren't always what they seem."

She looked up, and although it would've been the perfect time to tell her about Coop, I looked away. "Lizzy, I know it must be hard for you right now, but you'll get through it, and I will come help you if you need me to. Elise and I will go to the park and give you time with the baby . . . but I honestly don't think you should withhold things that El loves," I added quietly, "just to get her to use the potty. She'll figure it out in her own time—when she's ready."

"You're right," she said; then she smiled. "You would've made a good mom, Sal."

"Maybe," I said, smiling sadly.

"By the way, may I have a muffin too?"

"Blueberry or bran?" I teased.

"That's a silly question, isn't it, El?" she said, laughing.

"Booberry," El said, taking her cue from her mother and laughing too.

Chapter 31

The years slipped by, and before Coop and I knew it, six years had become ten. I continued working at the bakery and never gave another thought to teaching. I truly believe it was the customers who came into the shop for bread and quickly became friends that made me love working there. And of course, there was Abe. One October morning, when I came in early, he announced that he was thinking of retiring . . . and *selling* the place, and he was wondering if I'd be interested in buying it, adding—with a wink—he'd give me a good deal.

"You can't retire!" I said in dismay. "It won't be the same."

He shook his head. "I'm tired of getting up in the middle of the night, Sal. It's time to take a step back, sleep in, and go fishing *every* day. Besides," he added, "I know it will be in good hands and that will make it easier to let go."

"You know I'm going to change the name and add sandwiches," I said threateningly.

"That's okay. I actually think adding lunch is a good idea. I was just too tired to do it myself."

I shook my head—I couldn't believe he'd been putting off my idea because he was tired. "I would've done the work."

"Well, now you can," he said with a grin.

"Are you sure about this?"

"I'm positive. I still want to go to the Cape on Thanksgiving, though."

"I would hope so. If you didn't, I'd be really sad."

"Well, I don't want that to happen," he said, putting his arm around my shoulder. "So, what are you gonna call it?"

I smiled. "Cuppa Jo to Go."

"I love it!" he said. "It's perfect!"

I laughed and shook my head, wondering if anything in life was truly perfect.

While I was busy making the arrangements to buy the bakery from Abe for a ridiculously low price—even though I assured him I could pay more—Coop was busy becoming a well-respected and skilled master craftsman. Wooden boat enthusiasts from up and down the east coast were making pilgrimages to Nantucket to have their boats restored or to inquire about having a boat built by him. He'd become so knowledgeable about the restoration of classic wooden runabouts —from Gar Woods to Chris Crafts—that every New England magazine— from *WoodenBoat* to *Down East* to *Yankee* to *Vermont Life*—had featured the famous Nantucket boatwright on its pages, and because of all the publicity, he hardly had time for house projects—his or mine—but he always made time for me and, of course, Dimitri.

Life was good and we were getting ready to spend our tenth Christmas together when tragedy struck, changing our lives forever. The call came —as so many do—in the middle of the night. The weatherman had been predicting snow for days, but I don't think they really understood the impact the storm was going to have on eastern Massachusetts and the islands until it finally hit.

I was lying beside Coop, our bodies curved together under his quilt, sleeping soundly for once, when we were both startled awake by the brazen sound of the ringing phone. I glanced at the clock and felt my heart start to pound—it was two in the morning! *Who would be calling at this hour?*

I turned on the light, pulled the quilt around me, and listened as Coop answered in a voice still groggy with sleep. He cleared his throat and tried again: "Yes, this is he," he said, swinging his legs over the side. I waited, watching his tired, unrevealing face and then, suddenly, the color drained from his cheeks. "Oh, my God, no," he cried, his eyes growing wide. "How can that be? I just talked to her this evening and she said they were staying home." His usually steady hands started shaking and I draped the quilt over his shoulders. As I watched him, tears filled my eyes—I knew he had talked to Lily earlier in the evening because she'd called to tell him they were coming for Nantucket's annual

Christmas Stroll—little Liam had loved it so much last year, he couldn't wait to go again.

"What about their son? Is he okay?" Coop's voice cracked as he said this; then he nodded. "Of course. Please thank her for taking care of him. I'll come as soon as I can." He nodded and then realized the storm would prevent him from going anywhere. "I mean, I'll come as soon as I can get out. . . . ." he said, his voice trailing off.

He hung up the phone and covered his face with his hands, making a guttural, heart-wrenching sound. I put my arms around him. "Coop, what is it? What happened?"

He looked up and his face was dark with shock and anguish, making him look years older. "Lily and Daniel were in a car accident—they were hit by a semitruck on the Mass Turnpike."

"Oh no! Are they in the hospital?"

Coop shook his head as tears streamed down his cheeks. "They were killed."

"Oh, my God," I whispered. "Where's Liam?" I asked. "Was he with them? Is he okay?"

"The trooper said he's home. The babysitter's mom came over and she's going to stay with him until I can get there." He stood up and looked out the window. "I can't believe this is happening."

"Do you have family that will take him?"

Coop clenched his jaw and shook his head. "*I'm* his family," he said, wiping his eyes. "When they were here last summer, Lily made me promise to take him if anything ever happened to them—it's almost as if she knew." Tears continued to spill down his cheeks. "I can't believe they're gone."

I shook my head. "Poor Liam—he must feel so lost. He's too little to have something like this happen."

Coop shook his head, and as we listened to the wind howling around the house and icy rain pelting the windows, he said, "I need to go right now. Maybe I could take the launch. . . ."

I raised my eyebrows. "You can't go out in this. You'll be no help to him if something happens to you."

Coop ran his hand through his hair. "I don't know anything about helping him get through this."

"You just do what you have to," I said softly. "One day at a time."

After a long night of endless tears and cups of coffee, we heard the wind dying down. Coop turned on the outside lights and realized the snow had stopped, but there was still a foot of it blanketing the ground. Without a word, he pulled on his jacket and boots.

"I'm coming," I said, pulling on my boots.

"You don't have to."

I eyed him. "Don't be silly."

We shoveled in silence for over an hour and a half, trying to clear a path for the truck. "Good enough," he said finally, hurrying inside to grab the bag he'd thrown together and pouring fresh coffee into his travel mug. He gave me a quick hug. "Thank you," he said tearfully.

"Be safe," I said, searching his eyes.

And then he was gone—his mind already miles away, preparing for the tragic circumstances that awaited him, his own sorrow taking a backseat to the grief of a little boy, who had, in a heartbeat, lost everything.

Chapter 32

"What is man, that thou art mindful of him?" I murmured as I poured a second cup of coffee and sat back down at Abe's old desk to put the final touches on the new menu for Cuppa Jo to Go. The shop had been closed for all of January so we could remodel, and while Liam—who was slowly adjusting to life on Nantucket—was in school, Coop had been helping me—actually, he'd been doing the work and I'd been helping him.

We'd given a fresh coat of paint to the stamped tin ceiling; we'd stripped off old wallpaper and spackled, sanded, and painted the walls a lovely ocean blue; we'd installed wainscoting along the lower walls and around the new coffee counter, then painted it the same creamy white as the ceiling; we'd installed new glass display cases for the muffins and baked goods, and a new glass refrigerator for cold drinks, as well as stylish tables and chairs. As a final touch, I'd found some new retro metal signs with a coffee theme—my favorite being of a rooster crowing, with the words WAKE UP AND SMELL THE COFFEE! along the bottom.

Every afternoon at three, Coop headed over to the elementary school to pick up Liam. Then they came back to the shop so Coop could finish up whatever project he'd been working on. "It looks really nice," Liam said approvingly after I'd hung up the metal signs.

"Thanks, Li," I said, giving him a hug. "How was your day?"

"Okay," he said with a little shrug. "I only cried once."

"It'll get better," I consoled. "It takes a long time when you miss someone."

"I know," he said. "And it's going to take me twice as long because I miss two people."

I bit my lip. My heart ached for him. He was such a good little guy and his grief was so close to the surface it spilled over without warning—like a waterfall—anytime he thought of his parents. He tried so hard to keep it in, too—to take everything in stride—but his sweet blue eyes were always shadowed with sorrow.

"Want to help me hang this sign, pal?" Coop asked, looking up from unwrapping the new sign I'd ordered for the exterior.

Liam looked at the big wooden sign and nodded. "What's *Jo?*" he asked, frowning.

"*Jo* is another word for coffee," I explained, tousling his hair.

"Oh," he said, quietly reading the rest of the sign. "So people can get coffee to go?"

"Yes, coffee, muffins, bread, and lunch too."

Coop lifted the wooden sign. "Grab my tool

bag, Li," he said, nodding toward his tools. Liam lifted the heavy canvas bag and followed Coop outside.

The sudden loss of Lily and Daniel had had a profound impact on all of our lives. When Coop came back from Boston with his new young charge, they were both so heartbroken, they could barely muddle through. Coop tried to explain to Liam why tragedies happen—why his parents had been taken to heaven—but he could barely understand it himself. Why had his beautiful sister —whom he'd tried to protect his whole life—and her loving husband—and father of her child—been killed? Was this part of some greater plan, because if it was, he couldn't begin to see what it was. What possible good could come from orphaning a sweet seven-year-old boy?

I looked back down at my menu, trying to decide how much I should charge for the new items—sandwiches served on the customer's choice of any of the fresh breads we baked or on wraps. I'd already made the three different offerings—curried chicken salad with dried cranberries, apricots, and red seedless grapes; tuna fish with celery and thyme; or ham and Swiss—and put them in the fridge for our grand reopening the next day. I didn't want to have too many new options, and I didn't want to make them too expensive. I tapped my pencil, wondering if people would be willing to pay $3.00? I looked at the clock and sighed—it was already ten o'clock and I really needed to get the menus printed before noon. Finally, I jotted down a price of $2.50, drained my coffee, and stood up.

I was putting on my coat when I looked out and saw Coop's truck pulling in. I frowned. After everything that had happened—adjusting to having Liam living with him and helping me remodel the bakery all month—he'd been looking forward to getting back to work on his own projects at the boathouse, so when he climbed out, I was puzzled . . . until I saw Liam sitting next to him in the passenger seat.

"Not a good day?" I asked, holding the door open.

Liam shook his head sadly.

Coop put his hands on Liam's shoulders. "Mrs. Polley called and said they tried everything—it's just one of those days."

"It's okay," I said softly, pulling Liam into a hug. He nodded and buried his face in my shoulder. I felt him sobbing and looked up at Coop and he shook his head. The whole balancing act of caring for a child, dealing with his own grief, and running a business was overwhelming him—not to mention we hadn't slept in the same bed in weeks.

"Hey," I said, pulling Liam away to see his face.

"I was just going to drop off the new menu at the print shop—want to walk over with me?"

He wiped his eyes and nodded.

"Then we'll come back here and make some hot cocoa."

"My mom always made hot cocoa with whipped cream."

"Well, it just so happens that I make it with whipped cream too."

"Okay," he said, mustering a smile.

"Do you want me to give you a ride?" Coop asked. "It looks like it might start snowing any minute."

I shook my head. "No, a walk is always good for the soul, even—and sometimes, especially— in the snow. Besides, then you can get to work and Liam can help me finish getting ready for tomorrow."

Coop looked relieved. "Thanks, Sal. I don't know what I'd do without you."

"Oh, you'd probably be better off," I teased.

"I doubt it," he said, kissing the top of my head —which, except for fooling around in the kitchen when we were supposed to be remodeling—was the extent of our affection lately.

"I'll pick you up later, pal," he said, tousling Liam's hair. "Be good for Sally."

Liam nodded and reached for my hand.

Ten minutes later, we were pulling open the door of the print shop and noticing a handwritten sign in the window that said, *"Free kittens,"* except that the *s* was crossed out and it really said, *"Free kitten."*

We stepped up to the counter and Julie came out from the back. "Hi, Sal! Did you finish the menu?"

"I did," I said. Years earlier, I'd learned that all the business owners on Nantucket knew the goings-on of all the other business owners.

"Is tomorrow the big day?"

"It is. Are you going to stop by? I'm offering free samples."

"I hope to," she said, smiling.

She looked over the counter and saw Liam peering into the cardboard box in the corner. "Who's your little helper?"

"Liam—Coop's nephew," I said quietly, and from the look on her face, I knew she'd heard about the accident.

"No school today?"

"No—some days are harder than others."

"I know how that is," she said softly.

We talked about the menu and I explained that I wanted five hundred copies so I could replenish the baskets on the counter for people to peruse or even take home.

"I can do it while you wait," Julie offered, "and then you don't have to come back."

"Okay," I said, glad to have one less thing to do later.

Julie disappeared into the back and Liam looked up. "Come see the kitten, Sally."

I walked over and knelt down next to him. "He's cute," I said, stroking the kitten's soft fur, and Liam nodded.

"He's free to a good home," Julie chimed, coming back out with my copies.

"Can we take him home?" Liam asked hopefully.

I pressed my lips together uncertainly, wondering how Coop would react to having another responsibility added to his plate. "I don't know," I said. "I don't know how Coop will feel about having a kitten."

"He'd love it," Liam assured me, his eyes sparkling now. "He *loves* Henry and he always says he's going to bring him home to our house."

"And what if he doesn't *love* it?"

"Then he could live with you and Henry."

"That's just what I need," I said, laughing. "*Two* cats!" But when I saw the earnest look in Liam's eyes, I knew there was no way I was going to say no—if I'd ever been blessed with children, I would've been a total pushover and my kids would've been spoiled rotten. I stroked the kitten's soft gray head. A kitten might be just the thing for Liam, and if Coop wasn't up to the responsibility, Henry would gain a little brother.

"Okay," I said softly.

"All right!" he said, jumping up and down. It was the first time in a long time that I'd seen him truly happy.

Julie smiled too. "What are you going to name him?"

And Liam, who'd already scooped the stocky little kitten into his arms, thought for a minute. Then his face lit up. "Tomcat or Tom for short."

Julie nodded approvingly and slid the copies across the counter. "He looks like a Tomcat."

"He does," I agreed. "Can we take the box too?"

"Of course, and since he's the last one, you can take the kitten food too."

"Thanks, Julie," I said, pulling my wallet out of my purse.

Julie waved her hand. "No charge—it's on the house for taking the last kitten off my hands."

"Are you sure?"

She nodded, smiling, and then looked at Liam. "Good luck with Tomcat."

"Thanks," he said, slipping the kitten into the front of his coat.

I picked up the box. "Are you sure you don't want to put him in here?"

"I'm sure," he said. "He'll be warmer in my coat." And as he said this, Tom poked his head out between the buttons and Liam laughed.

Chapter 33

The first two years Liam lived with Coop, he spent a lot of time with me at Cuppa Jo. By the time he turned nine, he was able to ring up customers more efficiently than the teenagers I'd hired—he knew the price of every item without consulting the cheat sheet taped to the counter next to the register, and he was always first to make fresh coffee when the pots were getting low. He also made sure the floors were always swept and the counters sparkled. He was a conscientious little worker and I knew I was going to miss him when he announced, the summer he turned ten, that he wanted to help Coop at the boathouse.

"What?" I teased, feigning dismay. "I thought you loved Cuppa Jo, and now, after I've trained you to be the perfect employee, you're going to run off and learn how to restore and build boats—which, by the way, I've heard is *really* boring."

He nodded solemnly. "I think it's my calling."

I looked down, shaking my head and suppressing a smile. "I don't think Frankie can handle the counter by himself."

"Well, he'll have to step it up," Liam said of my current teenage employee. "And I'll still help on Saturdays." He knew it was our busiest day.

"Well, if you really think boat building is your calling, then I guess you better follow it."

"I'm sorry, Sal," he said, giving me a hug.

"It's okay, Li. I completely understand." I looked at Coop. "You're getting a great little helper."

"I know," Coop said, nodding.

"You're welcome," I added.

"Thank you," he said, smiling.

Liam looked up at him and grinned. "See? I told you she'd be okay with it.

"Just like you told her I'd be okay with a kitten."

"Well, I was right."

"You were," he said, tousling Liam's long, sun-streaked chestnut brown hair.

Liam *had* been right—Coop had immediately fallen in love with the kitten we brought home from the print shop that winter day. Tomcat was a true predator—mice and moles weren't safe when he roamed their property—and even though Coop claimed he loved that Tom was a hunter—and earned his keep—even more than he loved the cat himself, Liam and I knew better.

Liam was growing up, too, and he seemed to take everything about life seriously—almost *too* seriously, especially his job at the boathouse. When Coop and I had a minute alone—which wasn't often—he told me Liam was exceedingly helpful and observant, absorbing everything he could about the mystique and beauty of wooden boats. At the tender age of ten, he knew the language of boats, and any outside observer would think he'd been born on the water.

Liam wasn't just maturing emotionally, though. He was also growing physically—he'd grown four inches that year, and although he had his dad's angular chin and handsome features, he had his mom's eyes, and resembled Coop too. So much so, in fact, he was often mistaken for Coop's son—which Coop didn't mind one bit!

Kids are keenly perceptive, and Liam was no different. He watched Coop and me interact, laughed at our constant teasing and banter, and often wondered why we weren't a couple. One day, when he was helping Coop put up a new bird-feeder post for me, I overheard them talking.

"Coop, how come you and Sally never got married?"

Coop laughed and leaned on his shovel. "A wise man never gets married," he said, eyeing him. "If you can get through life without falling under the beguiling spell of a beautiful woman, you'll save yourself a lot of heartache . . . *and* money!"

Liam shook his head. "Wouldn't you want Sally to cook for you?"

"What?" Coop said, feigning indignation. "Don't you like my cooking?"

Liam laughed. "I love it, but I think it would be easier if Sally lived with us and did the cooking."

"I think you like her cooking better than mine," Coop teased.

"No, I don't," Liam said, trying not to grin.

"I can tell by the look on your face."

"No, you can't."

"Yes, I can."

"I still think you should ask her. Then maybe you wouldn't drink so much."

When I heard him say this, I looked up in surprise to see how Coop would react, but he just frowned. "I don't drink too much," he grumbled, and then plunged his shovel into the earth.

Liam watched him but didn't say anything.

"How come Coop drinks so much?" he asked quietly when he came inside a little later to get a chocolate-chip cookie, and I could tell he'd been stewing about it.

"Has he been drinking more than usual?"

Liam nodded and looked out the window as he ate his cookie, watching Coop fill the dirt back in around the new post. "Sometimes, it scares me," he added softly.

"It *does?* How come?" I asked.

"Because it makes him act different—like he's not even the same person."

"Well, he *is* the same person," I assured him, putting my arm around his shoulders. "It's just that he struggles with some memories from the war, and he thinks a drink will help him forget."

"Why does he want to forget? Did he . . ." Liam hesitated, as if he wasn't sure he wanted to know the answer to the question that had been weighing heavily on his mind. "Did he kill somebody?"

"I honestly don't know the answer to that, Li. He doesn't talk about it. I *do* know that a lot of his friends were killed, including his best friend."

"Oh," Liam said softly. "I didn't know that." He was quiet for a few minutes and then said, "I'd be really sad if my friend Jack was killed—I'd probably drink too."

"I hope not," I said. "Drinking doesn't solve problems . . . and it definitely doesn't bring someone back."

Liam nodded. "I wish Coop knew that."

"Me too," I said, squeezing his shoulder and making a mental note to talk to Coop.

Just then, he came into the kitchen. "I thought you were coming in to get some cookies," he said.

"I did," Liam said, smiling as he reached for another warm cookie.

"*And* . . . where's mine?" Coop teased.

"Right here," Liam said, holding out the cookie he'd just picked up.

Chapter 34

When I pulled into the parking lot of Temple Israel in my dad's vintage Bel Air, everyone who was walking inside turned to see who was driving the classic old car, and although I tried to look inconspicuous as I climbed out, as soon as Elise—now ten—saw me, she shouted, "Hi, Aunt Sally!" at the top of her lungs, freed herself from her mother's hand, and charged in my direction with Elijah at her heels.

"Hey, you two," I said, bracing myself as they barreled toward me at top speed.

"Where'd you get the cool car?" Elijah asked, stepping back to admire my dad's old car—which Coop had kept meticulously maintained over the years.

"It used to belong to my dad."

"How come we never saw it before when we visited you?" Elijah asked, running his hand lightly over the glistening chrome and silky turquoise paint.

"Because it's usually stored in a barn."

"Did he give it to you?" Elise asked, her eyes wide with wonder.

I nodded.

"How come *he* doesn't use it anymore?" Elijah asked.

I laughed, suddenly realizing why Lizzy always sounded like she was on the verge of losing it when I talked to her on the phone. "How come you guys ask so many questions?"

Elijah shrugged. "I was just wondering," he said, his voice trailing off.

"I'm sorry," I said, putting my arm around him. "You can ask as many questions as you like. My dad left this car to me when he died—that's why he doesn't use it anymore."

"Great Bubbe died too," Elijah said in surprise, as if it was the oddest coincidence that he knew two people who'd accomplished the same mysterious act.

"I know—that's why I came to see you today."

"I didn't know your dad died," Elise said, her almond eyes filling with tears.

I squeezed her hand. "It's okay, El—you don't need to be upset. It was a long time ago." She nodded but still looked like she was going to cry.

Lizzy came up behind them. "Hi, Sal," she said, giving me a quick hug. Then she eyed her kids, and scolded, "I don't think you guys looked both ways before running over here."

"Yes, we did, Mama," Elise protested.

"Not really, El—I was watching. Just because it's a parking lot doesn't mean a car can't pull out. Elijah, it's your job to look after your sister."

Elise looked down, obviously stung by the reprimand.

"Shouldn't it be the other way around?" I asked, putting my arm around her. "The big sister looking after her little brother?"

Elise looked up hopefully after hearing my suggestion, but Lizzy just shook her head. "I'm afraid that's not how it works in our house." And at this, Elise looked down again, obviously crushed.

"Thanks for coming, Sal," Lizzy said, turning back to me and mustering a tired smile.

I nodded. "I'm so sorry."

"Don't be silly," she said. "She was a hundred and three, for heaven's sake—she had a long, full life."

I nodded. "It's still sad to see an old soul go . . ."

Lizzy motioned to the car and smiled. "I didn't know you still had this! I'm sorry I couldn't pick you up."

"It's all right," I said, smiling. "My mechanic says I need to take it out once in a while."

"He's right, but I bet you had to pay a pretty penny to get it on the ferry."

"It's okay. It was fun."

Lizzy glanced at her watch and then at her kids. "We better go in." She gave me another quick hug and then ushered Elise and Elijah across the parking lot. "I'll talk to you back at the house—do you remember how to get there?"

I nodded, locked my car, and as I walked up the path to the front door, I thought about the abrupt and impatient way Lizzy had treated her children

306

—especially Elise. She was more like her own mother than she realized—and all I could think was how had that happened? How had my dear, nonconforming, freethinking, all-accepting friend evolved into a dim reflection of her self-centered mother? Are we all destined to become—as the saying goes—like our parents? My mom had died before I'd really gotten to know her, so I had no way of knowing if I was anything like her.

I settled into a seat in the back and listened to the somber, monotone reading of several Psalms and scriptures; then I watched Simon make his way to the front. Although I'd received a holiday card with a picture of their family on it every winter, it had been years since I'd actually seen Simon in person and I was surprised by how much he'd aged. His face was pale and he'd put on weight. He cleared his throat, and in a voice choked with emotion, he shared some childhood memories from the summers he'd spent on Nantucket with his grandmother. One memory was especially poignant and we were all capti-vated as he talked about it. Simon didn't even look down at his notes as he recounted the long-ago summer night when he and his grandmother had sat outside the beach house gazing at the stars. She'd pointed to the different constellations, telling her young grandson their names; then she'd quietly told him about being able to look up through the rafters above her bunk in the concentration camp and being able to see the Milky Way sparkling in the sky; in that moment, she said, she'd felt a sudden overwhelming peace and she'd known in her heart that God was with her—he was as constant as the stars. It was the only time, Simon said, she'd ever spoken of it.

Twenty minutes later, the service was over. After all the planning I'd done—making ferry reservations for the car, finding a hotel room for the night, and arranging for reliable help to keep Cuppa Jo open for the two days I'd be gone—the service was over. The celebration of Mrs. Cohen's long, triumphant life was over in a heartbeat, and we were off to see her laid to rest; and as soon as her casket was lowered into the ground and the Kaddish prayer solemnly prayed, we were off again—this time to Shiva, which was being held, because Simon's parents had moved to Florida, at Simon and Lizzy's house, confirming my belief that the Jewish people are thorough when saying good-bye to their loved ones.

When I pulled up in front of the house, I couldn't believe my eyes. Not that you could get a house painted in the short time between someone's passing and their funeral, but it looked like Simon and Lizzy hadn't put in any effort at all into getting ready to host Shiva—the house was desperately in need of paint, and the gutters were clogged and moldy; the grass was so long it had gone to seed, and the mower, sitting in the side yard, looked like it had died in its tracks, the grass behind it slightly shorter than the grass in front. I hadn't been to the house since Elijah was born, but I couldn't believe how—in the span of seven years—it had fallen into such disrepair.

I followed an older couple up the sidewalk and overheard them expressing the same sentiment . . . along with their reasoning. "I heard," the old woman whispered to her husband, "Simon's wife struggles with depression . . . and she drinks!"

What's this? I thought, frowning and tucking behind my back the bottle of kosher chardonnay I'd brought. *Was this the latest scuttlebutt being passed around Lizzy's world?* I waited silently behind them while they knocked on the door, and was surprised when they continued their conversation, seemingly unaware that I was behind them. "It's truly a shame Simon couldn't have found a nice Jewish girl to marry. If he had, he probably wouldn't have a retarded daughter." *Sheesh!* I thought. *If Lizzy is an alcoholic, I can certainly understand why!*

The door opened and the couple stepped politely inside. I followed them around in line and continued to listen as they solemnly greeted Simon's bereaved family—including Simon—who gave his grandmother's next-door neighbors, Mr. and Mrs. Rosenberg, long hugs and thanked them for coming.

"I'm so sorry," I murmured into Simon's

shoulder when it was my turn. "Your grandmother was a lovely lady and your eulogy was perfect."

"Thanks, Sally," he said. "She was very fond of you."

I nodded solemnly and then headed for the kitchen—where I knew I'd find Lizzy. "Hey," I said, giving her a hug too. I held out the bottle. "Am I tempting the devil?"

She frowned. "What?"

"Mr. and Mrs. Rosenberg think you have a drinking problem."

She rolled her eyes. "And they are entirely correct," she said. "Now, hand it over." I handed the bottle to her and she immediately opened it, poured two glasses, and handed one to me. "If I don't have a drinking problem now, I will by the end of this week."

"This lasts all week?"

She nodded. "We are expected to be prepared to receive guests at any time."

I shook my head. "The service was over in no time, but the grieving goes on for days."

"Exactly. Thank goodness we have plenty of food," she said, sliding a plate of cheese and crackers in my direction.

I reached for a hunk of cheddar. "Mmm, I'm starving." And then I looked around the kitchen and frowned. "Where are the kids?"

"Out back," she said, taking a long sip of her wine.

310

I looked out the kitchen window and saw Elise and Elijah sitting on swings, but not swinging. "Are they banished?" I teased.

"No, I just needed a little time to myself," Lizzy said, refilling her glass.

"Liz, I don't mean to meddle, but it seems like things—overall—aren't going that well. Is everything okay between you and Simon?"

Lizzy shook her head and laughed. "Did you get that impression from the state of our house or from the dark cloud of discord that hangs above it?"

"Well . . . both, I guess."

She took another long sip and sighed. "Simon lost his job and money is tight. We've burned through all our savings and we're behind on our bills, including our mortgage. On top of that, our credit cards are maxed out. There's no money to do anything—we can't even afford to fix the lawn mower."

I frowned. "How did Simon lose his job?"

Lizzy glanced over her shoulder to make sure we were really alone. "He was caught stealing from the hospital pharmacy," she said quietly. "He and another employee were involved in a scheme where they forged unnecessary prescriptions for patients, charged them to the patients' insurance, and then sold them—or in Simon's case, took them himself."

"You're kidding!" I whispered. "How did he get involved in that?"

"It all began when he hurt his back—at least that's what he tells me. Back then, he was prescribed painkillers, but his back never really got better; then he started missing work."

"How come you never told me?"

She shook her head. "It just spiraled out of control so quickly—he was suspended while they investigated, and then, without warning, he was fired. So, not only do we have no income, but we also have huge legal bills while he tries to fight their decision and not go to jail." She took another long sip of her wine. "It's a nightmare."

"What are you going to do?"

"I have to go back to work . . . although I don't know if anyone will take me. I have an interview next week, but I haven't worked as a nurse in ten years, so I'm sure I'm going to need retraining."

"That's going to take time."

She nodded. "I know . . . and we're probably going to lose the house." She refilled her glass again. "Now you know why I'm so short with the kids."

"I'm sorry, Liz. I had no idea."

She nodded. "I've learned you truly never know what another person is going through."

"Does your mom know?"

She shook her head. "No." Then she frowned. "I told you she's in a nursing home, didn't I?"

"No!"

"Yeah, she fell and broke her hip, and when she went to rehab, they discovered she had some sort of dementia going on and said it wasn't safe for her to live alone, and since there's no way she could—or would—live with me, we had to move her from rehab straight to a nursing home. She thinks she's going home, but her house is already on the market, and when it sells, the state will take everything because nursing homes are so insanely expensive."

I shook my head in disbelief. "Sheesh! Did you change your name to Job or something?"

"You'd think so," she said, laughing. "Our only hope is that Simon's grandmother left him something, but we won't know until Shiva is over and her will is read."

I took a sip of my wine. "I'll keep my fingers crossed. In the meantime, if there's anything I can do, please don't hesitate to ask."

She nodded. "Actually, there is something, Sal . . . and I wouldn't ask if I wasn't so desperate."

"Anything," I said.

"Yeah," she laughed. "You're going to wish you didn't say that!"

"No, I won't," I countered, thinking she was going to ask me for a loan—which I would happily give her.

"Well . . . do you think . . ." She paused, eyeing me. "Do you think you might be able to take the kids for a couple weeks—just until I can get my act together?"

"Of course," I said in the most positive voice I could muster while trying to hide my dismay—how in the world was I going to manage taking care of her kids *and* run Cuppa Jo? "But what are you going to do for child care after you find a job?" I asked, hoping she might see that a short-term fix like the one she was proposing wasn't going to solve her long-term problem.

"I guess Simon will have to become Mr. Mom."

I nodded. "When were you thinking?"

"Well, we have Shiva all week and my interview is the following Monday, but Simon has to go to court that day, so I was hoping you might be able to just take them back with you. It would be so much easier if they weren't here for Shiva."

I nodded. "Of course," I said, practically choking on my words.

"Are you sure?" she asked, eyeing me skeptically.

"I'm positive," I said, refilling my glass . . . to the rim!

The very next evening when I looked in my rearview mirror, Elise and Elijah were slumped on top of each other, sound asleep in my backseat, and although the sky, as we crossed the Bourne Bridge, was a glorious pink and orange, I didn't wake them. They'd been chattering nonstop since we left, and I wasn't going to ruin a good thing.

Chapter 35

"How is it?" I asked, looking over at Elise and Elijah and Liam. We were all sitting on a bench eating ice cream while we waited for the ferry bringing Lizzy to Nantucket. It was the exact same bench on which Lizzy and I had sat ten years earlier when she'd told me she was expecting Elise. Little did I know, back then, that I'd sit on the very same bench, ten years later, with three kids—one of which was that baby girl. Life certainly does take some interesting turns!

"Mmm," Elise said dreamily, seemingly unfazed by the melting strawberry ice cream dripping over her knuckles.

Elijah nodded as he tried to keep up with his chocolate.

"And you?" I asked, eyeing my other sidekick.

"Great!" Liam said, swiping his tongue expertly around the base of his black raspberry ice-cream cone and grinning. As always, he had everything under control.

"Can we play potsie?" Elise asked, eyeing the cobblestone walk that must've reminded her of a hopscotch board.

"When you finish your ice cream," I said, licking my coffee cone.

315

"I don't want any more," she said, holding it out.

"You've hardly had any," Liam said.

"Yes, I have, and I want to play potsie."

"Well, you have to wait till we're *all* done," he said, "so you may as well keep eating." I smiled and gave him a discreet thumbs-up, and he grinned and returned the gesture. I'd had Liam on loan all week, and he and I had been in cahoots, trying to keep harmony in my house—which hadn't been easy! I honestly don't know what I would've done without him. He'd been a godsend in keeping Elise and Elijah entertained and happy, quickly picking up on the little things that might set Elise off and running diversion to keep that from happening. At the same time, he helped me at the bakery, briefly forgoing his apprenticeship at the boathouse.

"I don't want any more," Elise repeated, holding out her cone, her hand covered with dripping strawberry ice cream.

"Okay," I said, pointing to a nearby trashcan. "Throw it in there."

She walked over, held the cone high above the can, and released it like a falling bomb, and it plopped onto the top of an empty bottle, splattering her shirt. She looked at her shirt and then her hand like it was a foreign object. "Sticky," she said in a despairing voice.

I popped the last bite of my cone in my mouth. "Let's go find a ladies' room," I said, ushering Elise to the nearby public restroom. "You guys stay here. We'll be right back."

Liam and Elijah both nodded.

Moments later, we reappeared and found Liam drawing a hopscotch board on the sidewalk.

"I wanted to draw it," Elise whined.

"You can," Liam said, holding out the chalk he'd been carrying in his pocket all week.

Elise took the chalk in her freshly washed hands and proceeded to draw the board while Liam and Elijah dug their favorite stones out of their pockets. When Elise finished, she reached into her pocket for her stone, too, but her pocket was empty and she suddenly looked like she was going to cry.

"Here, take mine," Liam said quickly, holding out his perfectly smooth stone.

"Thanks," she said shyly, taking it from him.

Meltdown averted, I thought with a relieved sigh.

Then, out of the blue, she stepped forward and, before Liam knew what was happening, kissed him right on the cheek!

I covered my mouth in surprise, trying not to laugh, but it was too late, and to add insult to injury, Elijah almost fell over giggling while Liam's face turned beet red. "What the heck did ya do that for?" he asked, wiping his cheek on his shoulder.

"Because I love you," Elise said solemnly.

Liam shook his head as if he'd never heard anything so silly. "Well, it's your turn . . . so go."

I bit my lip, still trying not to smile—I didn't want to betray my young friend, but if I were a ten-year-old girl, I'd have a crush on him too!

Ten minutes later, the ferry came into view and as it drew closer, we saw Lizzy waving from the deck. Elise jumped up and down with excitement, dropping Liam's stone, and when he saw it skip into the grass, he quickly picked it up and tucked it back in his pocket.

"Mommy!" Elise called at the top of her lungs.

Lizzy hurried down the ramp, and as her two offspring ran into her arms, Liam and I stood back, watching and smiling, utterly relieved that Lizzy was finally here to resume care of her children—it had been the longest two weeks of our lives!

"Hey!" she said, standing to give me a hug too.

"Hey," I said, hugging her back and then pulling Liam against me. "You remember Liam?" I said.

"Of course," Lizzy said. "Although I don't know if I would've recognized him without you telling me since he's grown six inches since the last time I saw him.

Liam grinned and politely shook her extended hand.

"Mommy," Elijah said, tugging Lizzy's sleeve. "Guess what?"

"What, hon?" she said, kneeling down, and although he whispered in her ear, we all heard what he said.

"She did?!" Lizzy said, eyeing Elise in surprise.

"I did not!" Elise protested.

"Yes, you did," Elijah insisted.

Lizzy looked to me for confirmation, and I just smiled and shrugged. "She takes after her mother."

While we walked along the sun-dappled street, Lizzy filled me in on everything that had happened since I last saw her. "So Simon's not going to prison," she confided. "It looks like he just has to do some community service."

"Well, that's good," I said. "It would be a little tough for him to be Mr. Mom from jail."

She nodded. "*And . . .*" she continued.

"What?" I asked, my interest piqued by the smile on her face.

"I got the nursing job!"

"You did?!"

She nodded. "It's not at Massachusetts General. It's at Somerville—which is actually better because it's closer and I won't have to commute. The only thing is the first two weeks are orientation at half pay."

"That's okay—it'll go by fast and then you'll be at full pay."

"And we'll have insurance again—another thing we lost with Simon's job."

"That's great, Lizzy. I'm so happy for you."

She nodded. "And I have one more bit of good news—Simon's grandmother did leave him a small inheritance—I know it's crazy, but it's just enough to get us out of the hole we're in."

"Thank goodness!" I said. "I don't know how many times I've heard stories about people receiving just enough by some odd chance when they needed it the most. They called it God's providence—but I've never known anyone whom it actually happened to."

"Well, I've been praying," Lizzy whispered in confidence. "I even dug out my rosary beads."

"Whatever works," I said, laughing.

"So now, Simon's home—hopefully mowing the lawn—and I can only stay till tomorrow morning," she said. "I start orientation on Monday."

I nodded, and as we turned into my driveway, she reached for my arm to hold me back as the kids raced toward the house. "Did Elise really kiss Liam?"

"Just on the cheek . . . but she also told him she loves him."

"No way!"

"Way," I said, laughing.

She shook her head. "God help me!"

Chapter 36

"All shall be well and all shall be well, and all manner of things shall be well," I murmured the quote to myself as I pulled into the driveway, praying Coop had misunderstood.

When Lily and Daniel were killed, Coop had been blindsided. At the same time, he'd been blessed with a child—the child he always wanted —the child I couldn't give him. Suddenly, he'd been compelled to look after someone other than himself and to see life from a different perspective. As the years slipped by and I watched how it changed him, I couldn't help but wonder if Liam coming into his life wasn't part of God's plan—a plan born of tragedy, but only possible *because* of that tragedy—a plan that was part of the wondrous tapestry of life that we humans usually find so difficult to see.

Liam had always been a good kid: He worked hard in school and at whatever job he was given; he was respectful and polite; and he was always first to offer a helping hand when one was needed—a trait that was made especially evident when he helped us serve dinner at the homeless shelter on Cape Cod every Thanksgiving. He had a good heart and loved to help people, and in spite of losing his parents, he had adjusted to living with his uncle and had grown up to be a generally good-natured—albeit serious and solemn—even-keeled kid.

But all that changed the summer he turned seventeen.

Every year, Coop told Liam to steer clear of all the pretty girls who flocked to Nantucket with their wealthy families in the summer. "They'll steal your heart and kick you to the curb," he warned, but Liam never seemed interested—he was too busy building boats—so it was never an issue. But all that changed when blond-haired, blue-eyed Cadie—Acadia McCormick Knox—walked into the boathouse with her father and stole Liam's heart.

"Reckless" and "damn fool" were some of the words Coop repeatedly used that summer, but Liam was undeterred. Even though Cadie's parents forbid her from seeing him, Liam took her out in his 1955 Chris Craft Sportsman—the one he and Coop had found in an old barn and restored together—at every opportunity. Coop was certain—from their sandy, tan, dreamy-eyed appearance when they returned—that they were spending time on Tuckernuck—the small, secluded island west of Nantucket.

"She's gonna break your heart," Coop warned, but Liam just shrugged. His head was playing no role in decision making that summer;

only his heart . . . and if you asked Coop, a lower part of his anatomy.

One evening, Liam and Cadie returned after dark, and as they neared the dock, they realized Cadie's father was waiting for them. "Get in the car!" Carlton Knox barked when Liam turned off the motor.

Cadie tried to say good night, but her father wouldn't hear of it. "Now!" he growled, throwing her bike in the Dumpster and declaring she wouldn't need it anymore.

The next morning, Cadie was gone . . . and Liam was devastated.

"The spin is unrecoverable," Coop said after Liam started skipping school that fall. "He's lost all direction."

And on a winter afternoon just before Christmas, Coop called me to tell me that Liam had enlisted, but as I drove to their house, I held on to the hope that he was wrong. As I parked my car—I'd finally broken down and bought a Subaru—I looked out through the gathering darkness to see if there was a light on in Liam's bedroom, but it was dark and I murmured my prayer of self-reassurance again: "All shall be well and all shall be well and all manner of things shall be well." Then I climbed out, hurried through the freezing wind-whipped rain, and knocked on Coop's door.

"You don't have to knock—he's not here."

I pushed open the door and Coop turned from the fire. Immediately, I saw a glass in his hand and my heart sank—as Liam had grown older *and* more perceptive, Coop had tried to drink less, but every now and then—when life got to be too much—he tumbled headlong off the proverbial wagon.

"Where is he?" I asked.

"Where else?" he answered derisively. I nodded, knowing the answer. Jack had been Liam's best friend since second grade. Jack had taken Liam under his wing when he first moved to Nantucket after losing his parents, and although Coop didn't trust him, Liam loved Jack like a brother.

"Glass of wine?" he asked.

"No, I . . . okay," I said, changing my mind.

"I don't know who the hell to blame," Coop muttered as he trimmed off the wrapper around the neck of the bottle—just as he'd taught me twenty years earlier. "Jack . . . or that damn girl!"

"Did Jack enlist too?"

"Liam said he did—they're going in together."

I watched him press the point of the corkscrew into the cork. "Maybe they didn't sign the papers yet," I suggested hopefully.

Coop shook his head. "Oh, they signed 'em all right—I saw the paperwork in his room."

"Do you know when they go?"

"After they graduate," Coop said, pouring a glass and handing it to me. "Assuming he *does* graduate. I'm beginning to have my doubts."

"Well, at least we're not at war," I consoled.

"Not at the moment," he said, taking a long sip of his whiskey. "The world is a crazy place, Sal—anything can happen." He shook his head in dismay. "Lily would never forgive me."

"It's not your fault. He did it without telling you."

"I should've seen it coming."

I stood in front of the fire and felt it warm my back. "Do you realize today is the tenth anniversary of the accident?"

"Shit . . . no," Coop said, shaking his head. "I didn't even think of that."

"Do you think he did?"

"I don't doubt it," he said, draining his glass and refilling it.

"He'll be okay," I said softly. "Maybe it will be good for him. Maybe he'll finally get over Cadie."

Coop chuckled. "I doubt it," he said. "We Cooper men fall hard . . . and we rarely get over it." He kissed the top of my head. "I've missed you," he murmured into my hair.

"I've missed you too," I said, turning to face him.

He pulled me toward him.

"When will he be home?"

"He's staying over Jack's. I think he's had enough of me."

"Well, I haven't," I said, moving against him.

He smiled, took my glass, and put it on the mantel next to his, and as he pulled me against him, my mind drifted back to all the times—before Liam had come to live with him—we'd lay in front of the fireplace, our bodies intertwined and warmed by the heat of the fire. And although we'd found other ways to be together over the years, it had been ten years since we'd lain here. . . .

Chapter 37

On July 5, 1990—two weeks after graduation—Liam and Jack left for Parris Island, and although the country was at peace when they left, one month later, Iraqi troops invaded Kuwait. Five months after that, Liam and Jack were deployed to Saudi Arabia as part of the first allied infantry group in support of Operation Desert Storm.

That very same night, Coop—with Dimitri's help—set off on a three-day tear. There was no talking to Coop after Liam shipped out, and although I worried, too, I couldn't help but think how nice it would be to have the house to ourselves when he went off to training. Being able to walk around in my underwear and Coop's old shirt; being able to have coffee together on Sunday mornings; being able to make love whenever we wanted—and basically, picking up where we'd left off—resuming the comfortable, easy habits of the unmarried couple we'd once been. Unfortunately, that was not to be.

As soon as Liam finished training, he shipped out . . . and Coop started drinking heavily. When he wasn't drunk, he was distracted; and when he was able to focus, it was on work, not pleasure. He threw himself into his work—claiming he had twice as much to do now that Liam wasn't there. He spent long hours at the boathouse, burning the candle at both ends until he was exhausted. He was afraid to fall asleep, though, because, if he did, a phone call or a knock on the door in the middle of the night might come and bring the unbearable news that something had happened to Liam . . . and for this, Coop would never be able to forgive himself.

Six months later, a phone call *did* come, but it wasn't in the middle of the night. Liam had been injured, the caller reported, and was being medevaced to the nearest hospital in Germany. Coop was beside himself and, frantic for more information, began calling everyone he knew in the military. Finally, a former commander returned his call and assured him that Liam would be okay. The boys had been on a mission with their squad to take Ahmed Al Jaber Air Base—thought to be the primary command post for enemy forces—but as they'd made their approach, plumes of black smoke from burning oil fields had stopped them. When they'd finally been able to continue under the cover of darkness, everything that could've gone wrong, had—they'd come under enemy fire and Liam had been hit in the leg and a second bullet had grazed his temple just below his helmet. Jack had been hit, too, but thankfully, both were alive and expected to survive. Coop hung up the phone, sank into his chair, and covered his face with his hands. Liam was okay—his boy was okay.

When Liam was well enough to travel, he was sent stateside. His injuries, although not life-threatening, were debilitating enough to make him eligible for an honorable discharge . . . *and* he would need months of rehabilitation in a vet hospital.

Coop could not have been more excited as we made plans to drive to Maryland to see him at the National Naval Medical Center. It was the one time I didn't care who saw us together—I was going!

Liam came home three months later, using a cane, but as time went on, he needed it less, and although his physical injuries were mending, his heart was still broken. He never talked about Cadie, but he also showed no interest in dating anyone else, and even though there were plenty of girls who were interested in dating him—including Dimitri's daughter Tracey—Liam just shook his head. Tracey was Jack's girl, he said, and then just continued working beside Coop, learning as much as he could about the restoration and construction of wooden boats.

Coop and Liam were two peas in a pod—driven by memories and heartache, they threw themselves into their work. The only difference between them was, at the end of a long day, Coop had a drink or two to unwind, while Liam went for a long run, forcing the ligaments and tendons in his injured knee to stretch and move. He wasn't going to let an injury stop him from enjoying *his* only outlet for unwinding.

Soon after Liam returned, Coop was commissioned to design and build a sailboat—an eighteen-foot sloop with a lovely green and white hull and a gorgeous varnished deck. It was for a man named John Alden, and he planned to call her *Pride & Joy*.

Coop and Liam talked endlessly about the design, and once the plans were finalized and approved, they became so caught up in the construction of *Pride & Joy* that I rarely saw them—only when one of them stopped by for coffee on his way to work . . . or if I stopped by the boathouse to see how they were doing— and of course, bring them some sustenance! As they carefully and meticulously steamed wooden planks and bent them over the wooden frames, I overheard Coop muse, "Wooden boats have a way of giving a man's life purpose. They symbolize the things that matter." And I knew it was how he truly felt.

Chapter 38

I couldn't believe Elise and Liam were turning twenty-five that summer, but even more unbelievable was the milestone Lizzy and I had reached—fifty! Since it was my turn to travel, I'd driven to Boston for our girls' weekend celebration.

"Where the heck has the time gone?" Lizzy asked as she sipped her cabernet in the Bell in Hand Tavern—it was only lunchtime, but as usual she'd convinced me we deserved a drink.

"I don't know," I said, laughing. "It's crazy! I definitely don't feel fifty."

"I do," she said, shaking her salt and pepper head.

Lizzy and I hadn't seen each other in a couple of years and I realized now, as she smiled, that she did look a little older—my dear friend was aging. Suddenly, it dawned on me that she was probably thinking the same thing about me. I smiled—our friendship had lasted over forty-five years—it was really quite remarkable.

"So, what's up?" I asked, searching her eyes. "You said you had something to tell me."

She nodded and took another long sip of her wine. Then she swirled her glass pensively. "Simon and I are getting a divorce."

"Oh no," I said, reaching for her hand. "I'm so sorry, Lizzy."

She squeezed my hand and smiled. "It's okay, Sal. Honestly, I'm not sad."

"I thought things were going better."

"They were . . . for a while, but he's hooked on pain medicine again and I just can't trust him. Things will never be the same." She shook her head. "To be honest, Sal, I don't love him anymore."

I nodded, my heart breaking for my friend.

"I've been waiting for Elijah to graduate from R.I.S.D. and find a job—which he's done—and now, I'm *done* too. I've found a place for Elise and me to live, and as soon as the divorce is final, we're out. Simon's buying my share of the house, and then he can do whatever he wants with it—it's so run-down I doubt he'll be able to sell it, and if he does find a buyer, he won't get much for it."

"Is he going to pay you alimony?"

She took another sip of her wine and shook her head. "He doesn't have any money, Sal. He's supposed to pay support for Elise, but he's not working, so I don't think he'll even be able to pay that. He's probably going to end up homeless, and at this point, I don't even care. He's turned out to be a total loser."

I sighed—it had been a long time since I'd heard Lizzy call someone *a total loser,* but it certainly sounded like Simon deserved it. It always amazed me to see how people's lives evolved. Some lives spiraled out of control, while others kept an even keel. And if a life was out of control, you could almost always look back and see where the wrong turn had been made.

I took a sip of my wine. "Do the kids know?"

Lizzy nodded and laughed. "Elijah asked me what took so long. He's so grown up, Sal—you wouldn't know him . . . and"—she hesitated—"not many people know this, but he's gay. He's been seeing someone for over a year."

"What?" I said, raising my eyebrows.

"I know—my mother's probably rolling over in her grave."

Just then, the waitress came over to see if we were ready to order, but we hadn't even looked at our menus.

"No problem. Take your time," she said, then noticed Lizzy's glass was empty. "Would you like another?"

"Please," Lizzy said, then looked at my glass. "C'mon, girl—ya gonna nurse that thing all day?"

I laughed. "I have to pace myself."

The waitress disappeared and Lizzy looked back at me. "Anyway, ever since he was little, I've had moments when I've wondered whether he was, but I always pushed the thought away. But you know what they say—a mother's heart always knows. And honestly, Sal, he has such a kind, generous soul—that's all that really matters. I love him with all my heart and I just want him to be happy."

I took a sip of my drink, trying *not* to picture Lizzy's handsome son kissing a boy.

"I know what you're thinking—it's wrong—it's not natural . . . but, Sally, it's as old as time. How do we know it's wrong? Who are we to judge? Just think of all the people in hetero-sexual relationships who aren't happy—me, for example . . . and you when you were younger. Look at all the mothers who aren't happy with the girls their sons bring home or the boys their daughters bring home—my mother, for example, who had a meltdown when I started seeing Simon. And look at all the divorces. Is anyone ever truly happy? Does it really matter who you love?" She shook her head. "If Elijah is happy . . . *and* healthy, I'm happy."

"What does Simon think?"

She shook her head. "He wants nothing to do with him."

"Oh no . . ."

Lizzy nodded. "Can you believe it? That was the last nail in the coffin. Elijah is twice the man he is, but Simon won't even look at him."

"Oh, Lizzy, I'm so sorry."

"Don't be," she said. "I mean, I'm sad for Elijah, but Simon is just proving, again, what an ass he is."

I took a sip of my wine and ventured, "What about the Bible?"

"Leviticus 18:22?" she asked with a smile. "Trust me, I've looked it up and it only confirms my long-standing belief that some teachings in the Old Testament should be taken with a grain of salt." She shook her head and smiled. "I'm not a theologian, but have you ever considered some of the laws laid out in the Old Testament? Do you know it says people who work on the Sabbath should be put to death? And that it sanctions selling your daughter into slavery?" She raised her eyebrows. "Do you think it would be okay if I sold Elise?"

"Of course not," I said, frowning. "It says *that?*"

She nodded. "Exodus 35:2 and Exodus 21:7. Don't get me wrong, Sal. I love Psalms and Proverbs and Song of Solomon—but other parts are a bit outdated. It says a person should be burned to death for wearing a garment that has two different threads . . . and stoned to death for planting two different crops together." She shook her head. "So many stories in the Old Testament are about sin and war and killing and revenge, while the New Testament is about love and forgiveness and spreading the good news. I honestly think God had a change of heart after He gave us His Son, and I don't understand how anyone can be anti-Christian when all God wants is for us to love and forgive and accept one another. How can anyone find that offensive?"

"I agree," I said, nodding thoughtfully. "You've always been more of a freethinker than me," I said. "Sometimes I think I'll always be stuck in the same rut."

She laughed. "No, you won't. You'll get there . . . although you are proving to be a bit of a slow learner." She smiled. "And don't get me wrong. I'm not returning to Catholicism either. I'm going to give the Protestants a try . . . and I can't wait to celebrate Christmas with the kids," she added, grinning. "I've missed it so much. One time, you asked me if I thought I'd miss it and I didn't think I would, but I definitely do. I'm so sorry the kids never got to experience the magic of Christmas when they were little."

Just then, the waitress came over with a glass of wine and set it on the table in front of Lizzy. She eyed us questioningly and we laughed and looked sheepishly back at our menus.

"Enough about me," Lizzy said, peering over the top of her menu. "What's new with the island girl? How's that cute boat builder?"

"Oh, same old stuff," I said, waving her off. Here we were again—Lizzy spilling her heart out about everything real and raw and true in her life and me staying mum. What the heck is wrong with me? What kind of a friend am I? I could so easily share, in this moment, how I knew what she meant—how my heart ached for Liam—

the closest I'd come to having a son—when Cadie broke his heart . . . or how angry I got when Coop drank too much. Instead, I closed up. It's been too long, I told myself—trying to justify my silence. If I told her now, after twenty-eight years, she'd never forgive me.

"Oh!" she said, interrupting my thoughts. "You'll never guess who I saw!"

"Who?" I said, setting my menu down and sipping my wine.

"Drew McIntyre."

"No!" I said, feeling my heart pound at the mention of his name.

She nodded. "I had to go to Medford to take care of some things related to my mother's nonexisting estate, and afterward, I stopped at the package store and he was in line ahead of me. I wasn't sure if it was him—because he looked really old—but then Jake Ellsworth came in and said hello to him, so I knew it was. I couldn't believe it! After he left, Jake got in line behind me and we chatted for a few minutes."

"I can't believe you saw him."

"I know. It was weird. If he'd said hello to me, I might've clocked him."

I laughed. "Yeah, right—I can just see you doing that."

"I would've," Lizzy countered.

"Did Jake know what he was up to?"

"He did," she said with a conspiratorial grin.

337

"He's living with Dana Jasmin *and* they have a daughter—I think she's fifteen. He also got a promotion at the mill—he's a manager or something now."

I took a sip of my wine and nodded, trying to picture Drew as a middle-aged man. Somehow, in spite of being legally bound to an estranged wife, he'd managed to muddle through—just as I had . . . and oddly, I found myself hoping he was happy.

"Ready?" the waitress asked, peering around the corner of our booth.

"One more for me," I said, holding up my empty wineglass, "and we'll be ready when you come back. Promise!"

She smiled. "You got it."

Ten minutes later, Lizzy and I were devouring chicken Caesar salads—after all the deliberation and indecision, we'd both picked our old standby. And after Lizzy had another glass of wine, we wandered out into the afternoon with our arms around each other, blinking at the bright sunshine.

"How's Elise?" I asked as we walked toward Quincy Market.

"She's fine. Did I tell you she's working?"

"Noo," I said.

Lizzy nodded. "That's why she didn't come today—although she wanted to. She works at the animal shelter and absolutely loves it!"

"Well, she always loved Henry, so I'm not surprised."

"Henry was such a great cat. How come you never got another?"

"Oh, I didn't think I'd be lucky enough to find another one like him. He was seventeen when he died and, right up to the very end, he put his nose against mine. He was such a sweetheart. I still miss him. I don't want to go through that kind of heartache again."

Lizzy looked over. "Did you ever consider there might just be another cat who needs a home and who would love you just as much? Elise is always talking about the sweet cats at the shelter that need homes."

"How come *you* don't get one?"

Lizzy smiled. "We *are* getting one—just as soon as we move to our new place. Elise has a little orange tiger cat all picked out—her name is Ginger."

I smiled, happy to discover that my dear friend seemed more relaxed and happy than she had been in years. "That's so great—Elise will love it!"

"I know," she said, smiling. "For the first time in a long time, I'm actually looking forward to the future. By the way, did I tell you Elise and I have taken up yoga?"

"No," I said, laughing.

"Yep," Lizzy said, nodding. "We love it!"

Chapter 39

"Oh, my goodness!" I whispered when I saw the copper-colored ball of fur in Coop's arms. "Oh, my goodness!" I whispered again as he placed the little golden retriever pup in my arms. I held it up against my cheek. "What are you going to call her?"

Coop smiled. "Liam thinks we should call *him* Tucket—Tuck for short."

I held the puppy so I could look into his sweet brown eyes. "You look like a Tuck," I said softly.

Just then, Liam came in the door and headed right for the coffee. "Oh no," he said with a smile. "Now we're never going to get him back."

"You might not," I said, laughing and cuddling the puppy in my arms. "Where'd you get him? Do they have more?"

Coop shook his head. "We got him over by Siasconset. He was the last one—they said he was the runt."

I pressed my nose into his soft fur. "You're not a runt," I consoled. "You're just the cute one." The puppy turned his head and licked my chin. "Yep, we're going to be great pals," I said. "You just come here anytime you want a little piece of bacon."

"Oh no," Coop warned. "No handouts or he'll turn into a beggar."

"Shhh," I whispered into the puppy's fur. "Don't listen to him."

Coop raised his eyebrows and I smiled. "So what are you guys up to today?"

"Taking the carburetor out of your dad's old Bel Air so I can find out why it's running like crap."

I rolled my eyes. "Don't you think I should sell that old thing?"

"No, I don't. You should hang on to it. It's in great shape and the older it gets, the more valuable it is."

I sighed. "I should just give it to you. After all, you've stored it and maintained it all these years."

He shook his head. "It was your dad's, and it's the only thing you have of his. You should keep it. Just think—his hands touched that steering wheel. Aren't you the least bit sentimental about it?"

I laughed. "I guess—when you put it that way."

In truth, I wasn't very sentimental about things. I had one pair of turquoise earrings that Coop had given me years ago, but I'd sold my mom's luggage at a tag sale, and although I still had her pearls, I never wore them—mostly because I never got dressed up. My wardrobe consisted of T-shirts and shorts in the summer, and jeans and flannel shirts over T-shirts the rest of the year. I didn't even own a dress! I was sixty-two years old—a fact I couldn't even begin to fathom, making Coop sixty-eight, and we never went out—never mind "out" together, so what did I need a dress for? I'd only kept the pearls because they were my mom's—and my great-grandmother's before her—and the earrings because Coop had given them to me, so I guess I was a little sentimental. I sighed—maybe Coop was right—maybe I should hang on to the car, too, since I didn't have anything else that had belonged to my dad.

"Okay, well, don't spend all day on it. I'm sure you have other things to do."

"Yeah," Liam said, sipping his coffee. "Like going to the doctor."

Coop frowned and Liam shook his head.

"Why?" I asked worriedly. "What's going on?"

"He hasn't been feeling well," Liam said, eyeing his uncle.

"What's wrong?" I asked.

"Oh, just some chest pain and numbness in my limbs," Coop said with a hint of sarcasm.

"Seriously?" I demanded.

"Would I kid about something like that?" he teased.

I looked to Liam for confirmation, but he just raised his eyebrows and pressed his lips together.

"If you're having symptoms like that, you *do* need to go to the doctor."

"See what you started?" Coop said, eyeing him.

"She's right. . . ."

"I already told you, it's nothing."

"It wasn't *nothing* the other day when I saw you gripping the picnic table at the boathouse."

I raised my eyebrows. "What?"

"You're making a big deal out of nothing," Coop said. "It was just indigestion."

I shook my head and handed the puppy back to him. "If you want to live to see this puppy grow up, you better get to the doctor and find out what's going on."

Coop rolled his eyes. "C'mon, Tuck. Let's go take a look at that car."

He turned to walk out and I looked questioningly at Liam, but he just shook his head. "I've tried."

"It's not nothing," I called after him. "My dad refused to go to the doctor and look what happened!" But Coop was already outside.

"I'll keep trying," Liam said, pouring a second cup of coffee. "Put these on our tab," he said with a grin.

"Ha," I said, shaking my head. "Your tab is maxed out."

As soon as they left, the first ferry of the Fourth of July weekend docked and Cuppa Jo became so busy I didn't have time to think—or worry—about Coop, but when I finally sat down that night, he was *all* I could think about. I poured a glass of wine—I'd discovered, over the years, that my abstinence had little to no effect on the amount Coop drank—or didn't drink—so I'd given up abstaining; then realized I enjoyed having a glass of wine in the evening. I tried to call Coop, but Liam answered and said he was out with Dimitri. "Are you on call then?" I asked, knowing Dimitri's wife, Fran, often called Liam to see if he would go round them up when it got late.

"Yep . . . and puppy sitting," he answered.

"Were you able to talk him into making an appointment?"

"No, he just gets angry."

I took my wine outside to sit on the porch, and as I watched the sun sink below the horizon, I tried to remember how long Coop and I had been together, and it suddenly hit me that it had been forty years—how had that happened?! I shook my head and looked up at the streaks of pink and purple clouds. If anything ever happened to him, I didn't know what I'd do!

Although Coop and I were rarely intimate anymore—the passion we'd known when we were younger had become a glowing bed of embers; and in its place, a spiritual intimacy—like that of an old married couple who knew each other's thoughts and finished each other's sentences—had taken its place. That's why I was so surprised when I heard his truck pulling into the driveway.

"Hey," he said, coming up the porch steps.

"Hey," I said. "Is everything okay?"

He nodded. "Everything's fine." He wrapped his arms around me and kissed the top of my head. "Can't a guy just miss his girl?"

I laughed. "Of course he can." He leaned down and kissed my lips. "Mmm . . . you taste like whiskey," I murmured.

"Just a little," he confessed.

"You were out with Dimitri and you only had a *little?*"

"Well, we were sitting at The Brotherhood and he asked me how long I'd had the boathouse, and I started thinking about it and I realized it has been forty years—which also means you've been putting up with me for forty years!"

I laughed. "Can you believe it's been that long?"

"I can't," he said, shaking his head. "Time goes by too fast."

"It does," I agreed, and as I rested my head on his chest, I wondered what had brought on this uncharacteristic showing of sentimental affection. Was he worried about his health too? Had he suddenly realized how much he had to lose? I listened to his heartbeat and silently prayed it would beat forever.

"Watch that," he whispered when I pressed against him. "You might get more than you bargained for."

"Really?" I teased.

"Mm-hmm," he murmured, kissing my neck. "Really."

Chapter 40

" 'Do not worry about tomorrow, for tomorrow will bring worries of its own. Today's trouble is enough for today,' " I murmured as I watched Coop reach down to pick up a tennis ball and throw it for Tuck. Over the last year—ever since Liam told me Coop hadn't been feeling well— I'd tried to get him to go to the doctor. I even offered to make the appointment for him, but the more I pressed, the more he resisted. He was just like my dad. "I'm fine," he'd say in an annoyed voice, and because I didn't want him to think I was turning into an old nag, I let up, but it didn't stop me from praying. To his credit, I never saw him show signs of distress—he always looked strong and healthy—but then again, I wasn't around him all the time.

Our moments of intimacy had continued to wane. We were more like old friends than lovers, but it didn't seem to bother either of us—we were content to just be together, quietly aware of each other's steady presence. Of course, I still loved it when he stirred the embers, but I didn't walk around on fire like I had when we were younger!

As I'd grown older, my prayer list had grown longer too—it seemed the older I got, the more people I knew who needed prayers. Needless to say—because my memory was going—I kept an index card with a list of names next to my rosary beads and I prayed for each person morning and evening. " 'Lord,' " I'd begin, " 'make me an instrument of your peace; where there is hatred, let me sow love; when there is injury, pardon; where there is doubt, faith; where there is despair, hope; where there is darkness, light; and where there is sadness, joy. Grant that I may not so much seek to be consoled as to console; to be under-stood, as to understand, to be loved as to love; for it is in giving that we receive, it is in pardoning that we are pardoned, and it is in dying that we are born to eternal life.' " And then I'd faithfully consult the card on which I'd scribbled names.

Even when I wasn't sitting in my chair—I could be kneading bread, stirring muffin batter, or weeding—my lips were constantly moving, saying the Lord's Prayer, the Prayer of Contrition, or whatever came to mind; then I'd murmur the names of people I knew who needed healing or guidance. I think anyone who didn't know me would probably think I was crazy—maybe even those who *did* know me thought so! But there was so much turmoil in the world, and with round-the-clock news cycles, the bad news seemed endless . . . and prayer seemed to be the only viable answer. It gave me comfort, but it also left me wondering if God really heard me.

So many times in life, I'd felt as if the answer I received to a prayer wasn't what I'd hoped—or asked for. I asked for healing for countless people who ended up dying, and I asked for guidance in countless situations but heard nothing. On more than one occasion, I pleaded, "Oh, God, where *are* you in this?" And I'd felt empty and hopeless, but when I looked back now—over the span of many years—I found I was able to see the rippling thread of God's presence. And that's why, when Lizzy called in late November to tell me in a terrified, tearful voice that she'd felt a lump in her breast, I began to pray feverishly. "God, this is your chance to prove you are really there and that you are really listening!"

For the next several weeks, I stormed the gates of heaven with my prayers. I was like the widow who begged the king for justice until he finally grew tired of hearing her voice and gave in to her demand. At first, I prayed Lizzy was mistaken and the lump was a benign cyst, and then, when her worst fears were realized, I prayed He would guide her to the right doctors and the right treatment. And finally, my prayer became a command. "Don't you dare take my best friend," I whispered tearfully, "because I will never forgive you." And then, worried that I might offend Him, I added: "Yet thy will—not mine—be done."

Chapter 41

" 'I can do all things through Christ who strengthens me,' " I murmured as I walked up the street to Lizzy's condo in Somerville—the home she and Elise had moved to after her divorce from Simon was final. All the parking spots in the visitors' area were full, and I had to drive around the block two more times before I found a space on the street. My heart pounded as I walked up to the door, clutching a bouquet of sunflowers.

I knocked lightly and held my breath. "Come in," a voice called, but when I tried the knob, it didn't turn. "Sorry 'bout that," the same voice called, and a moment later, I heard a click and the door opened to reveal a tall, slender figure.

"Elijah?" I said in surprise. It had been so long since I'd seen Lizzy's son I hardly recognized him. He was meticulously dressed in jeans and a button-down shirt, his hair was short on the sides and longer on top, and his eyes—behind stylishly square frames and long dark eyelashes— were still the same piercing blue that would knock any woman dead—if there was a woman in his life. Of course, the first thought that came to my mind was: *It's definitely true what they say about the cute ones. . . .*

"Hi, Aunt Sal," he said, smiling and revealing perfectly straight white teeth.

"I'm so sorry about all this," I choked, reaching up to hug him.

"It's okay," he said. "I'm glad I could take time off to help. Last week was kind of rough, but she's doing better." He stepped back so I could step in. "She's in the kitchen," he said, motioning down the hall. I'd been to the condo several times over the years, so I knew my way around. "I have to run out to pick up a prescription," he said, slipping his phone in his pocket, "but I'll be right back."

I nodded and walked down the hall to find Lizzy and Elise sitting in the kitchen with steaming bowls of soup in front of them.

"Hi, Aunt Sally," Elise squealed, jumping up and almost spilling her soup.

"Hi, hon," I said, giving her a hug. Then I stepped back and held her at arm's length. "Look at you!"

She beamed. "I know! I just had my birthday. I'm forty years old now!"

"I know!" I said, nodding, even though her birthday had completely slipped my mind. "That's why I brought you these," I added, holding out the sunflowers.

"Thank you!" she said, admiring the flowers. "I thought they might be for me."

"You're welcome," I said. "Maybe you and your mom can enjoy them together."

She nodded and then hurried off to find a vase.

I looked at Lizzy and she smiled weakly. I

leaned over to give her a gentle hug. "How're you doing?"

"I'm okay," she said. "I miss the girls," she said, touching her flat chest—a chest I'd once envied. I nodded sympathetically. Two months earlier, Lizzy had called to confirm the lump she'd found was cancerous, and then, in a whirlwind of the most aggressive treatment possible, had a double mastectomy. When she told me, I'd offered to come and stay, but she assured me Elijah had already said he would.

"Have you started chemo?"

She nodded. "It was brutal. I felt so sick . . . and my hair . . ." She reached up to touch her head. "It started coming out in clumps, so Elijah shaved my head and then he went out and bought this hat." She smiled, touching the soft pink hat on her head. "He's such a good kid. I don't know what I'd do without him."

"He *is* a good kid," I agreed, "and so handsome! I almost didn't recognize him."

"Did I tell you he and his partner have started their own company?"

"Noo."

She nodded. "They're designing Web sites. They're doing really well."

"Wow, that's good to know because I need someone to design a Web site for Cuppa Jo. I don't know the first thing about it."

"I'm sure he'd be happy to help you."

I looked down and realized she hadn't touched her soup. "You should eat."

She nodded. "Want some? Elijah made it—it's some kind of mineral soup. It's supposed to be very healing."

I shook my head. "He made it for you so you'll get stronger."

"It's really good," she pressed, but I shook my head. She looked around the kitchen. "How about a cookie?" she asked, pointing to a plate on the table heaped high with chocolate-chip cookies.

I smiled. "Did he make those too?"

"He did."

"Sheesh. You *are* definitely in better hands with him than you would've been with me."

She pushed the plate toward me and I picked one up and took a bite.

"How 'bout a cup of tea or a glass of milk?"

"Stop," I said. "I don't need anything *and* you need to eat your soup!"

She dutifully picked up her spoon, dipped it, and slowly lifted it to her mouth. "You should try it," she said with a smile, but I teasingly rolled my eyes and took another bite of my cookie.

Just then, Elise came into the kitchen carrying a vase. "Is this one okay, Mama?"

Lizzy nodded. "Maybe Sally will give the flowers a fresh cut before you put them in water."

"I can give them a fresh cut," Elise said, opening a drawer to find the scissors.

"The stalks are thick—be careful."

Hearing the concern in Lizzy's voice, I stood to help.

"How's Liam, Aunt Sally?" Elise asked earnestly.

"He's fine," I said, knowing Elise still—after all these years—had a crush on him. "He turned forty this year too."

"I know," she said. "I always remember Liam's birthday."

"*You* have a good memory," I said, helping her arrange the flowers.

"Does he have a girlfriend yet?"

"Not yet."

"I don't have a boyfriend either."

I smiled—Elise and I had this conversation every time we saw each other. Over the years, Liam—knowing how she felt, and never wanting to hurt her feelings—had gone out of his way to be extra friendly, which only made Elise love him more.

"He can be *my* boyfriend if he wants."

"I'll tell him," I said, putting my arm around her shoulders.

Lizzy smiled; then we heard the front door open. A moment later, Elijah appeared, bearing three coffees from Dunkin' Donuts and Lizzy's new prescription, which I soon learned—after Lizzy threw up the little bit of soup she'd eaten—was to help with nausea.

While Elijah cleaned up the mess, I helped

Lizzy get back to bed. "This sucks so much," she said weakly.

"It *does* suck," I said, fluffing her pillows. "I'm so sorry you have to go through it."

"You know what my mom would say?"

I laughed. "She'd say it's punishment for something you've done!"

"Exactly."

"Well, she'd be wrong," I assured her. I sat on the edge of the bed and held her hand. "It's just bad cells growing like crazy . . . for no reason—isn't that what you told me when we were little?"

She smiled weakly. "It sounds like something I would've said."

I nodded. "You did."

"Well, I was right."

I nodded. "You were *always* right."

"Thanks for coming, Sal," she said. "I always love seeing you."

"And I always love seeing you," I said. "You need to get better so we can go out and—" But before I could finish my sentence, she was sound asleep. I tucked her soft pink hat around her ears and pulled up her covers. "Oh, Lord, please help Lizzy get better," I whispered; then I lightly kissed her cheek. As I stood up, Ginger—the little orange tiger cat Elise and Lizzy had gotten from the shelter years earlier—hopped up on the bed and curled up next to her. I smiled, feeling oddly reassured that my dear friend would be okay.

Chapter 42

My change of heart wasn't triggered by some profound epiphany—I didn't suddenly see the light. Nor was I struck down and blinded by light like Saul on the road to Damascus. My change of heart was so gradual I didn't even notice it happening; it was so gentle it had taken a lifetime—a lifetime of living and witnessing just how messy life is—to finally realize that no one's life is perfect.

When I was young—and even as I grew older—I thought Lizzy's life was perfect. My best friend had always done everything right—from drawing with crayons to winning every game we played; from being our class valedictorian to getting a full scholarship and graduating from college, magna cum laude; from becoming a nurse to finding the perfect guy. Lizzy had done everything right, and as a result, her life was perfect—or so I'd thought.

My life, on the other hand, was a mess. I was the queen of sin and bad choices, and my imperfect life reflected every one of those bad choices. As I stood looking out the kitchen window, though, cradling my cup of tea, the sun broke through the clouds and made the raindrops glisten on every surface—just like they had on the day of my mom's funeral, the day I'd told my dad I wanted to go to St. Clement—and I realized I wasn't alone. I smiled wistfully. Did I regret my decision now? Would my life be different if I— at five years old—hadn't said I wanted to go to school with Lizzy? Would I now be living in a sprawling house with a handsome, successful husband? Would I be the mother of grown, successful children, *and* maybe even a grandmother to adorable, perfect grandchildren? Would I have spent my life teaching, or would I have been—because my husband was so successful—a stay-at-home mom who ran the PTA, volunteered in my community and my church, and ran my beautiful, smart, polite, perfect children to soccer practice, Scouts, and dance? Would my life, now, be somehow richer, fuller, happier?

I took a sip of my tea and pictured Coop, at that very moment, building a fire in the wood-stove at the boathouse. I pictured his calloused hands as they slid logs through the heavy iron door, struck a match, and held it to the kindling. I pictured him kneeling down, rubbing his hands together, and holding them to the fire. I pictured his eyes—eyes that had seen more than their share of tragedy—reflecting the glow of the fire, reflecting the trust and care he'd placed in me, and reflecting the memories of a life well lived. Suddenly, I knew, with every fiber of my being, that I didn't regret any of it. My life may not have been perfect, but neither was the life of anyone else I knew—not my parents' or Coop's or Lily's or Liam's . . . or Lizzy's. We'd all made mistakes, committed sins, had our regrets, and begged for forgiveness. We'd all known sorrow, joy, disappointment, and triumph. And we'd all pressed on.

I smiled. My cup overflowed—my imperfect life was rich and full of blessings, and I wouldn't change a thing. I'd known true love and I knew what it was like to *be* truly loved; my life had been touched by others' lives, and my life had touched theirs . . . and in the end, that was all that truly mattered.

The wisdom that comes with time is a blessing. That's why, on a morning in March—a day that was both rainy and sunny—I picked up the phone, whispered my "go-to" prayer—" '*Lord Jesus, Holy Father, have mercy upon me, a sinner*' "—and dialed the number on the card I'd been carrying around in my pocket for weeks—the number of an attorney who would help me begin the process of divorcing Drew.

Chapter 43

" 'Teach us to number our days,' " I said, four months later, as I pulled a large white envelope out of my mailbox, " 'that we may gain a heart of wisdom.' " In the waning light of the summer evening, I looked at the return address and felt my heart skip a beat. For forty-eight years I'd born the weight of guilt and shame for the things I'd done when I was a girl, and now, this envelope brought news that I was free—my divorce was final!

I'd begun the process of divorcing Drew on March 13th—the very same day Pope Jorge Mario Bergoglio—the pope who would quickly become known for his profound humility, mercy, and love—was elected. On that day, I'd felt oddly assured that all would be well—that I would find forgiveness in the eyes of the Church and in the eyes of God, and that I would be accepted into heaven when I died. And now that I was free, I couldn't wait to tell Coop.

I didn't know why it suddenly seemed so important to me. Would it somehow change the way things were between us? Certainly, we'd be able to live our lives openly, but did that really matter? We would still be the same people—the same couple—who'd loved deeply and been there for each other through all the joys and sorrows of our lives, so how would my newly found freedom change things? I didn't know the answer—I only knew that the thought filled my heart with joy.

I tucked the envelope under my arm and leaned down to pull a weed. The gardens were in desperate need of my attention, but as I knelt down to pull more weeds, I heard a truck pulling into my drive-way and I looked up. My heart pounded, hoping it was Coop—I couldn't wait to tell him the news, but when I realized it wasn't him, I frowned. What was Liam doing here?

I stood up, feeling my knees ache, and watched him climb out. His face was white. "What is it, Li? What's wrong?"

He shook his head and tears streamed down his cheeks, and he seemed unable to speak. I felt my heart start to race. "Tell me," I whispered, but he just shook his head.

I'm always surprised by the beauty and pain in the world. A good, full life is rich with both. Over the years, I've come to realize that hardly a day goes by when joy isn't mixed with a measure of sorrow, and with this knowledge comes the timeless reminder that we should make the most of each day. I have a favorite poem that reminds me of this too. Every time I'm bored with the monotony of everyday life, I think of Mary Jean Irion's poem "Normal Day." It reminds me to enjoy the loveliness of *every* day, even—and especially—the boring ones, because, all too soon, a day will come that's fraught with worry and sorrow—and my heart will ache for that simple, boring, monotonous day.

On the day Liam pulled into my driveway and stood in front of me, his broad shoulders sagging with grief, I suddenly thought of that poem. *Oh, please let me go back to the beginning of this day of making coffee, wiping down counters, washing dishes, baking bread, and pulling weeds. Please let me just be weary from a long day's work—let me go to bed and wake up to another boring tomorrow—just like today—with no surprises* . . . no sorrow. "Oh, please," I cried. "Please don't let this day end this way," I sobbed. "I want it back. I want all our days back."

Liam wrapped his arms around me. "I'm so sorry, Sal. I know how much you loved him. I know how much he loved *you*."

Chapter 44

" 'Trust in the Lord with all thy heart and lean not unto thy own understanding,' " I whispered as I followed Liam and Tuck down the winding path to the sandy beach behind their house. " 'In all thy ways acknowledge him and he will make straight thy paths.' " *Not this path, though!* I thought wistfully as we wandered along through scraggly pitch pine and beach plums.

Liam had finally managed to tell me, in fits and starts, what happened. . . .

He and Coop had finished work and Coop had tried to give him money for a couple of six-packs, but Liam had pushed the money away, insisting it was his turn to buy.

Coop had shrugged. "Shoot yerself."

And Liam had smiled. "I'll see you at home."

"Not if I see yer sorry ass first," Coop had replied.

When Liam got home a half hour later, he was surprised the house was still dark. Someone must've stopped by and they got to talking, he thought, but as it got later and later, he started to worry. Finally, he drove back to the boathouse . . . and found Coop lying on the cement floor with

Tuck beside him—the big golden retriever's head on his chest and his sorrowful eyes telling the whole story—Coop was gone.

"How about here?" Liam asked, stopping on a dune, his eyes full of tears.

Tuck sat down next to him—practically on his foot, and I nodded.

Liam and I both knew Coop hadn't wanted a service. Through the years, he'd made it very clear. "Just toss me in the water and be done with it," he'd said.

"Do you want to say anything?" Liam asked, wiping his eyes and opening the beautiful mahogany box he'd made from the wood of an old Chris Craft.

I cleared my throat, closed my eyes, and began softly, "Immortal God, Holy Lord, Father and protector of everything Thou hast created, we raise our hearts to Thee today for our beloved uncle and friend, Winston Ellis Cooper III, who has passed out of this mortal life. In Thy loving mercy—" Suddenly, I stopped midsentence, opened my eyes, looked up at the endless blue sky, and realized how weary I was of saying memorized prayers. Coop deserved more than that—he deserved a prayer that came from my heart.

"Dear Lord," I began again. "Thank you so much for bringing Coop into our lives and giving us so many years together. He has been a blessing to everyone who has known and loved him, and we miss him with all our hearts. We know he is with you, though. Now *you* have another master boat builder in heaven—and I'm sure he's already struck up a conversation with Noah and is asking him some technical questions about the ark. It would be just like him. Please continue to bless us as we carry on with our lives . . . and without our beloved Coop. Amen."

Liam brushed back his tears. "Thanks, Sal," he said softly. "That was perfect. It was just the right thing to say—I can just see him talking to Noah." He smiled sadly. "Are you ready?"

I nodded, and as I put my arms around Tuck's neck, Liam turned the box on its side and lifted it over the waves. We watched solemnly as Coop's ashes drifted through the summer air, sparkling in the late-day sunlight.

Chapter 45

" 'What are human beings that thou are mindful of them . . .' " I whispered, looking up at the vast August sky full of stars, " 'mortals that you care for them?' " I was sitting on the weathered, old bench Coop had made years earlier with a blanket wrapped around my shoulders. Every year, Coop and I had sat on the bench together to watch the Perseid meteor shower, but tonight I watched alone, determined to carry on the tradition—even if it made my heart ache. As I looked up at the sky, waiting for the first meteor, I replayed the conversation I'd had with Lizzy earlier that evening. I'd finally told her about my relationship with Coop, and instead of being angry, she'd chuckled. . . .

"I've always known, silly. Do you think I couldn't tell you were in love? I've asked you several times, over the years, about the cute boat builder, but you always seemed determined to keep it a secret. I figured you'd tell me when you were ready to, but, honestly, Sal, I never expected it to take forty-four years!"

"I can't believe you knew all this time!" I exclaimed, recalling all the times I'd felt miserable because I hadn't told her.

"Of course I knew. I know you better than anyone—probably than you know yourself. I don't know all the details. I'll let you fill me in over a glass—make that a bottle—of wine the next time we're together . . . and since I've been so patient, I expect all the details!"

I laughed, feeling utterly thankful and relieved that I hadn't lost my best friend! "Well, I've actually been thinking of writing a book."

"You should!" Lizzy exclaimed. "You always wanted to be a writer, and I think you've read every book ever written, so you should know how to do it."

"I haven't read every book," I countered. "In fact, I've hardly read anything lately. I can't seem to make out small print anymore and my eyes get tired in no time—not to mention, I fall asleep."

"I'll have to get you some large-print books," she teased.

"You might have to," I said, laughing. "Can you believe we're getting that old?"

"No, I can't," she said; then she grew quiet. "I'm really sorry, Sal," she said softly. "You must be devastated . . . and lost."

I nodded, suddenly unable to speak.

"I wish I was there so I could give you a hug," she said softly.

"I wish you were too," I managed to answer tearfully.

"I love you, my dear friend."

"I love you too."

I listened to the waves lapping the shore and my thoughts drifted back to Coop. It had been a month since Liam had pulled into my driveway and given me the devastating news, but the continuous ache in my heart felt as if it would never ease. I closed my eyes and tried to imagine Coop sitting next to me; then my mind drifted farther back—to the beginning. To the first time I saw him . . . to the first time we danced. . . .

I stood up and walked toward the water with my beer. It was then that I noticed the young man from the restaurant leaning against the bar. He was looking away, but when I walked past him, he turned, and for the first time I saw his face . . . and his blue eyes. He nodded to me and I smiled.

"How come you're not dancing?" he asked.

"I don't have anyone to dance with," I said, finding it hard to not notice his chiseled jaw and fine aristocratic features. He was tall, and although his T-shirt was tight around his shoulders, his faded jeans hung loosely from his hips.

"Dance with me," he ventured shyly.

I shook my head. "I'm not very good."

"I'm not either," he said, holding out his hand.

I put down my sandals and beer and, without saying a word, he pulled me toward him and we swayed slowly back and forth to Bob Dylan's "Lay Lady Lay."

"I love this song," I murmured.

He nodded, but didn't reply, and when it ended, I heard Lizzy calling. "I better go," I said, quickly pulling away and picking up my things. "Thank you for the dance."

He nodded.

I started to walk away, but when I looked back, I saw the sad half smile that I would never forget.

I started to softly sing Bob Dylan's haunting ballad "Lay Lady Lay," and as I did, tears filled my eyes. I hadn't heard the song in years, but now, as I sang it, the words came to me as if I'd heard it yesterday—and I realized how profoundly fitting the lyrics were. "Oh, Coop," I whispered, "you were always right in front of me."

I wiped my eyes and looked up at the stars sparkling in the endless sky. "Are you up there?" I whispered. "Are you keeping an eye on us? Do you know how lost I am without you? How lost Liam is? And poor Tuck is so despondent he won't let Liam out of his sight. . . ." Suddenly, a bright light streaked across the sky and I caught my breath. The majesty of creation—with

all its nuance and detail and timeless beauty—
always caught me by surprise. We'd watched
the meteor shower every year, weather permit-
ting, and it never failed to fill me with awe. I
continued to watch in amazement as one
bright light after another emerged from the
darkness and streaked silently across the heavens.

" 'What are human beings that thou art
mindful of them,' " I whispered again when the
meteors started to wane. " 'Mere mortals that
you care for us?' " As I said this, I pulled the
blanket around me and watched a single star—
not a meteor—grow brighter and I felt oddly at
peace. The God I knew—and loved—was as
constant as that star, and I knew He would
always love me—no matter what I did. He'd
already proven his enduring love with the life
he'd given me—my life on Nantucket—my life
with Coop . . . and I knew Coop would always
be with me, in my heart.

August

Sally woke with a start and blinked at the bright sunlight streaming through her bedroom windows. She sat up straight and looked at the clock—it was after seven! How could that be? She never overslept! Why hadn't her alarm gone off?

Feeling movement, Jax—from his sprawled-out position on the other side of the bed—opened one eye. "Why didn't you wake me?" she asked, flying from the bed and pulling on Coop's old flannel shirt as she hurried to the bathroom. Jax watched her curiously and then hopped lightly off the bed and peered around the doorway. "We're going to be late!" she
said with her mouth full of toothpaste. Jax didn't seem the least bit concerned, though, as he trotted after her to the kitchen and nosed around the closet door where his food was kept. "Out first," Sally reminded, opening the front door. "Make it quick and don't pee on my flowers!" But she may as well have said the opposite because the growing little Lab trotted right over to her black-eyed

Susans and promptly lifted his leg, releasing the first long stream of the day. "I said *don't!*" she called, but he just gazed up at her innocently and kept on peeing.

"Honestly, Jax, do you think you could listen?" she asked as he loped past her, wagging his tail, and headed right back to the closet. She opened the door and felt him trying to nudge past her and push his head into the bag. "You'd eat the whole bag if I let you!" she said, scooping a cup of kibble. She tossed a couple onto his bed, which he promptly gobbled, and walked over to the sink to add some water. When she turned around, he was sitting politely next to his water bowl, waiting. She put his food down, smiled as he gazed at it longingly, and whispered, "Okay!" and Jax bolted over and began wolfing it down. "You're such a Lab!" She glanced over at her coffee-maker, shook her head in dismay, and hurried down the hall to take a quick shower. Her coffee would have to wait.

Twenty minutes later, Sally parked behind Cuppa Jo and hurried inside with Jax at her heels. Liam and Tracey and the kids were already there, setting up. "Sorry I'm late," she said, hanging the clothes she planned to wear behind the door and kissing Tuck's brow when he hurried over to say hello.

"You're not late," Tracey assured as she cut lemon squares and arranged them on plates. "Besides, we have everything under control."

"Happy Pub Day!" Liam said, smiling. "Isn't that what you're supposed to say to famous authors?"

"I don't know and I'm definitely not famous," Sally said, "but thank you. I feel a little foolish. What if no one comes?"

Tracey put her arm around her. "Stop worrying, Sal. I saw Wendy last night and she said they've had a ton of calls and she's praying they ordered enough books!"

Sally shook her head skeptically. "We'll see."

"Come on outside and see the sign again," Aidan said, reaching for Sally's hand. "We added something."

Sally allowed herself to be pulled out to the front porch, and just as she looked up, T.J. plugged in an extension cord and a long string of tiny white Christmas lights sparkled to life. "Wow!" she exclaimed. "You guys are doing too much."

"It was Olivia's idea," T.J. said, politely giving his sister credit.

"Well, it looks wonderful! I don't know how anyone will be able to walk by without stopping to see what's going on."

371

"That's the plan," Aidan said, grinning.

They went back inside and Sally headed straight for the coffee. She poured a cup and then headed to the kitchen to help Tracey arrange cucumber, cream cheese, and dill finger sandwiches on a tray. "These look yummy," she said.

"You'd think we were having a grand opening for Cuppa Jo instead of a book signing," Tracey commented.

"You're not kidding," Liam chimed in as he dumped ice into a wooden bucket.

"Well, if people don't come for a book, maybe they'll at least stop by for some food," Sally said. "We definitely have enough to feed the whole island! Including you two," she said, looking down at Jax and Tuck, who were intently watching Tracey's every move.

Tracey laughed as she covered the trays with plastic wrap.

"What can I do?" Sally asked. "Job me."

"Nothing," Liam said. "You're the guest of honor."

"Oh, c'mon," Sally protested. "I'll go crazy if I don't have a job."

Just then, the bell on the front door tinkled, announcing a customer, and Liam looked up at the clock. "Why don't you go out front?"

"Okay," Sally said.

The next two hours flew by—the shop was busier than ever—so much so, Sally had to put the kids to work! Finally, Liam closed the front door, saying, "We just need a few minutes to get ready."

T.J., Aidan, and Olivia quickly covered the tables with crisp white linen tablecloths and set a beautiful bouquet of sunflowers in the center of each table while Tracey brought out trays of sandwiches and desserts. "Sally was wondering if you guys might like to pass trays too. What do you think?"

They all grinned and nodded.

"Good. Well, make sure you carry a little stack of these fancy napkins in one hand," she said, opening a package and taking them out, "and offer them to anyone who takes something to eat or drink." She turned and eyed Sally. "You better go get ready," she said. "Wendy said she'd be here by ten—*and* she's bringing more books."

Sally felt her heart start to pound—she'd never felt so nervous. It was suddenly dawning on her that she had put her whole life story out there for the world to read—and not just her story, but her innermost thoughts and perspective about life and faith and friendship, too—and it was too late to take any of it back. She'd spent most of her life keeping her life a secret and now she was exposing herself to the entire world! What if everyone laughed? What if they thought she was crazy? What if they criticized her and said her story was awful? The thought was almost too much to bear.

"Who's idea was this anyway?" she murmured as she stood in front of the bathroom mirror, pulling her old T-shirt over her head. She stepped into her new white linen slacks, slipped on the sea green linen blouse she'd bought especially for the occasion, and clasped her mother's pearls around her neck. As she put on the earrings Coop had given her, she looked at her reflection and reached up to tuck some loose strands of her silver hair behind her ears. "I am who I am," she said softly. "I've done the best that I can and I've spent far too much time worrying what the world thinks." She folded her T-shirt and shorts, slipped them into her bag, and softly whispered, " 'Hail Mary, full of grace, the Lord is with thee, blessed art thou amongst women and blessed is the fruit of thy womb Jesus! Holy Mary, mother of God, pray for us sinners, now and at the hour of our death' . . . and please be with me right now! Amen." Then she mustered a smile and opened the bathroom door.

"Wow! Look at you!" Liam said, grinning.

Sally looked down. "Do I look okay?"

"You look amazing!" he said.

"You look like an author!" Aidan piped.

Sally laughed. "And what, exactly, does an author look like?"

"She looks smart."

"I think I must be fooling you, or maybe it's my glasses," Sally said, reaching up to make sure they were still on top of her head.

"No, you definitely look like an author," Olivia confirmed while T.J. nodded.

Tracey put her arm around her. "You look stunning, and if you're nervous, just remember what you always tell us: 'All shall be well . . .'" And on cue, they all chimed in, "'and all shall be well and all manner of things shall be well!'"

Sally laughed and looked at each of them. "Thank you. I don't know what I'd do without you."

Just then, Wendy came through the back door wheeling a handcart with two more boxes of books on it. "Hi, hi, hi!" she said, smiling. "Have you looked outside?! I think the whole island is out in your parking lot."

"No way!" the kids said, running to look out the windows.

"It's just the free food," Sally said, laughing nervously.

"No, it's not," Liam said. "It's because they

want to get a signed copy of your wonderful book."

She laughed. "Did you finally finish it?"

"I did," he said, smiling. "I loved it. It's a classic."

"It *is* wonderful," Tracey confirmed. "I always wondered about you and Coop!"

"That reminds me," Wendy said, reaching into her bag. "I don't know if your editor e-mailed this review to you yet . . ."

Sally shook her head. "I've been so busy I haven't even looked at my e-mail."

"Well, this was in the *New York Times*," she said, handing Sally a copy of the Sunday Book Review. Sally scanned the review and shook her head in disbelief.

"What does it say?" Tracey asked.

She looked up with glistening eyes and then cleared her throat and looked back down. "Adams's lyrical debut novel, *Summer Dance*, takes a lifelong love affair and encapsulates it into the purposeful and easy-to-read frame-work of a lovely memoir. . . ."

"Wow!" Tracey said. "That's wonderful!"

"And that's just *one* of the glowing reviews," Wendy said. She looked out front. "I think we'd better get started."

Liam wheeled the cart to the table they'd set up with a display of books. Then he pulled the chair out for Sally. "Got your pen ready?"

She nodded and sat down, praying her hands would stop shaking, and Aidan, who was standing by the front door, looked over. "Ready?"

She nodded again and Aidan opened the door, and as people began filtering in, tears filled her eyes—she felt as if she was a guest on the old TV show *This Is Your Life*. Everyone from Lizzy and Elise—who had secretly traveled to Nantucket to surprise her—and Abe—who, at ninety, was living in a retirement community on Cape Cod—to Levi, Emma, and little Lily—who'd come over from Tuckernuck that morning; and from her editor and agent—who'd traveled from New York—to all the shop owners, friends, and customers on Nantucket had stopped by to show their love and support.

"I can't believe you came all the way out here!" Sally said, standing back up to give Lizzy a hug.

"Are you kidding?!" Lizzy said. "I wouldn't miss it for the world! Especially since I'm a main character!"

Sally laughed. "True, but that would be another reason to not come—you've already read it!" She'd absolutely made sure Lizzy had read—and approved—it before it went to press.

"That's not the same as having a copy

signed by the author," Lizzy said, hugging the book to her chest. "By the way, before I forget—Elijah wanted me to be sure to give you his best. He and Evan wanted to come, but they are swamped with work. He said he can't wait to read it."

"Well, please tell him 'thank you' and I completely understand. By the way, how're you feeling?" Sally asked quietly.

"You don't need to whisper," Lizzy said, laughing. "Remember—it's all in here," she said, tapping the cover.

"I know," Sally said, "but not everyone knows it's you."

"Well, maybe you should introduce me."

Sally raised her eyebrows. "I hadn't thought of that! Do you want me to?"

"No, no, I'm kidding. And I'm fine. I just had my follow-up, and although I'm still flat-chested, I'm in complete remission."

"Oh, Lizzy! That's wonderful!" Sally said tearfully, giving her another hug.

Lizzy glanced over her shoulder at the waiting line. "You better hurry up and get signing," she said. "You don't want to keep your fans waiting."

Sally took the book and opened it to the title page. Then she looked up. "I don't even know what to say . . . words don't begin to . . ." She shook her head. "I should've been thinking about what I'm going to write." She glanced at the growing line and swallowed. "Should I make it to both you and Elise?"

"No, no. Elise is getting her own copy . . . just sign it, Sal—no pressure! I know how you feel."

Sally tapped her pen, thinking, and then scrawled out the words: *To my dearest, oldest friend—I don't know what I'd do without you! All my love, Sally Adams.* She handed it back to Lizzy and smiled sheepishly. "It's not what I really want to say."

Lizzy shook her head. "The whole book is a letter to me, so don't even think twice about it."

Sally smiled and then turned to Elise and gave her a hug too. In fact, everyone got a hug and a moment of Sally's undivided attention—so much so that she spent more time standing than sitting. As each person got their book—or two or three—they all lingered, enjoying the fine food and finer company. No one wanted to leave—they all loved Sally that much!

Finally, Aidan pulled the last book out of the last box. "Wow, Sally! You sold all of them!"

"No," Sally said, looking up in surprise.

Wendy nodded. "We had just enough."

"This is the last one!" Aidan said, grinning.

Hearing this, everyone cheered and Sally

looked around. "My cup truly does runneth over!"

Late that evening, Sally sat on the porch with Jax curled up next to her and thought about the day and the lovely celebratory dinner they'd had at The Brotherhood. Lizzy and Elise, Levi and Emma—showing off her beautiful engagement ring—and Lily, as well as Tracey, T.J., and Olivia, had all come. She'd tried to get Abe to come, too, but he'd said he wanted to get home before dark. She said she understood and hugged him and thanked him for coming.

She smiled—it had truly been a wonderful day and evening, one for the memory books . . . and then she remembered the true highlight of the evening—Aidan calling Liam "Dad," surprising everyone and making Liam's eyes glisten. It really couldn't have been any nicer.

She felt the cool evening breeze whisper of autumn, pulled Coop's flannel shirt snugly around her, and realized another Nantucket summer was coming to an end. It made her feel a bit melancholy. "Where does the time go?" she whispered, smoothing Jax's velvet ears as she thought of the long winter ahead. Jax opened one eye, yawned, and nestled closer—he seemed unfazed by the passing of time—and she pictured him racing through his first snow and curled up in front of the fireplace on a stormy winter night—little things that would make the winter months cozier. "Life goes on, ole pie," she said wistfully, "and all we can do is keep going."

She felt her phone vibrate in her pocket and pulled it out to look at the screen. She'd received a text from her editor: ***Congratulations on a wonderful day, Sally!* Summer Dance *is going to be number seven on the* New York Times *best-seller list this Sunday! Soo—after you catch your breath —we need to talk about what's next!***

"Next?!" Sally said, laughing and shaking her head. "You just never know what the next chapter will bring, Jax," she whispered softly, and hearing his name, the little yellow Lab rested his head on her lap and thumped his tail in agreement.

Discussion Questions

1. As a girl, Sally always tried to be good, but by the time she was sixteen, she gave up. Why do you think this happened? How was her childhood affected by circumstances beyond her control?

2. For most of her life, Sally is consumed by sin and guilt and punishment. Who or what influenced her? Do you think it's right to place such a strong emphasis on these things?

3. Lizzy is much more willing than Sally to question the beliefs of the church—she even leaves the Catholic Church to marry Simon. How do these two women, raised to believe the same things, end up having such opposing viewpoints?

4. Sally doesn't tell anyone about her affair with Cooper—not even her best friend—but in the end, she writes a book and shares it with everyone. Why is she so reluctant to tell Lizzy? How does she change?

5. Why do you think Sally finally decides to divorce Drew?

6. Lizzy believes the Old Testament is outdated. What are some of the examples Lizzy uses to prove this point? Do you agree?

7. How has the Catholic Church changed to address the issues of today?

8. Toward the end, when Sally and Liam are spreading Coop's ashes, Sally starts to say a prayer by rote, but then she stops and speaks from her heart instead. What does this reveal?

Center Point Large Print
600 Brooks Road / PO Box 1
Thorndike, ME 04986-0001 USA

(207) 568-3717

US & Canada:
1 800 929-9108
www.centerpointlargeprint.com